FAYE, FARAWAY

HELEN FISHER

THORNDIKE PRESS
A part of Gale, a Cengage Company

LIBRARY OF CONGRESS CIP DATA ON FILE.
CATALOGUING IN PUBLICATION FOR THIS BOOK
IS AVAILABLE FROM THE LIBRARY OF CONGRESS.

ISBN-13: 978-1-4328-8790-2 (hardcover alk. paper)

Published in 2021 by arrangement with Gallery Books, a division of Simon & Schuster, Inc.

Printed in Mexico
Print Number: 01   Print Year: 2021

This story is for my children, Cleo and Dylan, who are good, kind, clever, and funny. Love always.

CHAPTER 1

The loss of my mother is like a missing tooth: an absence I can feel at all times, but one I can hide as long as I keep my mouth shut. And so I rarely talk about her.

It's a sad place to start my incredible little story, but please don't misunderstand me: I love my life. I'm quite an ordinary thirty-something woman with two daughters and a husband, Eddie, who's training to be in the clergy. He seems to think I'll make the perfect vicar's wife, but I'm not sure I'm up to the challenge. Compared to my husband I'm what you might call more rational, a little more scientific. But I suppose, after what I've been through, I should be able to believe in anything.

Eddie says I have all the necessary qualities, and I admit I think I'm a good person. For instance, you can tell me anything and I won't judge, and if I can't help raising an eyebrow, it will stay on the inside, to protect

7

your feelings. And I've always been completely truthful with Eddie, it's a thing between us, not a single lie. Until now.

Now I'm a liar. Now I'm a thief.

And I can no longer say hand-on-heart that I'm even normal. I'll let you make up your own mind. Lying to my husband makes me feel sick and I'm desperate to stop, but lies are like toes: where there's one, there's always more close by. My biggest confession is that I've been visiting my mother and lying about that, but I've also been scratched and scarred and lied about that too, so many things. If I told him the truth, Eddie would try to understand because he's a good man. But logically — *logically* — he's more likely to think I'm mad.

Maybe I'm being unfair to him, because as much as I love and need my husband, he loves and needs me, and over the past few months I've realized something important. I can't tell Eddie what's been happening, no matter how much I want to. Not because he won't believe me, but because he might.

And if Eddie believes me, he'll try to stop me.

Let me explain things from the beginning, although I wonder where the beginning really is. Time is not as easy to understand as I once thought.

It started with the photo and the box — but, oh, there's me saying "started," and that's the same as beginning. We'll make a deal: I could get philosophical about "the beginning" and what that really means, but I don't want to talk about that right now and I appreciate that you're not up to speed with the situation, so we'll hold off on that discussion (it will come up again later, I guarantee it). Let's just say this: the sensible starting place for my story is the photograph.

It's the kind of photo a billion people have in their possession. You might find it tucked inside a book you haven't opened for years, or it will fall out of an old album because it's lost its stick. I bet you have one in a shoebox somewhere, hidden among other bits of life debris: love letters, postcards, and christening pictures of unknown babies. Mine fell out of a cookbook. A cookbook with no pictures, but with spattering on various pages indicating best-loved recipes, chocolaty fingerprints, and a few handwritten notes. My mother owned this book and had a sweet tooth; the page for chocolate brownies is particularly smeared, as is the recipe for sticky toffee pudding.

The photo is of me. On the back it says

Faye, Christmas 1977. I turned it over in my fingers, and grinning up at me from thirty years ago was my six-year-old self: rosy cheeks, brown eyes, and messy curls. I'm sitting in a box in the photo, a box that had contained my Christmas gift that year: a Space Hopper. I remember sitting on it, holding on to the handles and bouncing around the garden. But in the photo, I am more interested in the box, and I look so much like a doll, I could be climbing out of my packaging on Christmas morning. I'm wearing a soft-looking pink dressing gown with a little rounded collar, and the Christmas tree behind me is heavy with colored lights and tinsel. I look so happy. Of course. I was a kid, it was Christmas morning, and my mother was taking that photo. It would have been a perfect, carefree day. My mother, whom I hardly remember, would have been soaking up this little girl's gaze of love. My love. I peered closely, trying to see beyond the photo, trying to see more than it was capable of giving me.

I work at the Royal National Institute for the Blind (RNIB) designing products for people with partial or no sight, and a year ago I was researching cameras, all very high-tech. There's this blind guy I work with, my friend Louis, and he was taking part in the discussions about cameras of the future and what they might be able to do. What he really wanted was to pick up a photo and feel everything in it, not just what you can see, but *round the back* too. He said he'd like to be able to put his arm round the shoulders of the people in the picture and felt sure one day it would be possible. He's always been blind and I think he thinks sighted people already get more out of photos than is actually possible.

I understand what he means though, because when I look at the photo of me in the box under the tree, I want to put my hand in and touch the face of my mother. She isn't in the picture, and yet she's there. I'm desperate to see her and touch her. I so very much want to climb in and spend a few minutes under that Christmas tree with her.

So you know I lost my mother a long time ago, and I told you I've been visiting her and that, if he knew about it, Eddie would try to stop me. But I guess you also know that if I were visiting her in the cemetery, Eddie wouldn't have a problem with that. Please don't give up on me when I tell you what I've been doing. Put yourself in my shoes and imagine telling your partner, or your boss, or your best mate. I think you'd lie too, because if you kept insisting it was the truth, you'd end up in a mental unit.

I hesitate in case you scoff or smile affectionately, or back away, slowly reaching behind you for the door handle. And I really don't want you to do that. I want you to keep a straight face, look me in the eye, and say, "Go on," and when you do that, I'll tell you the rest of my story.

I've been visiting my mother, who died when I was eight, and I'm not talking about the graveyard — I'm talking about flesh-and-blood, tea-and-cookies-on-the-table visiting.

So there you go, I've said it now. If you want to leave I'll understand.

The people I care about most in the world are Esther and Evie. Eddie's next, but it's not that simple because there's Cassie and Clem, my best friends, and they're like sisters to me; the sisters I never had, but if I could have chosen — or created — them, then they would be it. In a conversation we once had, which probably happened after two in the morning, we girls talked about who we would throw the last life belt to if we were on a sinking ship and the rest of us, including our children, were in the water. My hesitation in answering earned me a lot of abuse, including a cushion thrown with some force. The natural re-action is to throw the life belt to one of the children, but my thinking was: *Save the life of the one who'll save the ones you love.* I chose Eddie. "What about us!" Clem had wailed, and then she'd asked who I'd throw the life belt to if just she and Cassie were in the water, and — honestly? — *that* was the harder question. When you're a teenager with no real family, and you meet girls like Cassie and Clem at college, well then, sud-denly you *do* have family.

My life used to go like this: my daughters, Eddie, our friends, work, and domestic chores. That was about it, and it all pretty much worked beautifully. But then this thing happened, and it touched everything. My focus changed; life wasn't simple any-more.

Since I found the photograph I carry it with me everywhere, like a good-luck charm, a Polaroid tucked neatly into my wallet. I worry about losing it, but I'd rather have it with me than not. More than ever in my life, I've been thinking about my mother and what I missed out on. And as my children get older, I think about what she missed too; by the time I was their age, she was gone.

13

It was just the two of us when I was little. No father or family that I knew of. I have some fleeting images of my mother in my mind, but they're like butterflies: fragile, floating into my vision and out again before I'm able to get a proper look. And when she died, well, I don't have any clear images of that: a feeling of loss, but also expectation and disbelief. I thought she would come back, really believed I would see her again. She was ill, I knew that, a chesty cough and no energy, although she would always smile for me. I could go to her for hugs and kisses anytime: open door, feet padding on carpet, climb into her bed, open arms, warmth. All a bit vague, but a good feeling. And then one morning, I woke up and she was gone. I went to a house I knew down the road and knocked on the door — an old couple — and told them my mother was sick and I didn't know what to do. I stayed with them that night, Em and Henry, and stayed with them the next night too. They made phone calls, there were hushed conversations and a policeman, and they told me my mother had died, but I'd be okay. I ended up staying with Em and Henry forever, or rather, until college. They never gave me any details about that time, and I didn't feel I could ask. We drove to a churchyard on a few

Sundays to put flowers on her grave, but apart from that she was basically just gone from my life.

I had questions that could probably never be answered, and filled in the gaps with guesses. I guess cancer killed her, but I don't actually know, because why wouldn't there have been doctors, and why wouldn't she just have been dead in her bed? Maybe, like Louis, that's why I wanted this photograph to give me more information than it could, and the more I looked at it, the more I focused on the Space Hopper box and tried to think where I'd last seen it.

Not long after I lost my mother and was staying with Em and Henry, I went into my new bedroom, old-fashioned but comfortable, with lots of pink frills, and in the middle of the floor was the box that my Space Hopper had come in. It looked battered, but the sides had been taped up with brown parcel tape to strengthen it, and I opened the lid to reveal my things. Em and Henry must have finally decided that my stay with them was going to be long-term, and had gone to my mother's house to pick up some of my toys.

I lined up my Smurfs neatly on the carpet — there were about five of them, and they fell over in the plush pile — and then my

Slinky. There was a white plastic telephone on wheels, with eyes that rolled when you pulled it along, too young for me by then. There was my Little Professor, a handheld calculator with a clever face, like Einstein. I laid him next to my Major Morgan (a gift from Em and Henry) and they looked up at me like a pair of tiny electronic uncles; their happy faces made me feel sad. I switched on the Little Professor, and a mathematical question popped onto the screen. It was too easy for me, but I deliberately got the answer wrong. After three goes, he silently gave me the correct answer, and while a part of me wanted to smash him against the wall, I laid him carefully back down, next to the Major. A pack of Happy Families playing cards and my books were in the box, mainly Enid Blyton, *The Magic Faraway Tree* and *The Wishing-Chair,* and hidden between them like a stowaway was my mother's cookbook, the only one I ever saw her use: small and well-thumbed with a soft, pliable black cover, like an old-fashioned Bible. I opened it to a page covered in smudges, ran my fingers over what I guessed were her fingerprints, and traced some of the tiny writing in the margin, and the tiny tick she'd put next to one of her favorite recipes. I kissed it and tucked it away carefully with my other books.

In the bottom of the box was a pair of roller skates, and I held them to my lips; the metal of the wheels was cold and rough and embedded with tiny stones from the path outside. The skates were adjustable, and Henry would help me loosen them so they would fit. There were other things in the box, and I emptied everything onto the pink carpet. The Space Hopper itself was in the corner of the room; it had a smiling face painted on it, but its sinister grin upset me — it looked like it knew something I didn't — so I turned it to face the wall. When the box was empty I flattened it and stored it in my wardrobe. And when I moved out years later, I vaguely remember that box; I reinforced the sides with more tape, and it must have come with me for every house move I ever made.

The next time I saw that box after I found the photo was the day I made a cup of tea for Eddie and knocked on his study door; he turned on his swivel chair and took off his headphones, pressing Pause on the video he was watching on the computer. He stretched out his long legs and flexed his fingers, as he always does when he's been working.

"What are you doing?" I said, putting the tea on his desk and running my hand through his ruffled brown hair. Is it wrong to think Eddie is too handsome to be a vicar?

"Learning about the book of Revelation, and how it relates to certain services." He pulled me onto his lap and I straddled him, snuggling my head into the crook of his neck.

"You smell good," I said, and he wrapped his arms around me. He's so tall and I'm so petite I think he could wrap his arms round me twice. His thumb found the base of my neck and rubbed it. I leaned back to look into his kind brown eyes and he kissed me. Best kisser ever. I thought that the first time, still think it now. And I could feel him stirring.

"Revelation turns you on?" I said, smiling into his mouth.

"It's pretty weird stuff." He kissed me again.

"Want to get kinky later?"

"Let me think about that," he said, and I pinched him playfully behind the arm. As I rested my chin on his shoulder, I noticed a battered box in the corner of the room. Like an old soldier, it had outward signs of wear that suggested it had a story to tell. There was a faded image of a girl on the box, wearing long white socks, black shoes, and a yellow dress, impossibly short — seventies short — bouncing right at you on her Space Hopper. Some of the writing was hard to read, because it was obscured by brown tape, or had been torn away when tape was removed or replaced.

"Where did you get that box?" I said, sitting up slightly straighter in his lap.

"The attic. I was looking for some of my old textbooks, and I brought them down in that. Looks ancient, doesn't it."

"It's the one from my photo," I said, and I leaned back so I could look him in the eyes.

"What photo?"

"My photo, of me and my mother, except, well, my mother's not in it. The one under the Christmas tree." I got up and went to retrieve it from my bag, bringing it back like a piece of children's treasure: the thing that feels like treasure to the owner but not necessarily anyone else.

Eddie took it from me, and with his finger touched the face of me in the picture. "Look at you." He smiled, first at the photo and then at me. "You've fared better than the box," he said. "You still look perfect, but that box has seen some serious action. We should probably throw it out."

"What?" I said, getting off him abruptly and going over to it. I removed a couple of books from inside and lifted it up, holding it protectively. "How could you? This is in my photo. Part of the proof I was there."

"I only meant that given how bashed up it's getting, if you put something heavy in it, the bottom might drop out."

"Well, then, don't use it. But don't you dare throw it away."

Eddie held up his hands as if we were playing cops and robbers. "I won't, I promise. Sorry!" He grinned at me as though I was a nutcase he loved dearly, and I pulled a face to show him how crazy I could get if I really wanted to, and hugged that box a little tighter.

There was a quiet knock at the door, and I turned to see Esther standing there, holding her hands together in a little prayer.

"Hello, sweetheart," I said, and put the box down as she came and wrapped her arms round my legs, burying her warm face in my stomach. I stroked my hand over her glossy brown hair, tucked it behind her ears, and gently squeezed an earlobe. I always felt like I wanted to pop one of those earlobes in my mouth like a piece of gum. She pulled away from me and bobbed down in front of the box.

"I like this," she said, using her finger to outline the image of the little girl, who looked about the same age as her. I realized the girl on the box would be in her forties now, at least, and yet here she was, like a time traveler who had bounced from 1970-something into our attic and now into Eddie's study. Who knew where she'd end up next?

"Can I have this?" Esther said.

"No," I said, a little quickly, and Esther just said that was okay.

"What do you want it for?" I added, feeling bad, just as I did every time I said no to the girls.

"I was just going to cut it out or something — she's so lovely, isn't she?" Esther said, still looking at the girl from the past.

"Yes, she is," I said, bobbing down next to my sweet daughter who loved to cut out all the beautiful things she found in magazines and on cards. I once found her, aged six, tongue between teeth, with a tiny pair of scissors and a slim black out-of-date diary that she'd bought for ten pence at a yard sale and never written in. Every page of the diary was edged with shiny gold and she was trying to trim it off. When I asked her why, she said the gold was the best bit and

21

she wanted to separate it from the other part of the diary.

"You've got to take the rough with the smooth," I'd said at the time.

"I don't understand that," she'd answered, still concentrating on her cutting.

"I mean that sometimes the best bits are attached to the not-so-good bits, and we just have to accept that."

"I *know* what it means, I just don't understand why we can't just have all good bits. *We're* all good bits: you and Daddy, and me and Evie, and our house. There's no bad bits."

"What about when I tell you off?" I'd said.

And she'd stopped cutting and looked at me thoughtfully. "Even when you tell me off, that's a good bit, because I know you love me. If it was another mummy telling me off, then that would be bad."

"It really would!" I'd agreed.

But once Esther had trimmed off all that gold, the diary looked worse than before, and the little bundle of shiny strips didn't look any good either. She'd cried, and we'd cuddled, and I'd thought of my own mum and how Esther was right: how I would love for my mother to be here even if it was just to tell me off about something.

"This box is a bit important to Mummy,"

I said to Esther, and just then Evie came into the study, thumb in mouth, wrinkled from having been in there for so long, and her messy hair made her look like she'd just risen from a nap, when in fact she always looked like that: dreamy and warm. I sat properly on the floor and Evie climbed into my lap, head to one side, and stretched out her hand to touch the box as well. For a moment it felt like we were all connected to the box: Esther and Evie touching it, me touching it by virtue of holding Evie, and even Eddie, who was sitting there with arms folded, watching us as though we were a bunch of kittens, connected to it through the carpet that it was sitting on, radiating up through his feet.

"Why is it important, Mummy?" Esther asked, and Eddie leaned down to pass her the photograph.

"Who do you think this is?" he said, and Evie shuffled forward in my lap, her thumb loosening but still slightly wedged behind her teeth. The girls peered at it.

"Is it me?" Evie said around her thumb.

Esther looked from the photo to her sister. "It does look a bit like Evie, but that's not her dressing gown." And it was true, Evie was about the same age as me in the photo, and apart from a different haircut, we looked very much alike.

"It's me," I said, leaning forward and taking the photo gently, thinking they might pull at it or get spit on it. "And can you see what I'm sitting in?"

"The box!" said Esther.

Evie looked at the taped-up, battered box. "That's *old.*"

"Oi! Same age as me, roughly," I said, squeezing her and pretending to be offended.

"But that's just a silly old box," said Evie, "and you are our cuddly mummy." She snuggled into my armpit, and I felt a rush of joy at the warmth that was coming at me from all directions: from Esther and Evie, and from Eddie, watching over us. And as always, when I was in these moments, I felt an emptiness. As though there were a corridor inside me with a door at one end, and when the rest of me thought everything was wonderful and perfect, the door would open and cold air would rush through and I would remember what I'd always missed. My own lovely mother. My eyes filled with tears and I looked up at Eddie, who nodded and smiled like he knew what I was thinking, but he didn't, not all of it.

"So *can* I have this box?" said Esther.

"No," I said softly. "I need this, and I

don't even know why."

Evie — pouncing on the fact that she knew I hated to say no — picked just the right moment to ask for something.

"Mummy, can we have some popcorn and watch a film?"

"Now, *that* is a yes," I said, and the girls cheered.

Eddie put his headphones back on and turned to the computer. Going to the kitchen, I popped the corn, and the girls snuggled up on the sofa to watch *Mary Poppins.* Again.

CHAPTER 2

While my family were occupied, I decided to put the box back in the attic where it would be safe from scissors and bins. Upstairs, I stood on a chair in the hallway and pressed the hatch in the ceiling. It clicked and released a heavy ladder that flew down like it was worried I'd change my mind, metal scraping against metal as it descended, trying to take my fingers. I climbed up, the box dangling lightly from one hand while I used the other to grip the cold rungs. At the top I felt about for the cord and pulled it so that the single bulb gave a weak glow, lighting up first one side of the space and then the other as it swung about. Near the edge of the hatch was a chunky yellow flashlight. I turned it on and crawled in, dragging the box in with me.

The attic was warm — the summer sun was beating down on the roof — and it had a comforting smell like a mechanic's work-shop, both fresh and old, reminding me the attic is not a part of real, everyday life, but a place for storing the past: things we can't part with, but that we don't keep at the surface of our lives. Oh, and the Christmas decorations.

I sat cross-legged with the box in front of me, wearing a thin, baggy old sweater — one of Eddie's — and jeans. The sweater swamped me, but I loved it. I was barefoot but glad my arms and legs were covered, in case something brushed against me. I pulled my unruly hair into a messy ponytail and pointed the beam of the flashlight around the dark space. The attic is not a place I often go. Like the recesses of my mind, it was a part of my house that I felt reluctant to visit in case the remnants of the past opened something up inside me that was better off shut away. For me, the attic is a challenge, one I am usually happy to let Eddie deal with. But I didn't want to trust the box to anyone else, so I took it up there myself to make sure it was safe. And while I was up there, I decided I might as well look around. The first sign of a spider, I promised myself, and I was out of there.

The space became a series of snapshots as I used the flashlight to highlight objects in turn. There were stacks of plastic boxes with layers of books and papers inside. Brown cardboard boxes with writing on them like kitchen. A couple of small cardboard boxes, tied with string, that said important, do not throw out.

There was a plastic McDonald's container that looked like a house, but the size of a soccer ball, and when I pried open the roof part of it, it was full of marbles, all different colors. *Why do we keep this stuff?* I thought. But I admit, I didn't want to take it downstairs and trash it. There was a memory here, too hard to discard, too easy to keep.

When we go to the beach, Evie and Esther pick up stones and give them to Eddie and me. Finding the smoothest stone, a perfectly round one, or one that looks like a face, or a dog, or the shape of a heart, all these things transmit treasure status onto these small, ordinary objects. The moment they're picked up and admired — the longer they're held on to — the harder they are for the girls to throw away. The stones end up in my pockets, Eddie's pockets; and holding his hand in one of mine while rubbing the stones between my fingers in the other is the feel of the beach to me. When we get home, cardigan pockets misshapen by the weight of these stones, I don't know what to do with them. I can't throw them away. Eddie's happy to put them in the garden, but I feel like that's abandonment too. So I started having jars of stones around the house. I even bought some vases to display them. I just couldn't put them in the attic — it would feel like an insult to the girls and our days at the beach. But we do have a lot of stones. I guess one day they'll have to go.

We keep stuff in order to hang on to what's important, but it's an illusion. My pain at the thought of throwing away those stones is my pain at losing those days with my daughters. The pain of knowing that one day I will look back and they will be so far in the past that I'll feel like a balloon that has silently unraveled itself from the hand that's holding it, and drifted out of reach into the sky. As long as I have those stones, I can persuade myself that I still have those days. What I can't admit is that those days are already gone. Stones or no stones, the past is as far away from us whether we're talking about ten minutes ago or ten years. These objects are not bridges to the past, they're bridges to memories of the past. But they are *not* the past.

That was how I felt before I went into the attic.

29

By the time I left it, I'd changed my mind. The flashlight created a tunnel of light from me to the far side of the attic, and in truth, even then it was like reaching out to a different place and time. I saw a brown suitcase I'd taken to Greece as a teenager. Inside were the girls' baby clothes, too sentimental to give away. But now the idea of preserved clothes felt like Miss Havisham's stuff; it would have been better to pass them on. The suitcase had a worn-out sticker on it of Shaggy in his green T-shirt and maroon trousers, saying "Scooby-Doo, where are you?" My boyfriend at the time was a bit of a hippie. He had the same green T-shirt as Shaggy and the same haircut, and he'd smoothed that sticker onto my case, saying, "Send me postcards. This sticker is to remind you that I will be wondering where you are and what you're doing the whole time." I'd forgotten about that, and probably would have gone my whole life never thinking about it again if I never saw that case.

The tunnel of light fell on other things that made me smile: a proper old telephone, cream-colored with a rotating dial and heavy handset; a tennis racket with a wooden frame, must have been Eddie's; a basketball that looked a bit gray, but with a wipe might be orange again. I decided to take it downstairs with me; Eddie could put up a hoop at the back of the house. I'm a pretty good shot, and the girls would love it.

I have so little of my mother, missed out on so much. I don't blame Em and Henry, but I think they could have told me more, should have talked about her with me. When they took me in, they were already old and had no children. They were kind, and I was lucky that they were there for me, and later they adopted me. It was like living with sweet grandparents, and life could sometimes feel very quiet, but they treated me well, and what they did, I suppose, was try to ease my mother's death for me by never mentioning it. They said she became ill, which I knew, and then died, but I didn't know a person could die from a cough and a cold. When I get a cold myself these days, I worry so much that I make myself even sicker, wondering whether *my* children will grow up without a mother, when all I've got is a sore throat and a high temperature.

I realize now that it must have been something more serious, but at the time I allowed myself to believe it was as simple as that and I didn't question it. Maybe I had more memories of her at the time, but my mother was like a fairy tale to me, and as I grew up I suppose she became what fairy tales become to all adults: an illusion, a magical story that seems to say one thing, but mean something else. There were very few bridges to my mother. I suppose that's why the photograph was so important to me, even though she wasn't in it.

I sighed. I knew that coming into the attic would make me think, make me remember. Wanting to remember and *not* wanting to remember at the same time. All of a sudden I longed to be downstairs, back in the real world, the present, the place I understood, with my daughters, whose laughter I could faintly hear, and Eddie, whom I wanted to kiss again.

I stood up and lifted the box, wondering where would be best to store it, and whether to fold it up or keep it as it was. Being short, I could have stood upright, but I instinctively ducked as I went along, placing my bare feet carefully. I would paint my toenails later, I thought. As I stepped backward, I hit my head on the light bulb. There was instant darkness except for the flashlight beam, and a tinkling sound as the glass fell around me. I automatically squeezed my eyes shut, and when I opened them I felt my face. I was fine. I shone the flashlight on the floor. Tiny shards of glass were scattered everywhere, over the wooden slats and yellow insulation, all around my feet — surely this was more glass than makes a single bulb! If I moved, I knew I was bound to step on it, and pictured tweezering slivers of it from my skin. I set the box down carefully, and stepped inside it: a safe zone, a glass-free area.

I opened my mouth to shout for Eddie, hoping he could hear me with his headphones on — then closed it again before I made a sound. Standing in the box had given me the most extraordinary feeling of nostalgia. My photograph was still in Eddie's study, but I pictured it perfectly, myself as a child, grinning out over the edge of the box. And like that girl on the front of the box who was bouncing out at me from the past, here I was, the girl from the future, back inside the box of my photograph. The tiny child I had been would never have imagined that one day she would be standing in that very same box, too big to sit right inside it now, and having grown up entirely without the sweet mother she had loved so very much.

And then I felt myself drop just slightly to the right; the feeling was unnerving, like when you sit on a chair and one leg is a fraction shorter than the others, and the world feels completely off-kilter for a moment. But I was standing in the box, and there were no legs to be shorter than the others. Then it happened again; this time the left side felt like it jerked slightly downward. I realized the box must be on a weak part of the attic floor and I was about to fall through. I froze, I held my breath, I closed my eyes, but none of these things could make me lighter or levitate. And then, as Eddie had predicted, it felt as though the bottom fell out of the box completely.

I dropped fast, and I dropped vertically. My breath was whipped away from me so quickly there was no chance to scream. I shot straight down like a silk scarf being whisked from a hook on a wall. And it was pitch-black.

I knew I hadn't fallen through the ceiling — if I had, I would have hit the upper hall floor already. My legs scrambled in the air, instinctively seeking something to connect with. Sheer velocity yanked my arms from my sides straight above my head, and the rush of air pulled my sweater up and over my chest. It caught on my chin; then the wind ripped it over my head and away.

The air streaming upward flooded my nose and mouth; it was like trying to breathe in through your nose with your head hanging out of the car window (which I don't recommend, by the way). The roar in my ears reminded me of a time I stood behind a waterfall, intense, powerful. I know it's hard to believe, but the fact is that one moment I was standing in a box in my loft, and the next I was falling at high speed, in the dark, and showing no signs of reaching the ground.

I sensed a slowing; the air felt thicker and I was able to take a breath through my mouth. As the slowing increased, my legs took on a more graceful swimmer's kick. I was doing a front crawl, but vertically. A glimmer of light appeared below me.

Remember in the Disney version of *Alice in Wonderland,* when Alice falls through the rabbit hole at such a casual pace she has time to look at all the other things in the hole? I think there were lamps and clocks and playing cards. I was falling that slowly now, but there was nothing to see. Like a cave animal, I felt my eyes getting bigger in order to eke out any morsel of light available. Below me — a long way off — a multitude of colored lights spun like a lethargic kaleidoscope. I watched as those colors gathered, seeming nearer and more focused, and my feet continued to kick. For a moment I decided I must have fallen through the attic, hit my head, and passed out. Eddie would find me and revive me.

But just as I started to feel confident with the idea that I must be unconscious in the real world — surely the only explanation possible? — I found myself fighting for breath as though I had a corset on and it was getting tighter and tighter. I scrabbled at myself, trying to get my fingers between my skin and whatever was suffocating me. But there was nothing there. I couldn't breathe in or out. *Eddie, find me soon, otherwise I'm going to die.* The rushing sound of water vanished, and the silence was broken by another sound, soft and menacing: a rhythmic thud like wild horses running on a beach. Or the heartbeat of a giant when he's just swallowed you whole.

In my suffocating descent, I curled into a fetal position, my lungs ready to burst. I sped up again — free-falling — hair flying upward. The fear of not breathing superseded my fear of anything else. If I didn't breathe soon, I would die. I watched the colorful lights below as I spun: they charged toward me, and I squeezed my eyes shut again, expecting impact.

I hit the ground so hard I felt like part of me had gone through it. The force of the landing split my invisible corset and I took a noisy, desperate breath. I was in the fetal position; the muscles and bones on my right side shrieked, and I gulped in oxygen.

I managed to turn my head and look up from the floor. It was night. I had landed on a Space Hopper box — although this one looked newer — and practically crushed it, and above my head, twinkling festively, were the fairy lights of a Christmas tree.

CHAPTER 3

I didn't move for a few minutes. Breathing in and out hurt. I thought maybe if I just lay there, some explanation would make itself known. I've watched plenty of movies where the seemingly inexplicable was ultimately explained. I was hoping that would happen, right about . . . *now.* But it didn't.

I looked up into the tree, and the face of Father Christmas — glass bauble version — moved gently, close to me. His beard looked like shiny whipped meringue, his tiny pursed red mouth glinted through his mustache, and his scarlet hat glimmered in the tree lights. The holly around the rim of his hat gave me pause. I knew this face — correction, I knew this *bauble,* I had hung it myself on this tree, about thirty years ago.

I looked at the carpet, flat and gray, and as familiar as the bauble, more so. This was the carpet I had felt under my feet every day, a long time ago. I lay there, certain that

I was about to discover that I had died and gone to heaven.

Or something even more unbelievable to me than that.

A few minutes passed, I guess, and then I carefully eased myself out of the box. When I stood, pain shot through my hip like a bullet and it felt like my wrist was broken, though it wasn't. I looked around the room, turning on the spot like a damaged ballerina in a musical jewelry box that starts up when you lift the lid.

I knew this room. When I looked at the tree, I saw what was in my photograph, but it was the things that lay outside the border of the photograph that shocked me. *Too* familiar. Like my own bed, or my coat, or the smell of my children's hair; this room was practically a part of me. When people say that something is like *coming home,* it's that powerful sense of belonging, intensely normal. And here I was. Home.

People talk about what heaven is like. Some think it's clouds and angels playing harps; some think it's a golden city bathed in afternoon sunlight. I've heard some people say it would be the place they loved most on earth: a beach; a field; throwing a Frisbee to their dog and playing till they're muddy and running back to a warm kitchen where their mother and father are calling them in for dinner: hot, buttered rolls and chicken soup.

When my mother died, heaven was a blur to me, soft-focus, but I believed she was there, and if I'd had to describe it as a child I would have said it was most like the clouds-and-angels version. When I got older, I stopped believing in God and heaven, but when people died it still brought me comfort to imagine them somewhere else. So I visualized them sitting at a long bar, drink in hand, and then when someone else I knew died, I pictured that person joining the others at the bar, laughing, smiling, welcoming each other with a pat on the back. I even imagined a small TV on the wall of that bar with images of what was going on back on earth. I guess if there is a heaven, we don't get to choose what it is. But surely I was dead? In which case my heaven was my old living room.

I hadn't imagined that dying would be so difficult. I had imagined maybe a flash of discomfort, then a bright light, walking toward it, etc., then . . . nothing. But my passage into heaven, if that's what it was, had been a lot more strenuous than that.

As I rotated in the living room of my

40

childhood, I had to be honest with myself. I was quickly beginning to think that I might not be dead, but rather that I'd gone back in time. I know it's not possible, and usually when people travel back in time (I'm talking books, films), they don't get *hurt.* Don't they just walk into a cupboard and step out the other side? But the big difference was that this was real. Of course it wasn't going to be the same as storybooks and films, which after all are not autobiographical. The point is that at the time, in the living room, I was starting to think I wasn't dead. I didn't *feel* dead. Maybe you would expect me to wonder if I was dreaming, but I've had hundreds of dreams, and this was no dream. I tested it in all the clichéd ways — I even pinched myself.

It had always been hard for me to believe in things I couldn't see with my own eyes; I had always been skeptical about everything I read in a book. Nonfiction could be as fanciful as fiction to me when I considered that those books were written by people who were simply telling me something they'd read or heard somewhere else. I suppose it's why I've found it hard to believe in God, and share Eddie's faith. If I can't see it, I've got a problem with its existence. I mean, I believe in germs, even though I can't see them with my naked eye, because they are at least there to be seen under a microscope.

If only, *if only,* God could be seen under the microscope.

There were more abstract things I believed in, even though I couldn't see them or understand them, like electricity and how it makes bulbs light up, or aerodynamics and how those forces get an airplane off the ground, but the physical results of those things were evidence enough for me.

All this in an effort to explain that I had always, *always,* trusted my senses. I pressed my toes into the carpet and touched the needles on the Christmas tree. I jiggled one of the ornaments and heard the tiny bell ring inside it. I licked my lips and tasted salt, and a tiny bit of blood; when I closed my eyes and breathed in hard, I could smell my childhood home. A sensation that can't be described but is as distinct as the pattern on the wallpaper.

Never before had I mistrusted my senses in the face of such overwhelming evidence. If I could see it, smell it, hear it, feel it, and taste it, then it had to be real. But now my sense of reality was reversed; the confirmation of my physical surroundings was giving me proof of something that I knew simply couldn't be true. I had never had such unequivocal, solid proof of something being real, yet at the same time not believed in it. I wasn't sure I had enough faith to believe in what every single sense was screaming at me: that the only possible truth, impossible as it might be to accept, was that I had traveled back in time. *That* was the most reasonable explanation I could come up with. And for a woman who thinks God is farfetched, that was really something.

I considered the strangeness of my immediate situation: it was nighttime and I was in someone else's house, they were probably asleep, and if they found me it was going to be difficult. And when I say "they," I am of course talking about my mother. *My mother.* My heart stopped for a moment, skipped a beat, then it pounded hard. Would I see my mother again? Was she upstairs?

The issue of getting home again, by which I mean back to Eddie and the girls, hadn't hit me until I reasoned with myself that I must be in the past. I don't feel comfortable when my children are out of arm's reach or shouting distance. I'm only truly at ease when I'm in the same building as them. The only exception is when I know they're with Eddie, because he's the only other

43

person in the world who loves them like I do. And there, I suppose, is the most faith I have in the world: when I can't see my children but know they're with Eddie, for me, that's faith. A version of fear rose up and filled every cell of my body, a fear like no other that I might never see my children again. The times I had lost sight of them as they turned the corner at the end of a supermarket aisle; the time Evie wandered off in a shopping center and security locked all the doors, and I wailed, "What if she's already outside of those doors?"; all the imaginings I'd had, daily, of every possible thing that could go wrong, that might mean they were lost from me forever — *those* imaginings were nothing compared to this.

This time everything was different because it was me who was lost. They couldn't find me, and I couldn't reach out to them. If I became a prisoner in time, then my daughters — like my mother — would be relegated to memory only, and I would be relegated to theirs. I was suffocating with fear, which forced me to engage a level of faith I had never required before. The girls were with Eddie, but I was not in a different building or a different country, I was in a different year. The fact that I was thirty years removed from my daughters made everything go gray, and the air buzzed in my ears, and my arm swam about looking for something to hold on to.

I crouched down and pressed my hands to the floor. It struck me like a hammer that if I couldn't get home to my children, then I was like a mother who had died suddenly, leaving her most beloved to the care of others. And so I prayed that Eddie would be safe and well and strong, because my girls needed him. I tried to remember the last moments I'd spent with them: in the study; it was good. It would be a good memory for them, of me. I squeezed my eyes shut and pictured Esther and Evie in my mind's eye. "I'm going to get back to you," I whispered.

I stood slowly, my hands on my hips. I swayed, but I was okay. "I got here," I said out loud in a shaky voice, "I can get home again." I was being my own air hostess, the only woman on board who could reassure me that I would, at some point, make it back to the place I started. And I didn't quite trust her unsteady voice, but what choice did I have?

I felt the need to safeguard the box: it was my ride home, my ticket to see my children again — or so I hoped — so no wonder I had the presence of mind to protect it.

Although it was dark, I knew my way around the house; I took a right and went to the kitchen, unlocked the back door. The rush of freezing air bolstered my conviction that I was neither dead, in a coma, nor dreaming in any way whatsoever. I was in my bra and jeans and bare feet, having lost Eddie's sweater on the fall here, and I hobbled down a little path to the garden shed knowing the washing line was running parallel to my right. The bolt on the shed door had always been a bit stiff and I knew just how to wiggle it loose. I threw the Space Hopper box inside and bolted the door again before returning to the house. I didn't lock the kitchen door in case I needed to get out quickly. I braced myself by the sink for a moment, then did the thing my heart was longing to do: I went up the stairs to my mother's bedroom.

In her doorway, I hesitated. The room was dark, but predawn light bathed the room, making it gray rather than black. I was half in fear that she might be awake, and half in fear that it wouldn't be my mother in the bed; so that was 100 percent fear of one kind or another. I could tell from her

breathing that she was asleep. I'd been holding my own breath and it came out as a
shudder; my mouth was dry, palms damp.
Could I be about to see my mother for the
first time in thirty years, a mother I had
known in all that time only as being dead?
Hope rushed through my veins, while the
rest of me was paralyzed. I hoped, I prayed,
for the impossible.

Summoning movement, I padded round
to her side of the bed, crouching down.

My mother's sleeping face. I took a sharp
gasp. Her lips were slightly parted and her
breath touched me, soft and warm, the very
essence of alive. *This is my mother's breath,
remember this,* I thought. Her light-brown
hair swept across her forehead. She had
longish bangs and looked as if she'd
dreamed about standing at the front of a
ship at sea, letting the breeze do what it
wanted with her. I looked at the miracle of
her eyelashes, and her fingers that were
curled under her cheek. I leaned closer, to
smell her skin, and my eyes filled with tears:
her face cream, a hint of roses. I had smelled
the exact same scent on a lady in the
supermarket once, and had followed her for
a bit.

My face was an inch from my mother's. I
tilted my head forward a fraction, my nose

nearly touching her skin. Tears leaked from the outside corners of my eyes and I felt them meet under my chin. I wanted to wake her. A silent sob escaped me, and I wanted to shake her and say: *Mum, I'm here.* I whispered the words, needing to say them out loud. But I was older than her, by more than ten years, and I knew, despite my emotional unraveling as I knelt at her bedside, that I would scare her if she woke now.

I lifted the covers a fraction and felt the warmth of her sleeping body. The urge to crawl in beside her, as I had done many times as a young child, was overwhelming. But I was no child. And yet. And yet I was *her* child. And I had missed many years of falling asleep with her hand draped over my waist, with her falling asleep midsentence as she told me a story to chase away a bad dream with a good one.

She sighed, and I quietly stood, just watching her for a moment. Now was not the time for a reunion. I would have to think of some way to make that happen. I was still just wearing my jeans and a bra, so I slipped a sweater and some socks from her drawers and pulled them on, and walked backward out of her room, reluctant to lose sight of her.

I went to my bedroom, to look at me. And there I was, a beautiful child. I was more confident with my younger self than I had been with my mother, and sat on the edge of the bed, making it dip so that my sleeping self turned away from the wall and toward me. The action unwedged her little thumb from her mouth, and I could just make out tiny bite marks in the skin. I brushed her hair away from her face, *my* face; a curl disobediently bounced back. I stroked my thumb over her perfect cheek and whispered into her ear, "You are good, you are kind, you are clever, you are funny," which is what I whisper into my children's ears every night while they're sleeping. I don't know why I started doing that, although you may have already wondered if it's because I did it to myself when I was six years old.

It was getting lighter outside and the child's eyes flickered. She said, "Mummy," in a voice stuffed with sleep, and I kissed her — kissed me. I paused briefly on the way out and touched the spines of the books in my old bookcase — *The Magic Faraway Tree,* I had loved that — then went noiselessly downstairs.

I leaned against the kitchen counter, my heart thumping. My mother was alive and upstairs. Alive. *I was a child asleep upstairs.* What now? I bounced on my toes a little, took a few paces forward, shook my head, took a few paces backward: I literally didn't know what direction to take. I exhaled sharply, a long, thin, steadying breath. I stopped and held my palms in the air, as if quieting an excitable audience. I needed to get a grip. Despite everything, I had to be sensible, and I muttered aloud, "Get a grip." I needed to engage my brain, before my heart catapulted me back up those stairs and into my mother's arms.

Although it was cold outside, I couldn't stay in the house. So I quietly opened a drawer that I knew would be bursting with wrinkled plastic carrier bags, and pulled one out. I cut a couple of slices of bread; a whole missing loaf would be noticed. Doing everything as slowly and silently as I could, I took a knife and a jar of jam. There was always lots of jam in the cupboard, and I remembered it was because Henry had an allotment and made loads of his own. There were no plastic bottles to fill with water, although my mouth was dusty dry, so I drank straight from the tap. I wanted to take some water with me, but didn't know what to put it in. Then I remembered my mother cleaned and kept the empty jars to give back to Henry, so I filled a couple, screwed on the lids, shook them to make sure they weren't going to leak, and put them in the bag with the bread and jam.

I needed shoes. There were two pairs of wellies by the back door, a small yellow pair (mine) and my mother's, black. Clearly the absence of boots *would* be spotted, but right now my need was greater, and my mother would have other shoes. So I put them on, and went to the shed, to eat, wait, and decide what to do next.

CHAPTER 4

I shivered in the shed and sought re-assurance in the rough wood beneath my fingers, touched the cardboard of the damaged box and thought fleetingly how wood and cardboard never get really cold, like glass and metal do. Sheds are not the most comfortable of places, so I found a cushion to sit on; it had that oddly comforting smell, like the attic. Some of my aches were getting worse, but I only hurt from the waist up.

I messily broke off a piece of bread and dipped it in the jam. It tasted of the old days, except back then I didn't like the bits in it, and now I did. I leaned against the wall of the shed. My head was a mess: one thought chased another like a dim-witted cartoon cat trying to pounce on a gang of clever and very quick mice. I tried to make sense of where I was; how and why. Desperate to organize my mind, I mentally gathered what I could of my situation and tried to order it by importance, like some version of Maslow's hierarchy of needs. But my train of thought kept crashing before it left the station, so I felt like I could grasp only the very basics of my predicament. I could breathe and I could chew. I was safe, I had shelter and wasn't in any immediate danger, at least not that I knew of. Beyond that, I wasn't sure: I was in the past, but what if I was stuck here? I wanted to see my mother, yearned to reveal myself to her and have her understand who I was. But what about Eddie and the girls? I should get back in the box straightaway and get home — but I was here now, and maybe this was the only chance I'd ever have to be with my mother, the only thing that could fill the mother-shaped hole in my heart. I held my hands in front of me, watching them shake, strangely keen to see physical proof of my inner turmoil. I pinched myself, and laughed, more of a cruel snort at my own predictability. Such a cliché. If I'd had a bottle of alcohol, I would have looked at it accusingly.

I slapped myself round the face so hard that tears sprang to my eyes, and slapped myself again, about as hard as I possibly could, stinging my skin. Nothing changed; I was still in the shed. My mother was within reach, but inaccessible. No friend, no Eddie. No one. I was completely alone, even though my darling mother was in that house. I imagined myself running inside, shouting, *It's me, it's me.*

Gradually a cold, white light seeped through the cracks in the shed walls, and with it came the tinny sounds of distant voices. I looked at the house through a gap in the shed door. I couldn't see much, but after rummaging in a bucket of tools I found a scraper, which I used to widen the gap. The scraper was one of those flat metal things; I remembered my mother using it to scrape the old paint off the kitchen table. Now I could see her through the kitchen window in her blue dressing gown, her hair loose round her shoulders; the radio was on — that was what I could hear.

I pulled the sweater around me; it was long, black, and baggy, and helped against the freezing morning. But the real warmth came all the way from the kitchen window and the view of my mother. She was just so lovely. She had the power to make everything sweet, even this very moment. She leaned on her elbows and gazed out at the birds in the garden before turning away briefly; then she came to the back door and threw a handful of bread crumbs out.

Suddenly she turned fully and ducked out of sight, reappearing just as swiftly in the kitchen window with little me in her arms. I was laughing, throwing my head back in that slightly worrying way that looks as though it might have gone too far. My eyes were squeezed shut and then I opened them, using both my hands to hold my mother's face and press her cheeks together, kissing her lips. Then we both laughed — my mother and myself as a child — and I watched from the shed, wishing I were my younger self, feeling left out.

About an hour passed during which I saw nothing more of me and my mother, except the imprinted image of little me in her arms, which I played over and again in my mind like footage from a film.

I heard more old-fashioned morning sounds, distinctive mainly because of the lack of traffic. I'd thought the road we lived on was quite a main one, but it had been quiet enough to play on as a kid, picking up a ball or riding my bike to the curb now and then to wait whenever a car came by. And there was birdsong, lots of it, and some distant coughing and a dog barking. I wondered how I could approach my mother, speak to her. There was no easy way to introduce myself and spend real time with her. I thought about pretending to sell insurance, or maybe telling her she'd won a prize, but these ideas were so flawed. I only had one chance because I couldn't knock, get it wrong, and then knock again later.

I took in my surroundings, looking for anything that might help me. There was the usual shed stuff: a bucket of tools, masking tape, and a hammer; lots of nails and screws and unidentifiable pieces of metal; some glass jars, which used to contain jam, and some folded sheets spattered in paint.

I stared for a long time at the Space Hopper box. It was intact but rather crumpled from me landing on it, and I wondered about taping it up, to make it sturdier. And I knew that I would, because the Space Hopper box in my attic had loads of tape holding it together; I'd just never realized that *I* had put it there.

I suddenly remembered something and looked at my wristwatch, another way to check for evidence of my reality. Before the children were born, I went through a period of insomnia for six months, and it was torture: awake all night, with fitful sleep between 5 a.m. and 6 a.m. full of strange dreams. One day I discussed my insomnia with some work colleagues, and on the whole they were sympathetic; then one of them said, "You're probably sleeping more than you think."

"I'm awake all night," I said.

"You can't be sure," he said. "It probably just feels like that. But those long stretches in the night when you think you're awake, you're probably kind of dozing."

I felt furious with this well-rested know-it-all. "Are you sleeping now?" I asked him, my hostility quiet but sharp.

"Right now? No, of course not," he said.

"How do you know?" I said. "If I can be wrong about whether or not I'm asleep at night, then surely you can be wrong about being awake now."

He grabbed some paperwork and left, choosing wisely not to mess with me. After all, I hadn't slept for a long time and probably looked dangerous. More interesting was the response of another workmate, who told me there was a surefire way to check if you're dreaming or not. She said numbers don't work in dreams, they get all muddled up, so what you need to do is always wear a watch when you're awake and look at it a ridiculous amount of times. Every time you look at your watch, you must consciously ask yourself: *Are the numbers in the right place?* Then you must clearly answer *yes* or

57

no. When you've been doing this for long enough, it becomes such a habit that it leaks into your dreams, and then one day you'll look at your watch while you're dreaming and ask yourself the question about the numbers being in the right place, and the answer will be *no,* because when you're asleep they never are, and that's when you know you're dreaming. *That's* when you can do whatever you like in your dream. It's called lucid dreaming and is very good fun, because I've tried it. Give it a go, it works. I guarantee it.

My point is, two things: One, in the shed I knew I was awake, in the same way that you can be confident you're awake at this very moment. Second, when I looked at my watch, the numbers were all in the right place, even though it had stopped and the glass on the front was cracked. So we're definitely talking time travel or insanity; there was no other option.

The sound of a dog barking again just a short distance away had me mentally strolling in the direction of the sound. I could picture the little squares of lawn from this, my mother's garden, to the one next door, and beyond that all the fences in between, just low enough to peep over if you were a grown-up standing on tiptoes.

Now my mind's eye took me through all the gardens to Em and Henry's place, all the way down the other end of the street. Henry with his face like a sad puppy, and lovely Em; the couple who had taken me in when my mother died. In the quiet world I had inhabited with my mother as a child, few people had really made an impression on me. But Em and Henry had, and they had stepped in, and brought me up. Of course I should go to Em and Henry now; I would be able to get my foot through their door more easily than my mother's. After that, I wasn't sure, but it was somewhere to start. Before I did anything, I needed another glimpse of my mother; I was emotionally thirsty and she was my glass of water. Then I needed to get out of here without being seen.

The kitchen door opened and clattered shut, startling me. I scooched forward and pressed my face against the rough wooden door. My mother was putting a bag of rubbish into a shiny steel trash bin with a proper lid. She shouted, "Faye, get your shoes on, we're leaving," and then she paused, stood with hands on hips looking straight down the short, narrow garden, straight at me in fact, and took in a deep breath of cold air. She closed her eyes and smiled. She looked so content, and I realized I knew nothing about this woman, even though I loved her with all my heart. She didn't look like me, with her smooth brown hair and gray eyes. She was natural-looking, slim, and wore a belt pinching in the waist of a long sweater over a long skirt that made her look even slimmer, and brown leather boots. I saw little me come to the back door, open it slightly, and say something to my mother, who bent at the waist and cupped Faye's face in her hands. "Of course you can," said my mother in reply. They went inside and the key turned in the lock.

I knew they would go out the front door, so I unfurled myself. I was like one of the screwed-up plastic bags in my mother's kitchen cupboard, and it was hard to straighten up. I eased out of the shed, jogged cautiously down the side of the house, and peered round the corner. They were just coming out, my mother with a large brown satchel over her shoulder and little me wearing a puffy pale-blue and green striped jacket (how I had loved that coat!) with a chunky sweater underneath, and carrying a table tennis paddle on which I was bouncing a red rubber ball — small bounces — and counting each one. Little me got a rally of bounces, before missing one: it bounced on the ground and shot high in the air. My mother caught it, and I saw my young self look at her gleefully, shouting, "Five!"

They walked companionably down the street, my mother's long skirt thrapping her legs, and little me going at varying speeds, sometimes holding back, sometimes trotting, depending on what was required to keep the ball in the air. My mother chatted away and there was the odd interval of laughter. I had forgotten she was funny — I couldn't remember our conversations, but I guess that's true of many people. My friends remember a few lines their parents said to them when they were younger, the odd nugget of gold, and lots of nuggets of criticism, but nothing more than a small collection of well-worn anecdotes.

I walked behind at a short distance. I don't think it was obvious I was following or anything; we were walking toward town and there was nothing suspicious about another person walking to town. The sun was out now, and it was cold, but milder than you might expect considering people had their Christmas trees up.

When I neared Em and Henry's house, I

slowed to a stop and watched my mother and little Faye walk on ahead. My eyes stung and I felt that sense of loss that walks hand in hand with beautiful moments, with knowing that something is over even before it's begun. Knowing that one day all good things will be looked back on like dusty photographs, crackling videotape, and stones in jars. How could they be together now, when for me it was already over, already gone? How could I stand here and watch them walk away from me? I thought of how lonely Esther would feel if she saw me walking away from her when I didn't even know she was there. And for superstition's sake, I glanced over my shoulder to check she wasn't there.

CHAPTER 5

As I focused on Em and Henry's shiny red front door, my breath shuddered and I felt like crying with relief at the thought of seeing them, because I knew how these people treated strangers, and it was good.

I knocked and heard the muffled sounds of voices asking each other who could be knocking this early in the morning. Then the chain and a lock, a busyness of security behind a door that I could have smashed in with one hard kick.

"Hello?" Em said, and I saw Henry in the hallway behind her with a piece of toast in his hand. The comfort of kitchen smells enveloped me, and I wanted to just kiss Em on her soft powdered cheek and walk in as I had done a million times in my life. But this time she was blocking me, and her face, though friendly, was wary.

"Sorry to call so early, but I'm here from the . . . uh . . . *Sporting Gazette.* I understand you bowl, and I'm writing an article about . . . uh . . . recreation for adults in the area." Em and Henry looked confused, and I worried that maybe they hadn't got into bowling yet. I knew they played it when I went to live with them, but this would have been about two years earlier.

"You do bowl, don't you?" I wished I had a notebook to help play my part, where I could pretend to check details that had been passed on to me. But I had nothing. How convincing could I be without a notebook and pen?

"Yes, we do," said Henry. "Em, let her in, what are you doing leaving her on the doorstep?" He wiped crumbs from his mouth with the back of his hand.

"Of course, come in," said Em, opening the door wide and pressing her hands against her front as if to dry them.

The entranceway was welcoming, with thick carpet underfoot. The wallpaper was so familiar: pale-pink and cream stripes, but more notably, the walls were bare. They had always been covered with framed photos of me as I grew up there. I hadn't realized that, before me, there was nothing there.

I had always thought of them as old. But although they must have been in their mid-fifties, at least, they didn't really look old to me now. I would have just turned eight when they took me in, and anyone over thirty looked ancient to me back then. I knew Em's face like a wrinkled apple, Henry's saggy cheeks like familiar old battered cushions. But before me now their faces were quite smooth, and Henry had lots of hair; they were young to me now because I had seen them grow so very, very old. The only thing that seemed old about them now was their clothes: Henry with his baggy buttoned cardigan and leather slippers, and Em with her padded housecoat.

It would usually be my habit to simply walk into Henry's arms and get a big, strong hug, press my cheek against his chest and breathe in the scent of Brut and something else, vaguely smoky. But all I could do was stand and wait, feeling fraudulent and lost.

Em sprang into hostess mode and ushered me into the living room, where the lack of photos struck me again. I had always thought they had loads, but clearly, not until I came along. Crocheted doilies clung to the backs of recliners, and their familiarity drew me to them; I touched one lightly.

"Tea?" asked Em.

"Please," I said, wanting a cup of tea more than ever before in my life.

"Sit down," said Henry, and I did. Looking down beside the chair I saw a small pile of hardback *Beano* comics collections and smiled. They were Henry's guilty pleasure, and I had loved them too. I reached down and picked one up.

"Minnie the Minx is my favorite," I said, opening it up.

"I love the Bash Street Kids," he said, and we both chuckled.

"How did you get our names? Did you speak to Susan at the bowling center?"

"Uh, no," I said, quickly thinking that if they spoke to Susan they would be left wondering who on earth I really was. "I just, uh, got in touch with the club and got a few names and addresses of players."

Em bustled back in with a milk pitcher and teapot and flumped down into a chair. I really felt terribly conscious about not having anything to write on, or with.

"I have a few questions, but I seem to have left my bag somewhere. Maybe at the office. I don't have any of my things."

"Do you want to come back later?" Em asked. "We're here all day."

"I just need my notepad, but if you have some paper? I'm sorry, so unprofessional."

"Don't worry," Henry said, and he opened a drawer, handing me something to write on and a pencil. "You can rest it on that."

66

He pointed at the *Beano.*

"Are you all right, dear, you seem a bit flustered, and you seem to have a few scratches." Em looked at my forehead and touched her own to indicate where she meant. I felt above my right eyebrow and could feel some abrasions. There was no hiding them. I turned over my hand, and bruises were forming on my wrist.

"I had a bit of a tumble this morning, missed a step, landed on my hand, and . . . I didn't realize how much I'd scratched my head." Em looked at Henry with concern in her eyes, but whether it was concern for my fall or concern about whether they should have let me into their home, I wasn't sure. I was hurting, but the main thing was to keep the weirdness out of this situation; I wanted Em and Henry to keep me here, wanted to stay safe in their homey world, which transcended time and space, and even time travel. They were a port in a storm, a candle in the night when all others have blown out. And here they were, not knowing me, and I teetered on the edge of their welcome, needed them to pull me closer.

With the paper and pencil to anchor me and occupy my hands, I decided to get on with the interview, hoping to put them at ease. I asked them questions and made notes and somehow did all that while watching the faces of two dear people, younger than I could possibly remember them. All their old habits and quirks were like stitches that held the essence of them together, and it felt comical, as though I were watching someone do a very good impression of someone I knew really well. And Em, sweet Em, who had died ten years ago. The way she fussed over Henry, and touched his hand, and ended each sentence of her own with a "Didn't we, Henry?" or "Isn't that right, Henry?" as though he were an integral part of her truth; things weren't real unless they were confirmed by Henry. I knew how she felt, I still sometimes felt that way myself; his presence such a sturdy, reassuring comfort, now as then.

My piece of paper was full of quotes and information about bowling that I had barely any recollection of writing down. Em went to make more tea, and I asked if I could use the bathroom. I walked up the stairs on legs made of lead, trailing my hand over the bare wallpaper that only needed to wait two years before becoming a gallery of memories of me, a map of my progress from age eight onward. I flicked the old hook-and-eye latch of the bathroom door and sat on the closed toilet lid. The doll that covered the extra toilet roll made me smile and shake my head: basically a Barbie doll's upper body atop a big knitted dress that kept the toilet roll dust-free. I held her on my lap and tried to absorb the facts. The attic, the box, the past, my mother, myself, and now Em and Henry, me drinking their tea, using their toilet. I was just doing normal stuff now. But I did not belong. I was a visitor in a place not open to visitors. I had walked through the staff only door, the no admission door, the local access only. And I wasn't staff. In a minute, someone was going to find me out and . . . do what? Kick me out of the seventies? Again I tried to keep my thoughts contained, like a bag full of kittens. The thoughts that urgently whispered: *Are you sure that box can get you back to Eddie and the girls?* I gripped the top of that bag tightly and urged the kittens to keep still.

I had a pee and washed my hands — the smell of Imperial Leather soap took me back thirty years as surely as my Space Hopper box — and pulled the chain to flush. As I unhooked the bathroom door, I heard a knock downstairs, and again voices that I couldn't quite make out, but whose sounds were of pleased surprise and "Come in, come in."

I descended the stairs slowly and peered over the banister, gasped when I saw the back of my coat, the little blue and green one, me as a child, and the back of my mother's head, chestnut hair shining.

I paused where I stood. Em had come alive with chatter, and I could hear her insistence that my mother and little Faye have something to eat and drink. By the time I had followed them into the living room, they were all seated comfortably and I was an intruder, one person too many for this room. I smiled, but I felt like I didn't know how to do that properly anymore. When I looked at my mother, I had to look away, because it was going to be either a quick glance or I would be a deer caught in her headlights.

"I'm just leaving," I said, trying to keep it nonchalant.

"Ah, yes, our *reporter,*" Em said, puffing her bosom out.

"Stay," said Henry, though Em bristled slightly. I looked into his eyes, and whether or not he saw pain and desperation in mine, I'll never know. But he said it again: "Stay. You've had a rough day," and he gently touched my head, then gripped my upper arms. "Have another cuppa. You can meet our charming neighbors." He beckoned me to sit down and then left the room.

"What's your name?" little Faye asked, sitting wide-eyed, upright, and overconfident like some kind of hippie Shirley Temple.

"Faye," I said, the word like glue in my mouth, because I realized I should have thought to change it when I was halfway through my single syllable. I could have been a Dorothy.

"Me too! That's my name," said Faye junior, bouncing up and down.

Em took little Faye by the hand, possessively, I thought. "Do you want one of these?" Em said, gesturing toward the little silver Christmas tree hung with foil-wrapped chocolate bells. Little Faye jumped up, and she and Em were kept busy for a few moments.

My mother stretched her hand out toward me, and her bracelets slid up her arm, jingling. "I'm Jeanie," she said.

I opened my mouth to speak, and there was not a drop of moisture to lubricate my words. "Faye," I said again, the word still so sticky it could barely leave my lips. I watched my hand get closer to my mother's with the same awareness as if I were reaching out to touch an electric fence. But she didn't seem to notice; she briefly gripped my hand and shook it.

"Great name," she said, smiling and nodding at little me in the corner by the Christmas tree. "What paper do you work for?"

"Oh, the *Gazette,* it's like a supplement in the free paper," I said, flustered from the lingering sensation of my mother's hand on mine. Jeanie frowned slightly, and thankfully lost interest instantly.

"I only read novels, poetry, and cookbooks, I'm afraid," she said with a dismissive, easy smile. "Never newspapers."

Em swung little Faye up onto her hip and sat down in a chair holding the child in her lap. I saw *me* as a child lean into the comfort of Em's embrace, licking chocolate from her tiny fingers, the other hand absent-mindedly rubbing the fabric of Em's housecoat. I had no recollection of this happening to me and stared at the interaction between them as though it were video evidence in a trial of my memories. I know I shouldn't expect to remember everything, I know that I don't, and yet how could I not have some notion of it, especially when I could see how much this closeness meant to Em. She loved me, even then, and as she hadn't been able to have children of her own, I could see what a gift I had been to her.

Henry dispelled my reverie, returning with a cotton bag that clinked and handing it to Jeanie. "Jam," he said, as she opened the handles and peered inside, "and some homemade bread, and there's some of Em's scones in there too."

"What's this?" Jeanie said, pulling a bottle of something a little way out of the bag.

"Crème de menthe," Em said. "We don't need it, I don't even know why we've got it, just thought you might like it."

"Em and Henry always give us lots of treats," said Jeanie to me, raising an eyebrow.

"We *worry* about you, love, that's all," said Em.

"We're very grateful," said Jeanie. "But I don't know how I'm going to get through that crème de menthe on my own."

"Maybe it could go into a recipe, mint creams or something?" suggested Em.

"I'll put it to good use, don't worry," said Jeanie with a wink in my direction. She seemed to feel a connection with me, merely because we were the closest pair — age-wise — in the room. I could see she thought of Henry and Em as old, and wanted to distance herself from them; be in a gang with me.

"Faye's interviewed us about bowling. She

was asking us about what there is for people to do round here," Henry said.

"*Nothing* is the easy answer to that," said Jeanie, looking pointedly at me. "All we can do is go to the park, or play in the garden. You got kids?"

"Uh-huh." I nodded. *Your grandchildren,* I thought.

"Then you know, there's nothing to do. Unless you're like Em and Henry, older and got no kids, then it's bowling, and what else, Henry? Darts, right? If you're rich, there's golf."

"Gardening," said Henry.

"Crosswords," said Em.

"Oh, please!" Jeanie said, laughing at them good-naturedly. And they took it well.

"One day when you're as old as we are, you'll love those things," said Henry, smiling indulgently at her.

"Never!" She drained her cup. "I'm sorry, but we really can't stay, we just wanted to return some of your jars," said Jeanie, standing up.

Em looked disappointed. But Henry put his hand on her shoulder, and went to give Jeanie a hug.

"I really need to go too," I said, determined to stick with my mother. "Thanks for everything." I shook Henry's hand, and

Em's. "I'll let you know when it's going to be in the paper," I added, holding my notes in the air.

"Which way are you?" Jeanie asked as we neared the end of the path leading from Em and Henry's door.

I waited until we all turned left and said, "Same way as you."

It was midmorning and the sun was weak as we walked slowly in the direction of Jeanie's house. Little Faye got out her paddle and ball again and ambled dreamily a few paces behind us, trying to get a rally of consecutive bounces going. I could hear her counting but was tuned in to my mother's patter about Em and Henry. Jeanie swung the bag languorously, the weight of it giving a satisfying long arc as she strolled. I almost wondered if she would let it go at the height of its curve. I heard a rumble of traffic in the distance, and started to feel uncomfortable that I couldn't see little Faye all the time. If it were my children, I would be holding their hands, or at least have them within grabbing distance at all times, and so I found myself turning to look at my younger self frequently, and certainly whenever I heard a car.

As we rounded a corner, I turned and

walked backward, my eyes fixed on my younger self's bobbing mess of curls. The small red ball hit the paddle and shot upward; her eyes were on it, and so were mine. She missed, and the ball hit the pavement and the corner of a small rock, which sent it springing up in an unexpected direction. It was like a tiny meteor flying peacefully through space, only to collide with another meteor with a silent *boom* and fly off peacefully in a direction it had never considered. Little Faye reached out for the ball, but it glanced off her hand, sending it in yet another curious trajectory, at the mercy of the universe. Toward the road.

The little girl — little me — stepped casually into the street to follow the ball. But at that moment I heard the sudden roar of an engine as a car rounded the corner, looming behind the child and heading straight for her. I gasped as time lurched from a peaceful slow-motion to a raggedly rapid full-speed at the flick of some switch. I lunged toward the child and threw myself at her. Car, me, child, in that order collided in the cosmos, but the greatest impact was not me with the car, which only clipped my hip, but me with the road. Child in my arms, the sounds I could hear were the short squeal of brakes and the screaming of a woman.

But actually, it was the screaming of two women, and one of them was me. The road had cut like hungry teeth through my sweater and into my flesh, leaving a deep graze up my left arm and grit embedded in my face where my head had slowed my skid along the abrasive surface. Plus I had an instinctive and powerful grip on this six-year-old child, a grip I was making with a wrist that hurt like hell.

"Oh my God oh my God thank you thank you thank you," exclaimed my mother, as she flung herself upon us and peeled back my arms to see her child, cocooned and safe within, eyes wide like a small animal.

"Are you all right, baby?" my mother said.

"I think so," I said, assuming in the moment that she was talking to me.

"She smells like you," said my younger self, and I knew it was the sweater I'd taken, which smelled of my mother's perfume.

A man was standing over us: the driver. His shadow moved around a bit and there were apologies and the smell of smoke, and the twisting of a foot stamping out a cigarette butt on the road; apart from that I wasn't particularly conscious of him. I couldn't see him, I only had eyes for my mother. He drove away.

"You saved her life," my mother said, her words like a rush of wind. "And you're hurt." She gazed deep into my eyes with gratitude and concern; her fingers gently brushed over my forehead and cheek, and I could barely feel the pain when I compared it to the wonder of her touch. I almost forgot how to breathe. She held out her hand to help me up and — stunned — I let her heave me to my feet.

"I think you better come with us, my place must be closer than yours. You're not in a good way," she said, peering into my face, as though she realized she'd lost something there and was trying to find it.

And as we walked in the direction of her house I knew *all* the pain was worth it — more, if necessary. Plus, I might even have saved my own life. How fortuitous was that?

CHAPTER 6

My mother's hands waved in the air, reliving the position of me, the position of the car, analyzing all the what-ifs. Her voice broke and she stopped, cupping little Faye's face in her hands. She looked at me, and all the what-might-have-beens swam in her eyes.

"How can I ever repay you?" she said, barely audible.

"There's no need," I said.

I could have explained that my gain from preventing my younger self from being hit by a car was at least as great as hers. But I just let it tickle me, in a mind-boggling sort of way.

My mother took a deep breath and smiled. "We're okay," she said, as though reassuring herself of the truth of it. She chattered away as we walked, and I listened, mopping up her words like a piece of bread in the gravy. Her tone was familiar, at once calm and excited, like that of an adult telling a child a story that promises adventure. She told me what we would do when we got to her place, that she would look at my cuts and make some tea, and she thought she ought to run me a bath.

"It'll help get the grit out." She looked closely at my face again, and my arm, and grimaced. "I'll see to that when we're home, I'm a good nurse."

"You're a nurse!" I said.

"Not a real one, just a good pretend one," she said. "We'll take a look at it, and if it's really bad, I suppose we ought to get you to a hospital."

"Mummy doesn't trust hospitals, she says they make you sicker." Little Faye slipped her hand into mine and I felt something like an electric shock run through me. In that moment I remembered the stories where you shouldn't let your past self see your current self, otherwise something would happen, something bad. Ah well, I would have to discover the rules for myself, and hopefully not break any that mattered.

"Well, yes, I think that can happen, you can go to the hospital with one thing, and come out with something even worse," I said pulling a silly frightened expression at little Faye, and wondering if my mother's chest infections could have been helped if only she'd gone to a hospital. She gave me a sideways glance.

"It does happen," said Jeanie in a low voice, suddenly serious.

"What are we going to do?" I said, looking at little Faye. "We have the same name and we're going to get all muddled up."

She giggled. "I could be Faye One and you can be Faye Two, as you came along second."

Jeanie laughed. "Well, *technically,* she came along first," she said, nodding in my direction and winking at me as she had back at Em and Henry's. I'd forgotten my mother's winks, but they were so familiar that I must have kept winks in cold storage in my mind. I had also filed away the habit she had of sweeping her hair to one side and over her shoulder.

"We could call you by your middle name," said little Faye. "What is it?"

I started to say "Susannah" without thinking, but stopped myself just in time and said "Sarah" instead. It would be too much of a coincidence to have the same middle name.

"We have the same initials!" said little Faye in a reverent whisper, as though she had found treasure.

"Wow!" I said, bobbing down in front of

her. "We could be twins!"

"Well, she looks more like you than me," said Jeanie.

"Do you want to call me by my middle name then?" I asked. "I don't mind."

"No, I'll call you Faye, we won't get confused. And thank you for saving my life. I have a feeling we're going to be friends, don't you?"

"Friends? Me and you?" I pretended to look uncertain about that for a moment, then took her hand again and smiled. "I guarantee it."

"I have a top just like this!" Jeanie said, holding up the torn black sweater I'd taken from her drawer earlier that morning. "Mind you, I suppose everyone does." We were back at the house, in my mother's bedroom. I had taken off all my clothes and put on one of her dressing gowns. She'd asked me whether I wanted tea first or a bath, and I chose tea. But she'd suggested I get out of my clothes and into something warm straightaway. I was worried she'd see the boots — her boots — so I quickly put them in the bottom of her wardrobe; everything else I laid on her bed. My jeans were ripped, and absolutely filthy.

"You can have some of my clothes, after

your bath. I think these are ruined, don't you?" She frowned again at the sweater and then bundled it up, ready to throw away.

I nodded and gazed at my mother. I wanted to launch into a flurry of questions, ask her all the things you wish you'd asked your mother before it was too late. But I didn't want her to think I was nuts or nosy; I wanted her to like me. Also, that *normalness,* just being around her, was addictive. It was the luxury of taking a privilege for granted. Despite the events that had preceded this moment, I was wallowing in just being around this woman — a woman, frankly, I did not know. A list of facts about her didn't seem important just then.

I guess it's like this when you get out of prison and see a loved one for the first time in years. You feel a frantic urge to make up for lost time, but it's not doable, so you just ask if they want a drink and inquire how they are, as if you'd just seen them yesterday. A person can't stay in a perpetual state of excitement, no matter how exhilarating or profound the situation is. At some point, maybe quite soon after the monumental moment, the world settles back into a reasonably normal state. I thought of sand in a clear bottle of water, being shaken so the grains flew about and spun, only to settle before long into the place where they started at the bottom. We all return to some equilibrium — it's natural, homeostasis. I guess the moment we stop finding an inner balance in response to extraordinary events is the moment we go mad. But please don't think for a moment that the gravity, the sheer enormity of what was happening, escaped me.

And anyway, you know, I didn't necessarily want all the *big* questions answered. Not yet. It was the little things that fascinated me, like how she bit the corner of her thumb when she was pondering something. How she liked to cup Faye's face when Faye was telling her something. How sometimes she would interrupt Faye when she was talking, to tell her she loved her. "Mummy," Faye would say, "*listen* to me!"

And I was learning how my mother treated a stranger; I was seeing her through the eyes of an adult. And that was a new experience for me.

We sat at the kitchen table. I traced with my finger the outlines of small pink flowers and tendrils of green that decorated the tablecloth, and my mother dabbed my face with warm water and Dettol disinfectant on some cotton. The concentration in her eyes allowed mine to roam her features. I watched her hands working and urged myself to dedicate all details to memory so that I could, in the future, recall the white half-moons at the base of her nails. I observed her face as though I would be quizzed about it later: eye color; the flare of her nostrils when she sniffed; her perfect ears, with dangling silver chains in them; the peach tone of her skin; the freckle southeast of her left eye; the healthy white teeth and big easy smile. She smiled as if it was easier to smile than for her face to be at rest. She spoke as she worked, lifting my hand to examine it more closely, her face animated. She looked as though she were talking directly to my hand, and it gave me the opportunity to simply drink her in.

She poured tea. "You said you have children?"

"Yes. Two girls, Esther and Evie."

"Good girls or bad girls?" She winked again. My mother was asking about the grandchildren she would never meet.

"Esther is so sensible, she's like a teacher at home," I said. "She sets our dining room chairs out as if we're in a little schoolroom and makes me and Evie sit in them and calls the roll, and asks us questions. She even checks our fingernails like an old-fashioned schoolmarm, and tuts at us disapprovingly.

"Evie is so funny. She looks like an angel," I continued, "but she burps like a beer-drinking dockworker. She likes to shock old people by belching loudly when they've already said what a little darling she is. She's younger than Esther, but will thump anyone who hurts her sister's feelings."

Jeanie smiled wide. "I wish I had a sister," she said.

"Do you have any brothers?" I asked, knowing the answer already.

"No," she said, "I have no one."

"No family at all? Mum and dad?" I knew there was nobody, but I didn't know why.

"No one." She got up and walked to the fridge and opened it, sighing as though the emptiness there were part of the wider emptiness of her family. She swung the door shut and leaned against it. Her slender figure cut a striking image, her flowing skirts and floppy top not doing anything to hide her almost frail frame. "They're dead. Long time."

"How?"

"I was very young, my mum went into the hospital with an illness and never came out, she died; and then apparently my dad got sick straightaway, and he died too."

"Fuck," I said.

86

"My thoughts exactly. I've got a couple of old photos of them, but I honestly can't remember them. When I think of them, I just see the photos, not really them, and when I took Faye to the hospital once, the smell — oh God, did that remind me of them. And not in a good way, just reminded me of loss, confusion."

"And you were fostered?" I said.

"Yeah, just one place after another. You can't grow up quick enough when that happens to you, you just need to survive long enough to get out, and then, well, get out. And that's what I did.

"Anyway, Miss Journalist. How about you, where are your parents?"

My throat tightened to stop me blurting out anything ridiculous. "No brothers or sisters. My mum's around." I stared at her meaningfully. "I don't know my dad."

"What's your mum like?"

"Oh, I don't know her very well, which is such a shame. I don't see her very often."

"Pah," Jeanie said, batting her hand as if at an imaginary fly and pulling out a chair to sit down in front of me.

"What?"

"You don't need to *know* her, don't worry about that."

"What do you mean?" I said.

"People all make the same mistake, and I've given this a lot of thought." She took a long sip of tea and assumed the posture of an expert on the witness stand. "You cannot know your parents," she said. "And so you mustn't waste time thinking it's the most important thing. You can spend your whole life trying to know them. It's a *total* waste of time! Only three things matter when it comes to your parents." She stopped dramatically and drank more tea, very slowly.

"And they are . . . ?"

Her eyes sparkled. "So glad you asked. The first, most important thing is to know that your parents love you. Some parents go wrong here and assume that their children know it. But you have to be clear, tell your children you love them, and how much, and why. And if you're the child and you don't feel loved, you can forget bothering to know them. Love is the baseline."

I thought of little Faye upstairs, and my eyes went to the ceiling, where we could hear her moving about and playing in her room.

Jeanie pointed upward. "That girl knows I love her; if she knows nothing else, then she's going to be okay with me."

My eyes filled in an instant and my chin

creased up. I tipped my head and clasped my hand over my mouth to hold in a sob, shaking my head to deny the flow of tears, to keep back the flood. But the cork in the hole in my heart popped out and with it came salt water and emotion like lava, hot and spilling down my face.

"Oh, you poor thing, come here," Jeanie said, coming over and putting her arms around me. It was an awkward sideways hug, and she wasn't having it. She pulled my chair closer and put her arms fully around me, then drew back to look at my face and wipe away the tears with her thumbs. But there were too many. She held me close again, and I let myself fall into her arms, found a spot that fit perfectly, me inside my mother's embrace, my damp face in the crook of her neck.

"I'm sorry," I said, through a clogged nose and into her hair, which I was making wet.

"It's okay," she said, and held me tighter to prove that she didn't mind that a stranger was crying all over her, getting snot on her top.

After a while she pulled away, keeping a reassuring grip on my shoulders. "Is this about your mother?" she said.

I nodded.

"Shall we stop talking about this?" she

asked, almost a whisper.

"No," I said, my voice rough at the edges. "I want to know what the second important thing with parents is."

My mother returned to her seat and held my hand across the table.

"After love, the second thing that matters is just being with them. Time. Simple. Love, then time."

"Some people can't do that, don't get the chance for time with their parents," I said, sniffing wetly.

"I know," she said, "I didn't. And I don't know for sure that my parents loved me. I assume they did, but not really knowing hurts me."

"Time and love," I said.

"Yes, but not in that order. Love first, then time. There's no point in spending time together if the love isn't there. If you only have one of those things, love is the king. And that's it, that's all it really comes down to, the rest is all consequences of love and time, like protection and security and all that stuff. It's all important, but it's off-shoots."

"You said there were three things."

She batted the imaginary fly again. "Oh, that," she said. "Well, the third thing is getting to know your parents as people."

"You said that was a waste of time."

"I know, but the compulsion to do it is so strong, you really can't ignore it."

"That's a conundrum," I said, and we both laughed.

"You can only know your parents as parents, you can't know them as anything else. There's like a barrier to knowing your parents beyond that role."

"What about if you know they're your parent, but they don't know it?"

She frowned and puffed her cheeks out, seeming to think about it, then exhaled. "In what world?"

"Just hypothetically," I said. "Let's say you meet your mum and you know she's your mum, but she doesn't know you're her daughter. Can you get to know her as a person then?"

"Nope," Jeanie said, in a heartbeat.

"Because . . . ?"

"*Because,* the daughter still knows she's the daughter. She can only experience the mother as a mother, not as anything else. The mother thing is too strong, it's an impenetrable wall of unknowability. You can know some stuff, but you can't know her beyond knowing her as a parent, and that's a different kind of knowing. A sort of not-knowing. Get it?"

"Uh . . . yeah, I think I do."

"Heavy," she said, putting a lot of emphasis on both syllables and sounding like a doped-up hippie.

"Yeah, but that's okay," I said, "I can do heavy."

Jeanie took both my hands in hers and squeezed them. "You all right?" she said.

"Yeah," I said, and I was, at that moment I really think I was.

"Hey, neither of us has siblings, you want to adopt?"

"Huh?" I said.

"Adopt each other?" she said. "You wanna be my sister from a different mister?"

"Well, yes, but . . . we've only just met," I said.

"I already know things about you that it can take years to know. And I can tell you've got a good heart. Plus you threw yourself in front of a car for my daughter."

My face felt hot and my heart skipped. I thought of Cassie and Clem and how they were like sisters to me, how important a bond that was, and how maybe — for my mother — that was the kind of ally she needed. It didn't really matter what Cassie and Clem thought, yet I was certain they would like my mother if they saw us together now, and would agree with me that she was in need of a sister.

"Sisters," I said, and Jeanie released my hands momentarily, spat on her palm, and then gripped my hand, giving it one hard shake.

Upstairs I heard little Faye again. "She seems like a nice kid," I said, keen to find out what my mother would say about me as a child. I was fascinated and I was after compliments, I don't deny it.

Jeanie sighed and rested her chin on her hands, looking wistfully into the middle distance. "I couldn't ask for a better daughter. I feel like it's her and me against the rest of the world sometimes. And I feel like we're winning! I love her so much, I want to consume her. I want to be her, so I can feel what it's like to be loved *this* much," and she held her fists to her heart.

I stared at my mother, held my breath as she said these words, felt a tear slip over the edge and down my cheek. Jeanie put her hand over mine.

"You've had a hell of a shock today, what with the car, and you fell over earlier as well, didn't you say? Then there's me dragging up your past." She clapped her hands once, changing the tempo of the conversation. "Well, if we're going to be sisters, we need to get up-to-date, because we actually *can* get to know each other. Let's do Twenty Questions, okay?"

I wiped my nose with the back of my hand and nodded. Jeanie pulled a clean, folded tissue from up her sleeve and handed it to me; it was warm.

I asked first. Jeanie's favorite food was sticky toffee pudding; favorite color: blue; favorite thing to do: go to the seaside to play the penny slots and paddle and get fish and chips; favorite novel: *Rebecca;* if she had a lot of money she would take Faye to Spain for a holiday and buy a good TV; she sometimes felt lonely; she missed having a man around; worst job in the house: vacuuming; favorite things to do with Faye: bake, play cards, and hula-hoop. Her favorite subject at school was art; she was scared of spiders and heights; she got a chest infection every year; she had no family except Faye; she liked gin but not vodka; she knew the poem "The Owl and the Pussycat" all the way through by heart; she could cure hiccups; she'd stolen a pair of shoes once, leaving her old ones in the shop; if she could spend one day with her mother again, she'd spend it talking and holding hands; she hoped for her daughter that one day she would be happily married and be blessed with children; and the hardest thing she'd ever done was walk away from the love of her life.

"Hang on, what?" I said.

"No more questions for now." She wagged her finger. "It's my turn. You've asked me twenty. You'll have to wait if you want to know more." Jeanie lowered her voice. "And I can't talk about it in front of Faye, she doesn't know about him."

At that moment Faye came into the room, and slapped a pack of cards on the table. I recognized the image of animals on the front, Happy Families. I love that game; the illustrations of the families on those cards reside in the roots of my childhood.

"Shall we play?" she said.

Jeanie looked at me, eyebrows raised, and I said, "Why not?" Finding out what twenty questions my mother would ask me, and asking more about the "love of her life," would have to wait.

In fact, it was going to have to wait quite some time. We played a few games of Happy Families. I have always loved the Rabbit Family and Squirrel Family the best; they're so pretty. My mother, it turned out, had a soft spot for the Frog and Hedgehog Families, because nobody else seemed to love them, so according to her they needed more love. I don't remember who won the most games, or how many times we played, but I can still see my young face laughing and shouting, the good-natured mock-disappointment and accusations of "Cheat!" when someone was winning too often. I remember being conscious of the way I played with my hair and pressed my nostril with my finger when I was thinking, the same way little Faye did. I remember feeling caught in a moment in time that existed unattached to any other, like a bubble in space. I remember watching my mother smiling, laughing, *living,* and love caught in my throat.

The day darkened, and Jeanie switched on the kitchen light.

"Do you need to get home?" she said. "Will your husband be worried?"

"Not yet," I said. "But he'll worry soon. I better think about leaving." I didn't know what would happen next or even if I would be able to get home. My palms were suddenly damp at the thought of what might or might *not* happen when I got into the Space Hopper box again. And if I left my mother now, would I ever see her again? What if it was the last time? Again.

I longed to hug her with the luxury of knowing for certain that I would see her soon, or talk on the phone. I longed for a

96

telephone that spanned the space and time between us. Instead, I would hold her now in the knowledge that it might be my last chance. It was worse than not knowing, and yet, there was hope. I pushed myself away from the table, and she stood too and opened her arms to me.

"Who knows how this day would have ended if it hadn't been for you," she said softly as she embraced me. And she didn't let go. "I'm blessed that you came into our lives, and I have a good feeling about you, Faye. You're a kindred spirit."

I said nothing, my face in her hair.

"Will you come and see us soon?"

"Yes," I said, remembering that somewhere I had read that a promise I might not be able to keep was better than no promise at all.

"You okay to get home?"

"I'll be fine," I said. Then looked at my feet.

"Where are your shoes?"

"I don't know," I said, pretending to look round for them.

Jeanie brought me a pair of her brown calf-length boots, and I pulled them on.

"I'll bring them back," I said.

I gave little Faye a hug, and after the thank-yous for the clothes and everything, I left. The memory of walking away from that house as a child, knocking on Em and Henry's door, and never seeing my mother again replayed in my head as I took one step after another away from my mother's arms. I looked at my feet in my mother's boots and felt I was following in footsteps no daughter should have to take more than once in her life. Leaving behind a mother I loved, maybe forever. And the tears streamed down my face.

CHAPTER 7

I felt sick about getting in the box again. What if I couldn't get home? I desperately needed to see my girls. Was Eddie wondering where I was? Would he have called the police? Had I disappeared from the present day while I was here, or was I lying unconscious in the attic? But that would mean I was in a coma. I wondered how much time had passed, whether it would be the same there, or a different amount. If it were the same, then I wasn't sure how I'd explain my absence. But when the children in *The Lion, the Witch, and the Wardrobe* disappear, they live their whole lives in Narnia, then return home to England as though no time at all has passed. I started to consider all sorts of various dreadful possibilities: like getting home to find that Eddie was an old man, telling me about our grown-up daughters and their lives I had missed.

I pondered all this as I sat on a low wall

behind a hedge, waiting for the cover of complete darkness. But the immediate vital question was only this: Would the Space Hopper box take me home? I could only deal with one mammoth philosophical conundrum at a time, and right now, despite the churning in my stomach that came from leaving my mother behind, I was even sicker at the thought of not getting home. What would I do if I stood in that box and nothing happened? Maybe it would take me somewhere completely different, to a world somewhere between the only two I knew.

And I wondered how much it would hurt.

When everyone in the street had closed their curtains, I crept back to my mother's shed. I felt for the door and unbolted it, but couldn't see what I was doing, and kicked over the bucket of tools and nails in the dark, before carefully feeling for the edges of the box; I didn't want to step on the side and damage it any more.

I stood in the box. I waited. Nothing happened.

"Please, God, make this work, please take me home, please, please, please take me home," I whispered.

I don't know if my words had any effect, but as I said "home," it felt as though someone grabbed my left foot and yanked me down. The bottom of the box — the ground — well, it was like they didn't exist. After the uncomfortable first pull, the rest of me came through smoothly.

When I went through the box, there was pressure on my ankle as though it were being gripped, and I was spinning round and round on what felt like a horizontal plane.

Like a fairground ride, at first I could deal with the sensation (if not the actual fear), but it became more and more intense, faster. I may have yelled "Stop!" But I can't be sure. I don't think my lips could move. I was definitely thinking *Stop the ride, I want to get off!*

And it did stop: no gradual slowing, no easing me back into the atmosphere I was accustomed to. No. Whatever — *whoever* — was gripping my ankle let go and I went spinning into space, finally releasing a scream into the void. It was dark and the air was cool, and I continued to spin as I propelled through nothingness. I was just beginning to wonder if this was it — if my life would be spent whirling through space between the past and the present — when I "landed." Not an elegant landing; not what you'd want if you were doing a dismount in gymnastics. My spinning momentum was halted when my body met the wall of the attic.

I was more or less in the box, though I had crushed it and broken one side again. And I was in a messy heap, cramped up against the end of the attic, hurting as you would if you were thrown against a wall.

Relief flooded over me as I heard Eddie's voice from below. I detected concern as he called, "Hello?" up the hatch. I didn't know at that moment what his concern was, because I didn't know how long had passed in his world during my visit to my mother. If no time had passed, Eddie would likely have heard a loud noise, removed his headphones, noticed the loft ladder was down, and wondered what I was doing up there.

But time *had* moved on, as it happens, and he was concerned for my whereabouts. I'd spent about twelve hours with my mother in the past. But arrival time back home with Eddie, it turned out, was three hours on from when I'd left. Long enough to puzzle him, he told me, but not long enough for him to call the police. Apparently Eddie had stayed at his computer for another two hours, but when *Mary Poppins* finished, the girls came in to him, climbing into his lap and singing "Let's Go Fly a Kite." He decided to stop studying and only then noticed I wasn't around. Although Eddie is capable of cooking dinner, I normally do it, and it was teatime, and I hadn't said anything about going out. He'd looked for a note on the fridge, he said, then rang my mobile (which vibrated across the kitchen counter), and then put some fish sticks in the oven and played a quick game of hide-and-seek with the girls.

He told me that later he stopped with surprise and relief on the landing when he saw the attic ladder was down, and climbed up to find out what I was doing up there; but it was empty, and then he was confused, he said, disappointed that I wasn't there, but not overly worried. What confused him even more was spotting my flip-flops by the front door, which I almost always put on if I'm just popping out.

So Eddie wasn't overly anxious, but he'd given himself a deadline for worry and planned to start calling my friends if it got to 7 p.m. and I still wasn't back. When Eddie heard the thump in the attic, he was on edge because he'd already looked there and knew it was empty. So, the concern in his voice was a small fear of the unknown.

"Hello?" he called. His voice entered the attic like an echo from the past.

"Eddie, it's me." My throat was dry, but

my relief equaled my pain. I was home. *Home*-home. In fact, scrap what I just said: my relief outweighed my physical pain by a long way. I would see my daughters again.

Eddie climbed the ladder and poked his head through. I could see his knitted expression clearly, but his eyes hadn't adjusted to the dark and he squinted in my general direction. "Faye, is that you?"

"Of course."

"What are you doing up here? Where have you been? Come down."

"I can't move." My voice sounded like sandpaper, my throat raw from screaming as I spun through space. I felt utterly exhausted. I could have slept right there. "Can you put the girls to bed and then come and get me? I'll wait here."

"No. What's going on? Just come down, the girls are in the living room."

I tried to move but was incredibly slow. I thought I had splinters in my forehead where I'd skidded into the wall of the loft; my head had really taken a pounding. It took me so long to move that Eddie just came up and got me.

"Have you broken something?" he said, crouching in front of me, using the light from his mobile phone to illuminate me.

"The light bulb," I said.

"No, I mean you, have you hurt yourself?"

"A few bruises, some scratches. I'm all right, I think."

"How are we going to do this?" he said, grappling to get his arms around my waist in the tight space. He got me so I was sitting on the edge of the hatch with him standing below me, then encouraged me down the ladder a little way before carrying me like a baby into the bedroom.

"What the hell have you done?" he said.

As I lay on the bed, the present day seemed brighter and more colorful than the past, and fresher, less cluttered. Then again, the seventies have always seemed a bit untidy in my memory. It was still light outside, late July here, and the evenings were long. I could hear the girls laughing, and Eddie looked out the window.

"They're in the garden in their nighties," he said.

"I love that."

"Me too."

"I don't want them to see me," I said, touching my forehead. It was bleeding.

"You look like you've been dragged through a thornbush," he said. "I don't understand — I looked in the loft and you weren't there, you weren't in the house.

Then an almighty bang and there you are in the attic."

I didn't speak because I couldn't say anything that would make any sense. *I've traveled back in time, and it was a bumpy ride.* Could I have said that?

"Where have you been? Did you go out, get hurt, and then get into the attic? I mean, how did you get into the attic when you could barely get out of it? Are those your boots? Did you find them up there?"

I opened my mouth to speak, and shut it again.

"What's going on?" I could hear anger in his voice.

The tears slipped out of my eyes and I turned my head so the pillow blotted them. I looked at Eddie as he knelt by the bed.

"I haven't done anything wrong," I said. Which was the truth.

Then I lied.

"I went up to put my box somewhere safe, and I hit my head and must have fallen, knocked myself out."

Eddie just stared at me. "What was all the noise I heard?"

I shrugged.

"You've done more than just bump your head, you're a mess."

He looked at me the way he looks at one

of the girls when she says she hasn't had any chocolate milk, except there's a line of it right across her top lip. He pulled me into his arms. "You always tell me everything," he said into my hair.

Will you do something for me? Next time you're alone with a person whose opinion you respect, or someone you love and care for, I want you to tell them that you've been time-traveling into the past, that you have met with a deceased loved one from back then, and met your younger self. I want you to tell them that while you were there you got hit by a car, played cards, drank tea, and then returned home via a box. Do this for me, and don't make a joke of it; tell them you're serious. You'll be at an advantage because it hasn't actually happened to you, and you won't need them to believe in you, you won't be desperate to share your unbelievable reality, because it won't be true. But if it *were* true, think about how they would react.

I'm guessing at best they'd laugh it off. But at worst?

What would it be like, at worst, if you kept insisting it was true? Soon enough I think you'd see a little less of that person; they'd glance at you sideways, whisper about you to someone else, and steer clear.

How could I tell Eddie? If I told him what had really happened, he would think I was making up a stupid story to hide some horrible truth. Or he would think I'd lost my mind.

And then there was the possibility that he might believe me — I mean, he *might.* After all, he believes in God, and that takes faith. He might have faith in me. And if he believed me, he'd want to protect me; he wouldn't want me injuring myself and ending up lost who-knows-where in the dark spaces between there and here. I think he might destroy the box for my own safety, and I can't let that happen. Because being safely home again, all I could think about was my return trip to see my mother.

Therefore the truth wasn't a good option.

But who was I kidding? He was never going to believe me.

Eddie was cross with me, I could tell. He read to the children and tucked them in. Meanwhile, I kept a safe distance, evading his questions and suspicious looks. I got into bed, and lay there, looking at my mother's boots, which were standing near the wall, and drifted off to the sound of my family winding down for the night.

It felt like only seconds later that I woke to Eddie brushing a strand of hair away from my face. It was dark outside, a lamp was on, and he was gazing at me.

"Is my photo still in your office?" I said, feeling uncomfortable that it was not in my wallet, but exposed and free to be picked up or moved.

"I guess so," he said, not moving.

"Can you get it?" I said. But he just stared at me. "Please."

He sighed as he got up, and when he returned I almost snatched it out of his hand, and stared at it. There was the tree, there was the box, in the best condition it was ever going to be. I had been there, in the photo, *just now.* I shook my head, my thoughts spinning about in there like a bag of marbles that had been tipped out and were bouncing off each other, rolling in one direction, then hitting something and going off in another. When you look at a photo that you remember being taken, you remember the moments around it: the argument that erupted as soon as the smiles could be dropped; the dispersing of people from the group to the bar, the garden, or the bedroom; or the moment just after the photograph was taken — that moment when everyone relaxed, laughed for real, and looked their absolute best, but the camera had already clicked and captured the lesser moment: the one before. But a picture of a truly happy child is different. I tapped the photograph as though my genuine, smiling face were not imprisoned in time and on paper, as though my younger self were on the other side of a pane of glass, reachable, tangible. Eddie slowly took the photo from me and placed it on my bedside table, where my eyes followed it.

Eddie touched my cheek to turn my face to his. "I've run you a bath," he said. I went to get up, but my limbs felt stiff when I tried to move them. "Let me," he said, and peeled back the duvet, gently straightened me out, and carefully removed my clothes.

"I don't recognize this top," he said.

I was mute.

He sighed. Resigned. "Okay."

When I was naked, Eddie picked me up as he had before and carried me to the bathroom, lowering me into the tub, for my second bath of the day.

The warm water was heavenly. Eddie drew the little wooden stool to the side of the bath and sat on it; we had bought it a few years ago to save our backs when bathing the children. He leaned his elbows on the rim of the bath and stared at me. I kept shutting my eyes, unable to keep eye contact with him. He didn't speak, but took a sponge and some body wash and washed me, lifting my legs out of the water and sponging my feet and knees. He was more careful the higher up he went and dabbed at my face, which stung.

"How did you do this?" he said. I think by now he hardly expected an answer. "Can you talk?"

"Yes."

"Should I call the police?"

"No!" My body jerked in the water as I tried to sit up.

"Okay, okay," he said.

"I don't want to talk about it," I said. "Nothing's happened."

"Well, if nothing's happened, there's nothing to talk about." Eddie exhaled slowly and looked into the distance before refocusing on me. "I'm thinking that whatever it is, you think it will hurt me. And you refuse to lie to me, so you can't even make up a good story. In the absence of feeling you can tell me the truth, you're telling me nothing."

"Is that okay?" I said. "Can we leave it at that?"

"No, it's not okay. I love you, I want to know what's going on. We always talk." He rubbed some dirt off my cheek with his

111

thumb, his brown eyes creased and intent. "But you're here, and you're safe, and whatever happened to you didn't kill you, although it looks like it nearly did."

"I'm not having an affair, I'm not seeing anyone," I said. Why I said that, I don't know. I guess I hoped at least to reassure him that there was nothing obvious to worry about. "No one tried to hurt me, it was an accident."

He frowned, and I wished I could just shut up. I was making no sense, not even to my own ears.

"You'd need a lot of faith to believe in what happened to me today," I said, vowing to myself to stop talking now.

"Now, faith I'm pretty good at," he said.

"Not me," I said. "I wish I could believe in God, but I don't."

He looked at me as though searching for words in a word search, trying to make sense among the jumble of letters. Sometimes a thought is so strong that it feels like people can read it above your head in a speech bubble, or in subtitles, but it's just as well they can't.

"You do a lot of things that God would like," he said.

"But I don't believe in him," I repeated.

Eddie closed his eyes. I saw the gentlest of

smiles light his face, and I knew a good memory had passed behind his lids. He opened his eyes and looked at me. "The day Esther was born, I remember you held her in your arms and said, 'She doesn't even know us, and yet we love her more than anything in the world.' Do you remember that?"

I nodded. The moment was as fresh to me as though it had happened yesterday. We were in the hospital and she was in my arms, bundled in a white blanket, her tiny face screwed up like the world had a bad smell, and Eddie encircled us both. In the boundless universe, we were a very tiny, very important speck.

"It doesn't matter if you don't believe in God," Eddie said, drawing my fingers to his lips and kissing them. "Because he believes in you." He kissed my fingers again. "When he needs you to believe in him, he'll give you a sign."

I felt a surge of overwhelming love for my husband. My chest felt tight with a cry of emotion that I wanted to let out, something guttural that had everything to do with him, and the children and my mother and me. Me as a child whom I had seen and touched, and saved. The *me* I so pitied because she was going to lose her mother soon. My mother, for whom my heart ached with the pain of what she was about to miss out on, the pain of losing her the first time, the pain of leaving her today. Could God be involved in anything that was happening to me? If he was going to give me a sign, then surely this was it?

And yet I battled against any reasoning that said God was there for me. It was easier to think of my journey as a split in the fabric of time, or more like a passage *through* time that I had accidentally found the entrance to. If I accepted that God would let me know when he needed me to believe in him, then that would be like saying I do believe in God, just *not right now,* and I'm sorry, but I just couldn't do it. I wanted to, but couldn't. I touched Eddie's cheek. "Eddie, I think it's crazy that you believe in God."

"Tell me why."

"Because there's no proof, you can't see him. And the rabbits. *Watership Down,*" I said, feeling weighted down with drowsiness. I was overcome with the events of the day and wanted to sleep, just wanted oblivion. What I really wanted was to tell Eddie that I had been back in time, in fact fallen through time and landed hard and that's why I was injured, and that I had met my longed-for mother, and my younger self, and I wanted to ask him what it all meant and what I should do. Eddie always knew what to do.

"Well, I believe in lots of things I can't see, Genghis Khan, for instance," said Eddie, and I frowned, making the cuts in my face sting. "I believe that Jesus rose from the dead because he was the son of God. People there, at that time, saw him, and I trust in the things they wrote about that."

I decided to get out of the bath, and as I raised myself up Eddie grabbed a big towel and carefully dried me, patting my scraped shoulder and face, and tutting at the purple marks coming up around my ribs and arms.

"Anyway, what's this about *Watership Down*?" He wrapped the towel and his arms right round me and I leaned into his chest; the warmth of the steamy bathroom and the strength of my husband beneath my cheek were comforting.

"When I was a little girl," I said, my voice slightly muffled by the towel, "I believed in God, and when my mother died, I assumed she'd gone to heaven. I was about eighteen, I think, when I read *Watership Down,* and those rabbits believed in their own God. And I knew that there was no God for rabbits; it was a charming thought, but ridiculous. And I realized that if a higher being was looking down on me, and saw that I believed in God and heaven too, the higher being would think of me in the same way I thought of those rabbits. Deluded."

"Except that the *higher being* would presumably be like God," said Eddie.

"Only if you think of humans as gods compared to rabbits."

"Oh yeah," he said, putting an arm under my knees, lifting me again. "You're not the first person to query these things in this way. A lot of time and effort has gone into the study and debate of exactly this. Lots of people have written stuff about animals believing in their own kind of God, and a world beyond the one they see every day."

This was so sweetly distracting that I hoped Eddie would do what he often did, and carry me away on a train of thought that would remove me from my inner turmoil for a few miles of thoughtful contemplation. He would do beautiful sermons.

He took me back to bed, carefully pulled a baggy T-shirt over my head, and drew a sheet over me. "Wait here," he said. When he came back he was carrying a slim volume, light gray with a circle of thorns on the cover. He perched on the end of the bed. "Now, shut your eyes and just listen," he said. "Rupert Brooke wrote this over a

hundred years ago, using fish in a stream to
look at the way humans want to believe in
something beyond their immediate surroundings. It's called *Heaven:*

Fish (fly-replete, in depth of June,
Dawdling away their wat'ry noon)
Ponder deep wisdom, dark or clear,
Each secret fishy hope or fear.
Fish say, they have their Stream and
    Pond;
But is there anything Beyond?
This life cannot be All, they swear,
For how unpleasant, if it were!
One may not doubt that, somehow, Good
Shall come of Water and of Mud;
And, sure, the reverent eye must see
A Purpose in Liquidity.
We darkly know, by Faith we cry,
The future is not Wholly Dry.
Mud unto mud! — Death eddies near —
Not here the appointed End, not here!
But somewhere, beyond Space and Time.
Is wetter water, slimier slime!
And there (they trust) there swimmeth
    One
Who swam ere rivers were begun,
Immense, of fishy form and mind,
Squamous, omnipotent, and kind;
And under that Almighty Fin,

The littlest fish may enter in.
Oh! never fly conceals a hook,
Fish say, in the Eternal Brook,
But more than mundane weeds are there,
And mud, celestially fair;
Fat caterpillars drift around,
And Paradisal grubs are found;
Unfading moths, immortal flies,
And the worm that never dies.
And in that Heaven of all their wish,
There shall be no more land, say fish.

I was close to sleep, and in my mind I saw rainbow-colored trout and neon minnows gliding in shallow water so clear I could see the pebbles beyond them on the riverbed, and I saw children's fingers picking up those pebbles and passing them to me. I tried to think that the fish were silly to think of a heaven of their own. Then I tried to visualize my ideal heaven — my own creation — and what would be in it, and I knew that there would be rivers and fish there. And as I floated into oblivion, I realized that fish don't need a heaven of their own, because if my heaven existed, then I would take them with me. And all the rabbits too.

CHAPTER 8

The next few days I'd catch Eddie looking at me, the same way he sometimes looked at the crack in the plaster that ran from the corner of the fireplace to the corner of the ceiling. Except when he looked at me — a frown between his eyes over the top of his cup — he didn't say, "I really need to fix you." But I could tell he was thinking it, or something like it.

I was tired the way you're tired after exercising when you haven't done it for a long time — muscles protesting, every bone begging me to lie down — so that's what I did.

"Are Cassie and Clem coming over today?" Eddie said, as I shoved lunchboxes into bags and found the girl's school shoes. Every Monday after the school run, we ladies have coffee together, and I just knew he hoped I would talk to them, tell them what had happened to me, and then, if it was something serious, they'd make me talk to Eddie, or tell him themselves. I suppose most couples have those friends each person calls his or her own, the ones they would take with them in case of divorce. But Cassie and Clem — though mine — were loyal to Eddie and always had been. If he and I ever split up, we'd have to have joint custody, because I don't think they could give him up.

We'd all known each other since college days: they were in the same course as him — something financial — and when Eddie and I started dating they stepped in like two protective aunts. Before they became like sisters to me, I thought of them as Aunt Sponge and Aunt Spiker from Roald Dahl's *James and the Giant Peach,* though both infinitely better-looking and nicer than in the story. Clem was big and beautiful, as was everything else in her life — husband, house, and baby — while Cassie was tall and slender, with an ethereal look that we all agreed meant she could be related to aliens. She'd been stopped in the street before and offered modeling work, but said she preferred accountancy.

Now, in my experience, girls can bond over a lot of things, but periods, diets, and slagging off boyfriends were standard topics in most familiar female company. In those days, however, I was at a disadvantage, because the moment I said anything detrimental about Eddie, Cassie and Clem would start cooing and bustling like a couple of matronly pigeons, shooing me away from any notion that he could do wrong.

We were a lot older now and all with children, and the idea that Eddie was perfect had mellowed and shifted. They'd seen his temper flare up on the rare occasion, the odd bout of jealousy, and some choice swearing when we all got drunk; enough for them to realize that he was just a man after all. But still, they considered him a better man than most. Until he announced he wanted to be a vicar. They didn't like that.

So when Eddie was at work and I was back from dropping the girls at school, Cassie and Clem knocked on the door and breezed into my house as though they owned it. They kissed me on the cheek and pressed on through the hallway, continuing their conversation, as Clem — baby on hip — tested the weight of my kettle and flicked it on.

"Don't you agree, Faye?" Cassie said, crossing her willowy arms and seeking my approval for the side of an argument I knew nothing about; a position I had found myself in so often that I'd developed a set of stock answers.

"No, I'm sorry, on this occasion I have to agree with Clem," I said, winking and holding my arms out for the baby. Clem hefted him over to me as casually as a bag of potatoes, and I nuzzled my nose in the soft down of his head.

"Of course she agrees with me," said Clem, looking at me earnestly. "By the way, you look like shit."

"Thank you," I whispered into the baby's head.

"We're talking about Eddie," Cassie said. "Clem thinks this whole vicar thing is practically grounds for divorce."

"Deal breaker," added Clem. "If Dave did it, I'd kill him." She busied herself, efficiently fetching out cups, tea bags, and milk. "He's not just changing *his* life" — she turned on Cassie, waving her hands like an Italian mother — "he's forcing a complete lifestyle change on Faye and the girls. And not really giving them any choice in the matter."

This had become a regular subject, more pointed and intense as it became clear that Eddie was seriously intending to train for the clergy.

"Yes, but not grounds for divorce," said Cassie. "Is it?" She looked at me, her huge almond eyes full of confidence.

"It's a pretty big thing," I said. "I didn't sign up to be a vicar's wife. I'm not sure I'm sensible enough, for a start."

"See!" Clem threw tea bags into the cups with gusto. "Isn't that what I said, Cassie? She's too juvenile for this role. No offense."

"Juvenile!" I said. "Is that meant to be a compliment?"

"Oh, you know what I mean," Clem said. "You're going to have to be on your best behavior all the time. Forever. It's too big an ask. Eddie's being selfish."

"He's following a calling, hardly selfish," said Cassie.

"It is a *bit* selfish," I said, and finally they both stopped talking and moving about and just looked at me. "I wouldn't dream of getting Eddie involved in my job, but I don't think I'm up to being a vicar's wife. Plus, I don't know how much it matters about the God part."

"Does Eddie know you don't actually believe in God?" Clem said.

"I've told him, he knows, we've talked. But it's amazing how religious you can start sounding when you just say that you believe in compassion, peace, and helping others. I think he thinks I'm going to learn to believe in God."

I felt tired again and handed the baby back to Clem; they followed with tea and cookies as I headed out of the kitchen into the living room. Cassie and Clem shared a small sofa with the baby, and I lay down on the larger one, opposite them.

"I just want to know, Faye, tell me the truth, is it going to break you up, this clergy thing?"

"Don't worry. I'm not leaving Eddie, even if he becomes a vomit collector at a fairground." And we all laughed, because in college we used to joke about the worst jobs in the world, and this was one of them. To change the subject, I showed them the photo of me in the Space Hopper box.

"So cute!" Cassie said, and Clem took the photo, holding it out of reach of small sticky hands.

"Where was this taken?" Clem asked.

"In my mother's house, Christmastime, obviously. It was taken by my mother. I would have been six."

"How old were you when she died?" Clem said. "Wasn't it quite soon after this?"

"Eight."

"That's why you're kind of stuck, sort of

immature in some ways."

"Shut up, Clem," Cassie said.

"Part of you got stuck when your mum died. It happens, it's a thing. Evie will be eight soon, and after that, you don't have a role model for motherhood. Esther's definitely more sensible than you."

"Jesus, will you shut up?" said Cassie, elbowing Clem and looking at me apologetically. "Esther's more sensible than all of us."

I just nodded and closed my eyes. I didn't want to open them. My friends' voices retreated to nothing but background noise, and I wanted to be alone because even in their company — at this moment — I felt utterly isolated, and the silence that hovered underneath the noise they made was just waiting for me anyway, I might as well face it.

It suddenly struck me that this weariness I felt could be something like grief; a type of grief I hadn't been capable of before. Em and Henry hadn't known what to say or do with me when it came to helping me through my loss and suffering; back in the seventies, everyone thought the least said, the better. Wanting to protect me from further pain was understandable, but by today's psychology, it had to be counterproductive.

I didn't remember asking Em and Henry a lot of questions about my mother. What I did recall was that I felt I *shouldn't* ask. I searched my memory as if it were a messy drawer, trying to find an image, some mental recording of a conversation, something to explain exactly *why* I'd felt so alone in dealing with losing my mum, when Em and Henry had been so supportive, so caring, in every other way. I could see Henry's face in a memory so coated with dust I could barely picture it. It was his face with a worried look, glancing over at Em, as I asked her a question or said something about my mother. What would it have been? *I miss my mother. I want to see my mother again. Do you think my mother was happy?*

I had seen those looks of his, and I'd filed them away. I hadn't thought about it, but now I realized what they were: he didn't want me to upset his wife. Em was a lovely woman, and she cared for me like her own. I trusted her completely; but maybe when I came to her, while she would never have wanted me to lose my mother, maybe it had suited her. I thought of how possessive she'd seemed when she played with little me at her house, with the chocolates on the Christmas tree, as though I were a doll that she wanted. My mother's loss was entirely

Em's gain, and it must have been easier for her to pretend I was all hers and put my mother behind her, behind *me.* I bore her no ill will; Em had been good to me. She was selfish in her love for the daughter she'd always wanted, that's all.

But as a result, for me there had been a void, an emptiness, a sad silence. When I cried back then, it was on my own and into a black hole, an abyss, the unknown. But now I had just lost my mother *again.* So was I grieving again? A more normal type of grief? Or rather, a grief that was easier to cope with, because this time I had said good-bye, embraced her, and now had some hope of seeing her again, as I might if I actually had faith.

Cassie and Clem were talking, ignoring me; I'd been quiet for a long time and I knew Cassie would be keen to steer away from the emotional stuff. They were arguing happily about something else now.

I thought about what Clem had said, about me getting stuck around the age I was when my mother died. Something about that felt true, although when I was with my mother a few days ago, I did feel older than her, not just because I looked so much older, but probably because I knew more about the situation.

I swung my heavy legs over the side of the sofa and sat up. "What do you think of time travel?" I said, when my friends paused for breath.

"What?" Cassie said, taking a bite from a cookie.

Clem looked at me blankly for a moment. "Impossible, obviously. UFOs, questionable; little green men, improbable; God" — she sighed — "dubious; time travel, well, that's just for nutters, novels, and the movies." Her eyes slid back to Cassie and she turned absently away, resuming her previous line of conversation, hardly missing a beat.

I didn't push it, or defend time travel; I'd just wanted to try out the words in my mouth. In the instant before I asked my question, I'd imagined I would be able to pursue the topic a little further, though I was aware that anything I said might reach Eddie's ears. But Clem, with her brutal gauge of irrationality, and Cassie, with her bored silence, were as definitive as a door slammed in my face. I was the unwelcome salesman and I didn't feel I could knock again.

CHAPTER 9

I was thinking of going back in time, could think of nothing else. But this time I'd be prepared. My mother would let me in and know me as the adult who had saved her daughter's life. I would have my questions ready for her, all the things a person wished they'd asked before it was too late. I would make the most of it. Absorbed in my thoughts of her, I sometimes caught Eddie looking at me with eyes full of questions he knew I wouldn't answer. Daydreams of seeing her again were like brown paper parcels tied with bright ribbon, and I could happily have spent my days planning and thinking, but I needed to go back to work.

I do experiments at the RNIB to test product designs on blind, partially sighted, and sighted people. Then I write reports on whether the thing being designed is likely to be as easy for blind people to use as the developer claims it is.

This one experiment I'm doing involves participants wearing rubber gloves and feeling plaster-cast heads of Mozart and Bach. Sighted participants wear blindfolds, and everyone has to describe what they can feel. I'm trying to find out if they can get enough information from what they're touching to give a meaningful description of the thing.

I could tell you why I'm doing the experiment, but it's not part of this story.

I had thirty participants: ten blind, ten partially sighted, and ten sighted, and my friend Louis was one of them — he's the one who wanted to feel inside photographs. Whenever I do an experiment or a focus group, Louis gets involved; we've gotten to know each other over the years, and we go out for lunch most weeks.

I think of Louis as a Big Gay Bear, because he's gay, and big, and very lovable. He's a snappy dresser, always in expensive-looking shirts, and has a neatly trimmed beard. And he smells great. He's been blind since birth and says the thing that irks him most about being blind is that he can't look after a guy on a date the way his sighted friends do. He'd like to be able to go out with someone and then make sure he gets home safely, by driving or walking him home, but he says it's just not like that for blind guys. His protective streak is forcibly suppressed by his lack of sight.

He's a sweetheart, but frustration can make him argumentative after a couple of pints. We were in the pub across the road from the RNIB one day after work, and he went to the bar — he insists — and got us a couple of beers. On the way back to the table, some guy was walking backward as he finished a conversation with his mates and knocked Louis's arm, getting beer down his front. Concentrating only on his beery T-shirt, he started the predictable "Oi, watch where you're going mate, what are you? Blind? You've ruined my shirt!" When he looked at Louis and saw that he *was* in fact blind, he started apologizing madly. Well, Louis was having none of it.

"Come on then," Louis said, relishing the novelty of the upper hand. "What do you want to do? Take it outside?"

"Nah, mate, no harm done," the guy said, retreating like a slug touching salt.

"No harm done? I don't think so!" my Big Gay Bear said. "Your shirt is ruined and I've lost half a pint. The question is, whose fault is it?" He raised the arm holding the offending pint, slopping more of it on the wilting bulldog of a man. And for the record, he had initially spilled only a fraction of a pint.

"It's okay, I'll buy you another, I'll buy a whole round, what're you drinking?" Even Louis couldn't argue with that.

Louis sat down next to me. When the guy came over with another couple of beers, he set them in front of us, saying *sorry, sorry, sorry.*

"That was nice," I said to Louis after the guy had gone. "Him being so apologetic for you spilling beer all over him."

"Nothing to do with beer. He was apologizing because I'm blind and he's not, so whatever fight we get into, he's already the winner." I squeezed Louis's hand, because the upper hand for him, like any dream, is just an illusion. I squeezed his hand because he was so right.

When Louis came to the rubber glove experiment, I hadn't seen him all week. He was feeling the head of Mozart, and there was something surreal and soothing about watching my friend carefully caress the contours of the musical genius. His sightless face tilted toward the ceiling, and his fingers walked and glided over the manmade contours of hair and facial features.

"I've never seen him before in my life!"

"Louis, you're supposed to be doing a

description." I stopped the recording and rewound. "Ready?"

"Okay," he said, and I switched the machine back on. There was a long pause, and then he said, "The head I'm feeling is meaningless to me. I have no idea if it's a man or a woman. I can tell there's a lot of hair, but it feels nothing like real hair. It feels like waves carved in stone, which is as far away from hair as you can get." Louis stopped.

"Is that everything?" I asked, and he nodded. I stopped recording again. "Not exactly what I was expecting," I said. "But it's all valid, really interesting, actually."

"What have other people said?"

"Mainly an account of the features of the face, you know, the shape of the nose, whether it's bigger than average. That sort of thing."

Louis grunted. "This thing is not a head," he said.

"It's not?"

"It's a solid cast in the shape of a head. What's the point of me feeling this? I presume it's supposed to tell me roughly what a head feels like. Well, I can feel my own head. Or yours, if you'll let me. Nobody feels a stone head to get to know what a head looks like. This is for the eyes, not the hands," he said, tapping it.

"Let me press Record again. Ready?" I said.

"I'm sick of sighted people doing this," he said. "When I was a kid, I can only have been about six, this expert gave me a test." Louis used sarcastic fingers as inverted commas around *expert*. "I don't know what he was trying to find out, but he gave me some braille pictures, raised outlines. One was a cat, I found out later. But if you've only ever felt a real cat, would you draw it in the standard way a sighted person does? A cat in my world is different from the cat in your world; nothing about it is sharp, apart from its claws, because a cat is predominantly a bundle of fur. But this outline the man gave me was sharp: hard pointed triangles — *ears,* apparently — and a smooth round body like the base of an hourglass. I got it wrong, I don't know what I said, but it wasn't 'cat.' The guy thought I was an idiot. Then he asked me to draw an egg, and I couldn't. He said, 'Just the simple shape of it will do.' But I'd never held an egg. My mother spoon-fed me, to avoid a mess. So I drew a blob because my experience of egg was only a soft blob in my mouth. Then he asked me to draw a bus, and when I finished, he said, 'What is this, young man?' and I said, 'It's a bus, like you asked.' And he said, 'This is just a few random lines.' I had drawn a long vertical line and, to the left of it, three short horizontal lines."

"Hang on," I said. "Let me try to work it out." I drew the lines as he'd described with a pencil on the back of an envelope.

Bus. Vertical line. Horizontals.

I closed my eyes and imagined getting on a bus.

"Got it," I said. "You drew the handle you held as you got onto the bus, that's the vertical line, and three horizontal lines, they're the steps that lead up to the driver. A bus! Correction: *your* bus."

"I knew you'd understand. In a practical sense, my world extends as far as my arms can reach. Yours is as far as your eyes can see. But we both know, in our hearts, that our worlds are actually far bigger than that. You know that, don't you, Faye?"

I did.

I picked up the keys for the room and shoved my chair back. "Let's get out of here," I said. "I'll buy you a coffee."

It was a beautiful day, the sun was out, and Louis and I sat outside the Turkish café that was just a little way down the road from the entrance to RNIB. I put a folder on the wooden picnic table between us, so if any of our colleagues walked by, it looked more like work than chitchat.

"What's going on with you?" Louis said.

"What do you mean?"

"I feel like I haven't seen you for ages, and your voice seems lower."

"I've had a sex change."

"Not that low!" he said. He waited. "See, normally you'd laugh at that."

"I don't know." I shrugged. "I'm down, I suppose, lonely."

"You? Really? Well, join the club," he said. "But you've got Eddie, and the girls."

"I know, but . . . I've got stuff going on. Secrets I can't tell," I said, pretending to be mysterious, brushing it off.

"Oh yeah, I've got that one all sewn up. I felt like that for years until I came out to my sister." He stopped, and I said nothing. "Are you gay? Is that what this is about?"

"No," I said. "You know I'm not."

"Is it about Eddie, and you entering the world of Vicar's Wifedom?"

"If only that was my problem now," I said.

"Just spit it out, stop being so fucking mysterious."

"I can't. You won't understand."

"Oh, here we go: lonely, middle-aged,

136

overweight blind guy can't relate to lonely, middle-class sighted white girl."

"You're white too," I said.

"Am I!" he said, feeling his face.

The tiny click of spit that sometimes accompanies a smile gave me away, and he said, "That's more like it."

"And I wouldn't call you middle-aged," I added.

"But overweight?"

"Cuddly," I said, and gently pinched his cheek. "You're perfect." I looked at my friend. "It must be especially hard being gay when you're blind."

"Everything's harder when you're blind."

"I know. But especially dating, I imagine."

"Yeah," he said. "First there's finding someone who's okay to go on a date with a blind guy, then you've got to weed out the ones who want a charity date."

"Sympathy is not a big turn-on," I said.

"Not to me, or you. But I think a lot of people get off on it. I'd like to meet someone who sometimes forgets I'm blind."

"That ever happened?"

"I had a few dates with a guy I got on really well with — we always had such a laugh, my stomach would be hurting by the end of the night."

"What happened to him?"

137

"He said he wished I could see him. He said that sometimes when we were out, people would stare at us with a knowing look, a look that said that if *I* could see *him,* I wouldn't be going out with him. He got insecure and eventually said I should find someone more like me."

"More blind, or better-looking?" I said.

"I don't know." Louis tented his fingertips. "So, what is going on with you? I can hear it in your voice, something's happened. If you can't tell Eddie, it must be bad. Tell me about it. Come on."

Blind people are not possessed of superpowers any more than the rest of us. But Louis knew me well, and prided himself on observation; he knew something was up, and I knew he could be like a dog with a bone. He wouldn't give up until I gave him something. I traced the outline of one of the sticky circular stains on the tabletop.

"I visited my mother," I said.

"Go on," he said, after a short hesitation. "Was it disappointing?"

"Uh . . . no. Definitely not disappointing, but unexpected."

"Too vague," he said, waving a hand in the air.

I ran a finger along the gaps in the wood of the picnic table and looked at Louis's fingers, lovely, well-manicured; he was careful with his fingers after years of getting them hurt by not being able to see what he was putting them into. "Okay," I said. "Well, I haven't seen her for a long time. And I knew she wouldn't recognize me. So that was difficult. I turned up unannounced, but actually, as circumstances would have it, we did have a lovely conversation, and it was a good visit."

Louis didn't say anything. He just waited, a tactic of his to get a bit more information out of people; and even though I knew what he was doing, I couldn't resist. "While I was with my mother, I got hit by a car."

"Shit," he said, as a waitress put our coffees on the table. Louis raised his hand and gently brought it down in the air, carefully locating his cup before gripping it with his other hand.

There was a comfortable silence between us, and I played with the foam on the top of my coffee while I waited for Louis to ask about the car accident.

"But your mum's dead, right?" Louis said, and I looked at his vacant, milky eyes, which looked straight back at me.

"Mm-hmm," I said. And we sat in silence. No one else was sitting here; it was late morning, and the sun was hot on my legs.

People walked past, a conveyor belt of suits, and more than the national average of guide dogs and white sticks. A small brown sparrow landed on our table and pecked at some crumbs that hadn't been swept away. I watched the jerky sideways movements of its head and its tiny, bright, black eyes; I think it was watching us. I didn't tell Louis the bird was there, although normally I would.

"So you visited your dead mum and got hit by a car." He stated it as a fact.

"Mm-hmm," I said again.

"Anything else?"

"Yeah, I saved my six-year-old self. I threw myself between her and the car."

"Excellent!" he said, and chuckled to himself. "You making this up?"

"No," I said.

"Okay. Tell me more. How did you get there?"

"You believe me?"

He picked up his coffee and brought it carefully to his lips. "Life can be pretty dull, Faye," he said. "Even duller if you're blind. Don't let the blinkies tell you otherwise, or the do-gooders, who think we can live as full and exciting a life as sighted people. If there is any color in my life, it's because of people like you. So, do I believe you? Well, I

140

don't know. Does it matter? Just tell me what happened, and if there's any raunchy bits, don't hold back."

"There are no raunchy bits," I said, with a smile in my voice.

"Oh, now, that is disappointing," he said. "Tell me anyway."

And so it was that I told Louis everything.

CHAPTER 10

You can imagine the relief I felt simply telling someone the truth about what had happened. The itch to tell Eddie subsided; so much of my twitching desire to share my burden had been unloaded just by saying the words out loud to another human being.

Telling Louis was like a drug that hid the pain. But I knew it was only a matter of time before it wore off; because telling Louis wouldn't be enough. I needed Eddie. I knew if I didn't confide in him, sorrow would seep into my life like water into clay, making it heavy and misshapen. Yet I *couldn't* tell Eddie, even though I felt salvation depended on him; that was the whole problem. However, the day I spoke to Louis, none of that mattered; like an addict, I was on a high. I didn't feel alone anymore, and that was enough at that moment. I came home like a woman who had finally put down a load she barely had the strength to carry. I felt physically lighter. And I knew this too: I had to go back again. I had to go back to my mother, and soon.

Talking to Louis had brought up a number of practical and emotional issues that I needed to address. I found him surprisingly logical and, well, *useful* about the whole thing. Most — though not all — of his suggestions made total sense. He listened, and he helped, none of the predictable questions regarding my sanity. He suggested I get the Space Hopper box out of the attic and put it somewhere that would be less damaging to me when I returned home — somewhere that would provide a softer landing — and also somewhere that didn't make so much noise. He thought my return trip should be made in the middle of the night, when Eddie was asleep (which I thought was risky), or when he was away (which only a bachelor would suggest; I couldn't leave two children alone in the house). He said I should wear clothes appropriate to where I was going, both in terms of weather and decade, and to bundle up around the parts of me most likely to get broken: ankles, arms, neck. He wondered if I should wear a crash helmet, but I just wasn't sure about that.

You know what, we stayed at that Turkish

café for hours. We had lunch, and more coffee, and then moved on to the pub and had a cold beer. No one from work rang to ask where the hell we were, and we wondered how many hours or days it would take before someone noticed we were missing. I popped back to the office about an hour or so before I was due to go home, and my boss smiled at me, bright and guileless.

"How'd it go?" she asked. She was tanned and too skinny, and I wanted to take her home and feed her.

"How did what go?" I asked. I put my bag on the desk and searched for chewing gum in case the smell of beer reached her.

"The experiments," she said. "Rubber gloves."

"Oh yeah." I'd forgotten about them. "Good, but they took longer than I thought, I'm going to need an extra day or two." Lying was getting easier. I didn't even feel bad about it, as long as it wasn't Eddie.

"No problem," she said. "Why don't you take off early? You've been working so hard."

I smiled to myself: get in late, leave early, and have a long lunch. Sometimes you just need a day like that to get back on track, and it was a great start to the weekend.

By the time Eddie got home that night, the

144

girls were in bed and I'd made us some dinner and opened a bottle of wine to breathe. I got out the cards and the eggs, as I always do when we play. I have a wooden bowl, smooth and shallow and beautiful in its simplicity, that Eddie bought for our fifth wedding anniversary. In the bowl I keep ten eggs I found at a yard sale: some wooden, some marble, all roughly the size of a real chicken egg. Whoever wins a card game takes an egg from the bowl, until there are none left. Person with the most eggs is the overall winner. It stops us watching too much TV.

When he saw the bowl, he loosened his tie. "Feeling confident tonight?" he said.

I put my arms around him and kissed him long and deep.

"I've already won," I said, looking at his handsome, kind face, and he pulled me into a stronger embrace. He burrowed his face into my neck, and we were like two animals reunited, animals who didn't have the words to say they were happy to see each other again. His touch told me that he'd missed me, because I'd been distant.

While he went to look at our sleeping daughters I put a bowl of chili on the table, some salsa, and homemade tortilla chips to dip. I spray tortilla wraps with oil and sprinkle them with sea salt, then cut them into triangles with a pizza cutter and put them in the oven for a few minutes. The best. Eddie's favorite.

He'd put on a sweatshirt and some jogging bottoms and took a large mouthful of wine as he sat down, grunting happily as he scooped up chili in a chip.

"Good day?"

Eddie nodded and kept nodding till he swallowed. "I had some one-to-one interviews," he said. "I think they like me, hard to tell."

"How could they not like you?" I said.

"You're biased, but thank you. They have an important job — it's not just about them liking me; they need to decide if I'm right for this sort of work. The role of ministry is about serving other people *well,* not just about me thinking I'd be good at it and therefore being allowed to train for it, and then simply doing it. My calling is not the job. The job is an instrument to help me carry out my calling. But it feels like they like me, which makes me feel better."

Eddie wanting to train as a vicar was not like applying for any other kind of job. Apparently God calls you (I'm thinking not literally), and you feel it, and then after a lot of discussion with your vicar, if you feel

146

it strongly enough, you can apply to the Diocesan Director of Ordinands, and they'll decide if you can take it further and have a role in the church.

Eddie had his calling from God a few years ago, but didn't do anything about it. Apparently it got stronger until the point he had to act on it. I guess it must feel exactly like being "called," because everyone uses that expression, don't they? I had never asked Eddie what it was like. Was it *literal*? Did he hear God as clearly as a parent calling his children in for dinner, or was it a feeling, a strong emotional one, like finding out you've won a prize? Or a strong physical one, like badly needing to pee?

"What was it like when you got your calling?" I said.

He took another swig of wine and dealt the cards. Seven each. Rummy.

"It was a voice, in my head," he said, looking at his cards and rearranging them in his hand. He looked at me, and I guess my face had the kind of expression that makes you want to reword your last sentence.

"It was *my* voice — my inner voice — and it was when I was quiet, alone, praying. Especially in church. When I'm there I feel . . . right, a sense of fulfillment, contented. It was natural. Good. The voice I heard was a bit like when you're cycling uphill and want to give up; when your inner voice says: *You can do it, just a bit farther.*"

I picked up a card, laid one down, took a chip.

"But one day I was in church," he said. "I'd been praying silently. The whole place was candlelit, the choir had just finished singing Allegri's *Miserere,* and it felt like someone laid a hand briefly and gently, but very definitely, on my shoulder and I heard a quieter voice, and I wasn't conscious of producing that inner voice myself, so it was more like someone else's voice that time, and it said, *Your purpose.* And that was it."

"That was your calling?"

"It was a *part* of my calling, I suppose. It's been gradual, taken years. And I guess I always knew, always felt it in me, but hadn't put a name to it. But at that moment, when I felt the hand on my shoulder, it became more real. I felt God was nudging me, simply giving me a clearer sign. I couldn't ignore it or keep it in a separate box anymore." He picked up, smiled, laid down; he was after hearts. "I'm going to get the first egg," he said.

"I guarantee it," I said, looking at my cards. "I've got a hand like a foot." I had a pair of threes in my hand, but nothing else that went together. I hesitated, let my hand hover over the card he'd just laid down, wondering whether to pick it up and make something of it. Changed my mind, and went for the deck.

"Why didn't you ever tell me about this calling, if it started years ago?" I asked, munching another tortilla chip.

"I don't know. It wasn't a case of keeping it from you, or anyone. I suppose I didn't say anything because I thought, *This is ridiculous, who am I to be called by God?*"

"I always imagine the voice of God to be a bit thunderous," I said, thinking about the clear, quiet voice Eddie had described.

"Well, in the Bible it's often quoted as being a big voice. But God was only talking to me in the church, he didn't need to shout." Eddie looked at me. "See, it makes me sound conceited and ridiculous."

"No, it doesn't," I said, putting my hand on his. "I'm just sorry I didn't ask you sooner."

"Now was always the time for us to have this conversation. The things we need to know will reveal themselves when the right time comes."

He was talking about the things I still hadn't told him. He was telling me he would wait until I was ready, even if it was hard on him.

"How do your parents feel about it?" I asked. "I mean, your mum?" Eddie's parents live in France, have done for the past fifteen years or so, and his dad, always a quiet, lovely man, has dementia. Eddie's mum looks after him at home. She says he's like a lovely pet; she feeds and cleans him, and during warm days she sits him in the garden with a blanket, while she potters with the flowers, vegetables, and bird feeders. On cooler days she makes up a fire, and he does much the same thing, but indoors. She reads to him, although his hearing is not that great. Every day they go for a walk, every Thursday morning they go to the shops, and every Sunday they go to church. She's certain that their simple, regulated, wholesome life keeps her husband content and helps him enjoy his life as much as he can. She's a good woman.

"My mum wasn't surprised, and that doesn't surprise me. We've always been a family that quietly believes in God, his presence. He's always been a part of our lives," he said, laying down his cards faceup and taking an egg.

"Beginner's luck," I said, and started stacking the cards together to shuffle them.

Eddie watched me deal and looked thoughtful. "Funny thing," he said. "If I'm honest, I kind of wanted Mum to be a bit surprised, or at least seem really pleased. I should be happy that she isn't the kind of mum who thinks I'm making a terrible mistake, and throwing my life away. She accepted it, and that's great. But she accepted it like getting change back when you've paid for your groceries. It was just another thing that she took in her stride. A little too expected. I suppose she made it seem ordinary, when it felt more important to me than that."

"You wanted to shock her!" I said. "Like someone who comes out as gay to their parents, and is all prepared for the drama of the moment, but instead they just say, 'Oh yeah, we've always known.'"

"Something like that," he said.

"Shame on you, it could have been so much worse."

"You're right. She accepted it as though it was nothing. The good things about that outweigh the bad."

"She's too hearty to be shocked. *I* was shocked," I said. "Still am. I hope that's some consolation."

He laughed and poured more wine into my glass. I opened a drawer in the table, took out a candle, and lit it.

"I think most people have to come to terms with balancing what they have always hoped for from their parents, with what they actually get," he said. "I've been luckier than most. I know a lot of people who are more than a little disappointed with their parents. A lot of people won't get the answers they dream of from their mum and dad, even if they get round to asking them."

"And what are the right questions?" I asked.

"Exactly," he said. (I'd hoped for a more literal answer to my question.) "And some of us never even get the opportunity to ask." He looked at me and held my gaze; we never really talk about my mother, although Eddie tries to encourage me now and then.

"Wouldn't it be amazing to be able to go back in time and ask the questions we never thought we'd get the chance to ask, of the people most important to us?" I said, laying the pack facedown and forgetting about it.

"Yes, it would," Eddie said, shaking his head sadly. "I know you must feel like that about your mum, but I also feel like that about my dad. It's too late, and yet . . ." He hesitated.

"And yet what?" I said.

"And yet, even knowing that one day,

152

maybe very soon, it may be too late to ask my mum all the things that only she can tell me, I'm still not asking her those questions. Why is that?"

"What would you ask her?"

"I don't even know. Lots of things."

"Make a list," I said.

"I will." He nodded firmly, and I knew he would actually do it.

"And then go to France, as soon as possible, and ask her those questions before it's too late," I said. I suddenly felt both urgent and passionate that he should do this. My words were a softly spoken and determined order. Eddie needed it, perhaps we all do: a reminder to minimize regret while we still can.

"Okay," said Eddie, and again, I just knew that he would.

The chili was almost gone, and only one egg had been claimed. "I can hardly see the cards anymore," I said, holding them closer to the candle.

"Shall I turn on a light?"

"Let's go to bed," I said, and he blew out the flame, took my hand, and led me up the stairs. In the dark we had no need for anything beyond our tiny world, insignificant and yet so important, our connection, so vital to us. Right now I only needed him, and the knowledge that my children were safe in their beds nearby. I didn't need to see, I only needed to hold him in the dark, and be held, and know that he loves me. But I knew that soon this world alone would not be enough; I was already hankering after another.

CHAPTER 11

I'm glad you're here, still listening. It was a relief to talk to Louis, but you're so important to me. All this stuff I'm telling you happened a few months ago, so you and I are still in catch-up mode. I told you that telling Louis my story was like a drug I knew would wear off. Well, telling you everything is distracting me from the withdrawal symptoms, the pain of not being honest with my husband. I still need to bring you up to speed, but I *will* tell you that at this very moment in time from which I am telling you my story, I still haven't said anything to Eddie about what's going on. And so I need you — very much — to hear me, and believe in what I'm saying.

The day after the cards was Saturday and we took the girls roller-skating. When I was growing up, roller-skating was by far my favorite thing. My first pair of skates had metal wheels and straps that tied over my shoes. I used them on the pavements and you could hear me coming from a mile away. Then a skating rink opened in the town where I lived, and that's where everyone went at the weekend; by then you could rent skating boots. Kids with money had their own, but I wasn't one of them, and I didn't know anyone like that. Anyway, skating with Eddie and the girls is so much fun; we're usually there for a couple of hours and we always go for burgers afterward.

I was feeling happier, and I could tell Eddie was too, even though I knew he must still wonder what had happened when he found me in the attic a few weeks ago. We were definitely back in a good place, talking about stuff, working things through; I was trying to understand him and he was listening to me. I was thinking a lot about my mother, and my younger self; I felt the pull of them, and a desire — which got harder and harder to resist — to return to them. I yearned to see my mother again. After a little taste of her company, she was almost all I wanted, but the thought of what I had to go through to get back to her tightened my throat and made me sweat. It was like having to go on the most frightening roller coaster in the world, one that might kill me, in order to get to the sweetest destination imaginable. I had to go back, I wanted to help them — my mother and me — but I didn't know how; while I thought about how to do that, real life kept me busy.

As often happens when we four go skating, I do a few circuits on my own, while Eddie and the girls take a less graceful approach to it all: stumbling into each other, picking each other up, bashing into the far ends and setting off again; they laugh and enjoy it. I love it too, but I get lost in my own thoughts as I circle the rink, and this Saturday more than ever. As I glided around, I grew intensely conscious of my breath coming out of my nostrils and felt ultra-aware of my immediate place in the universe: alive and present. I felt governed by a deeper sense of calm and focus than I had ever felt lying in bed at night pondering the madness and wonder of my time-travel.

I guess most people experience something similar when they perform any repetitive physical activity at which they are proficient: the body is fully engaged, and if the skill is mastered then the mind is completely available for exploration of itself. I glided round the rink and the other people there were blurred and irrelevant to me: simply obstacles, easily avoided, like rocks on a path.

Even my own family. I was vaguely aware of the sandy-colored, polished wood flooring and the hum of the wheels as they spoke the language of easy movement: of wheels and weight unimpeded running on a smooth surface. On the walls around the large skating rink were electronic posters at eye level, and they made a vague Technicolor impression on me as they advertised travel in beautiful locations. I was barely aware of the bright images showing mountains and rivers, as I circled round and round in lazy, easy rotations.

My body was busy roller-skating, my eyes were occupied with beautiful visions, and in my head I was free to meander through a maze — a visual maze — of thoughts that came unbidden: I softly glided between high green walls of foliage, and in my mind I saw Eddie, surrounded by tables full of cakes, biting into a slice of Victoria sponge and smiling. "You can do this," he said, looking at the teeth marks he'd left in the cake and then back at me. "In fact, you can do better." Being a vicar's wife, as I would eventually be, was going to involve some twee practicalities: I would attend events that I would normally avoid, and bake a lot more; I wouldn't be able to ignore the call to provide homemade buns and cookies. There was going to be no more genuine private life for us. We would become public property. We would be on call, on show. But if Eddie were a politician, or a celebrity, life would present me with the same demands. Religion worried me, partly because of its intangibility, but cakes were tangible, fundraising was tangible, kindness could be tangible. I could do this part of it, I could take this on and do it well.

I continued skating, still gliding, vaguely conscious of a pleasant ache in my thighs and conscious too of being in control of my surroundings; I found relief in feeling that I was rooted here on earth, and not flying through the atmosphere to another time and place. Soon I was back in the maze of my mind — turned a few corners in there, watching my hands ahead of me brushing the leaves as I passed between carefully crafted topiary. I saw my mother and actually stumbled on my skates briefly — saw the floor come into sharp focus for a moment. In a beat I was steady once more, and my inner eye watched my mother in the maze. Her smile was one-third apology and two-thirds amusement. "I'm sorry, but this is all I've got to give you," she said, handing me a glass jar and her leather recipe book. "This should sweeten the savage," she added dreamily, and I looked down and saw that the book was open on the page for sticky toffee pudding. "Come and see me, I'm your mother," she said, but when I looked, she was gone, and I heard her echoing voice say: *"Now you see me, now you don't!"*

I thought I heard the rushing of a river, but it was the thrum of my wheels on wood. Without any effort my mind sifted thoughts and worries. Is this what meditation is? Because I've never done it, I've never even done yoga, but if I had to guess, this was meditation. I continued to float through my cerebral maze while my body remained on the roller-skating rink, in a zone, unaware of anything around me. I felt wisps of my tied-back hair blowing in the breeze generated by my speed of motion.

The green of the maze was alluring, I wanted to breathe it in, but I started to get the same nervous feeling I associate with being lost. The visions of Eddie and my mother had come unbidden; they were there for me with messages, and not too cryptic. I struggled both with my mother and with Eddie, and my responsibility to them, and what they needed or wanted from me, what I needed and wanted from *them.* But I could work through it. The loneliness of the maze was now harder to bear than my more obvious responsibilities; a loneliness that felt like hunger.

The maze had more to show me, I felt sure, but before the center could reveal itself to me, I hit a wall, or something like a wall. I had been totally mesmerized by my weird dreamlike visions, and eventually something was going to get in my way and disrupt them. It happened to be a wide-bottomed man who had entered the rink and got into difficulty. Too far from the edge to hang on, he'd opted to steady himself against the floor and was rolling along slowly, bent over as though trying to touch his toes. I hit him at speed and rolled awkwardly over his arched back, landing hard on my coccyx. The jarring in my back was nasty, and the shock of being yanked out of blissful meditation and back into the real world of pain, people, and verbal interactions was unwelcome, to say the least.

Eddie had been with the girls having a drink, but when he saw me go down, he came and pulled me to my feet. I was fine, and I navigated myself against the flow of skaters to join Esther and Evie, while Eddie helped the guy I had leapfrogged.

"That was horrible," I said, rubbing my

bum and sipping the icy lemonade that was waiting for me on the table.

"He really broke your reverie," said Eddie.

"He broke my cool," I said, looking at the girls, "which is far more serious." They giggled.

"Seriously, you have been skating round in a daydream for half an hour."

"Half an hour!"

"At least," he said, checking his watch. "You must be exhausted."

"Thirsty," I said, draining my drink. I gave the girls some change and asked them to get me another; they loved getting the drinks on their skates — dangerous waitressing.

"You were in a world of your own," Eddie said. He looked gorgeous in a black crewneck sweatshirt and jeans that sat low on his hips. The belt he was wearing I'd bought him for our leather wedding anniversary. I can't remember which number that is.

"I was," I said. "I was daydreaming. Meditating, I think."

"Out there?" Eddie said, with more than a hint of disbelief. I looked back out to the rink; from here it looked as far from a place of meditation as it's possible to get.

"I must have shut the world out. I was

alone with my thoughts."

"Penny for them."

"I thought about you, about being a vicar's wife, the role I'm going to take on when you're ordained one day and how I'll cope. I thought about my mother, and how I wish I could see her."

He held my hand. "And you did all that thinking out there?" He jerked his head in the direction of the noise, the music, and the mayhem of what looked like too many limbs per person.

"You must have experienced being so lost in thought that you didn't notice anything around you?" I said.

"I've been lost in thought, but usually in peaceful places."

I looked over at the girls, who were at the counter ordering my drink. Evie was like a baby deer on ice as she fumbled with money and tried to hand it to the man serving them. I winced.

"They'll be all right," Eddie said. "Don't look! We're too far away to catch them if they fall."

I shook the ice from the bottom of my cup into my mouth and crunched it.

"It's a skill to be able to block out all this interference and concentrate on your inner world, Faye. Finding peace amid the havoc

163

of daily life is something to aspire to."

"It's dangerous, is what it is," I said. "I nearly killed a man."

The girls returned, and I drank half my drink and let them share the rest between them; they're rarely allowed fizzy drinks. Then I clapped my hands. "More skating?" I asked. "Or is it time for burgers?"

We all voted burgers, and I remained in the real, outward-facing world for the rest of the day. It was heavenly.

CHAPTER 12

France happened, which meant I didn't have to lie to Eddie or sneak around in the middle of the night in order to get back to the seventies. He decided to squeeze in a trip before the end of the summer holidays and take the girls. At first he assumed I'd go with them, which was slightly awkward, but I told him I could really use the time to myself, I would love some me-time, I said. He stared at me as though trying to read my mind, but then he just said he understood. I mean, we all need me-time; you, I'm sure, have felt the need for it. Having young children makes you hungry for the opportunity not to be constantly and intently alert, it makes your mouth water at the thought of not looking at the clock or even knowing the time. So it wasn't an unreasonable request. And I could picture Eddie and his mum talking into the night in their own private way, after the girls were asleep, without me there spoiling their opportunity to be completely frank with each other. I think people underestimate how much their presence interferes with the way things would be if they weren't there, and I knew that Eddie's visit with his mum, this time, would be better for him if I wasn't there.

And of course I wanted to be alone to visit my mother. Being selfish is so much easier when you convince yourself it's better for others.

Every time I went in to work after my revelations to Louis, he would contact me, wanting to talk about it. I wanted to talk about it too, but for me it felt more serious. Louis was delighting in it all a little too much, as though it were a game, a trivial and challenging conundrum, as opposed to a life-threatening voyage into the unknown. But I can't criticize him really, as I do love him. It's just that he took the logistics seriously, but not the emotional side. I *knew* how to get back to my mother, my body could take it, I thought. But my heart?

When Eddie went to France, I was so relieved. Getting a good opportunity to visit my mother had been my priority, and with that sorted, the dangers of it all began to strike me; other really frightening things played on my mind. Frightening in a different kind of way than never going back to her, I mean. Because that was a worry: never getting back to her. But then, anyone who has lost their mother has to deal with that.

Risk of injury was high on my list of concerns. First of all I got the box out of the loft and put it on my bed. I stared at it, rubbed my chin, then heaved the mattress onto the floor and surrounded it with pillows; landing on that was going to be a lot easier than landing in the loft. No splinters, for a start. Then I pulled out armfuls of clothes from the wardrobe on their hangers — I needed something that might be good for time-traveling — and piled them onto the bed base. Louis had suggested bundling up, which was a great idea, but my bottom layer of clothing would need to be acceptable in the 1970s. I had a floral skirt and blouse, but a skirt didn't seem like good time-travel attire, too flimsy, so I put on a pair of light-blue flared jeans and my white pumps. I added a long-sleeved sweatshirt with green arms and white torso, and I looked retro enough, but it was too thin to protect me on the journey; I needed something spongy and thick, and started squeezing sweaters between my fingers. When I remembered Eddie's ski suit, I smiled. It would be huge on me, which was a bonus, plus it had a hood.

So it was that I found myself standing in my bedroom one sunny August evening, about eight o'clock. I was too nervous to eat but I drank lots of water because good hydration always seems sensible. I wore the everyday 1970s-style clothes with a coat on top, because I was guessing it would be January or February in the past. Over that I wore the big red ski suit. I pulled on a balaclava and then put the ski suit hood up and pulled the toggles to form a puckered peephole. Louis had suggested gloves, and I pulled some on: ski gloves in my size that secured at the wrist with Velcro and were made of something stiff and synthetic. I turned to the full-length mirror and saluted myself: I looked like a spaceman with a desperate uniform made up from charity-shop items, or a very conspicuous, fashion-challenged burglar. A trickle of sweat ran down my back. I stepped slowly toward the box: a make-believe astronaut ready for takeoff.

I tried not to think about what might be about to happen as I stepped into the box. To think I used to be afraid of flying in a nice safe airplane. To think I was afraid of spiders, for goodness' sake, when there was

168

so much more to be frightened of. My mouth was dry as I stood in the cardboard box, despite my efforts at hydration. The mattress was an uneasy platform, and I worried that I would split the bottom of the box.

I waited there, sweating — one-third heat, two-thirds fear — and imagined, as I had once before, Eddie finding me passed out while I dreamed that I was back in the past with my mother. How would it be for him to find me here like this when he returned in a week? Like a riddle: *A woman is found wearing an oversize ski suit in the middle of summer, in a cardboard box on a mattress on the bedroom floor. What happened?*

He would struggle to find a logical solution.

Anyway, that wouldn't happen: I wasn't dreaming, this was real. But I didn't seem to be going anywhere. When I'd been in the box maybe a minute (time is relative and it seemed longer), I started to panic. The delay was giving me too much time to reconsider. Waves of hot and cold washed over me, and I thought of an octopus I saw on a nature program whose colors rippled and changed. I tried to decide whether I had time to get out of the box before it ripped me away from my family and my home, and suddenly realized I should have left a note for Eddie in case I never returned. No matter that my words would have seemed like the ramblings of a crazy person. I had to leave him something; otherwise it was too cruel. He was in France all week, so I didn't have to rush this, and decided I just had to write a letter. But as I shifted my weight to get out of the box, the world opened up under my feet and I fell through it like a trapdoor.

The speed with which I fell is beyond adequate description. You have probably fallen yourself at some point, or missed a step as you're coming down the stairs, or stepped off the curb when you walked too close to the edge. That sickening lurch, the flood of adrenaline, the shredding of nerves. But those moments last only a fraction of time. Less than a second. When the falling goes on and on, that's what I can't describe. I had thought about it and hoped that if I fell for long enough, maybe I would become accustomed to it, and it would feel more like falling with a parachute. But the plummeting nothingness was relentless. I felt like a baseball that had been thrown from an airplane.

But the least I could do was try to breathe. This I had practiced. The rush of air had made it almost impossible the first time, but the squashy ski hood tied up around my face helped. I panted, taking fast, shallow breaths. My breath was hot and I was reminded of being in a cold bed in the winter, head under the covers, trying to produce heat. I remembered the midwife saying "Pant" as I gave birth, and as I rushed between one space and another, I thought: *Is this more like giving birth, or more like being born?*

I hugged myself. The first time I'd fallen through the box my arms had shot above my head, and the force had stopped me bringing them down. This time I clutched myself and shot through the air like a bobsled crew member with fresh air for a track, or a madwoman with a straitjacket on.

So I panted and held on to myself tight. Simply knowing what was going on helped; knowing that I would see my mother again made everything worth it. As before, I began to slow down. I tipped forward and started to descend headfirst. Last time I had seen fairy lights speeding toward me, but this time there was a lightening of the gloom, but no kaleidoscope of colors. I guessed it was because this time I was heading for the shed and not the Christmas tree in the living room. It was impossible to keep my

171

arms around me as I fell headfirst, and they shot out, as though I were diving: nature will insist on sacrificing the arms for the brain. I felt the tightening around my chest and tried to keep calm when I couldn't breathe; I knew it would stop — but there again, nature programs us to be alarmed when breathing is threatened. I stretched my arms out, desperate to reach my destination, knowing it would mean air to breathe, and stillness, and my mother.

Then I came into the world arms first. The box broke on one side and a panel neatly flattened out from the rest as I skidded forward across the bottom of the shed at speed; one of my sleeves caught on something and peeled up as I shot across the short space, exposing my arm, allowing splinters in. Then, much too soon, my head met the shed door with a crack. There was a dull ringing in my ears, and I kept still for a few long seconds, trying to assess the damage before I dared to move. I must have looked like a discarded puppet that had been thrown against a wall, but I was panting and conscious and, it seemed, had no broken bones, and that was good enough. I righted myself gingerly until I was sitting in the gloom, legs outstretched, with my back against the door. I put my fingers inside the puckered hole of my hood and pulled it open, happily taking lungfuls of air, stale though it was. I tasted blood and pulled my gloves off to touch my lip, which I'd bitten. Patting myself down revealed only bruises, and I stood cautiously, grateful for my lack of serious injuries, but still hurting from the impact and feeling disoriented. In the cramped space I unzipped my ski suit and pulled it down, struggling to get it over my feet. Standing on one foot wasn't necessarily the wisest move, as my shoe caught on the elasticized ankle cuff and I pitched forward, like a drunk woman bobbing for apples. In the fraction of a second it took to reach the tipping point and know I would fall, I hated myself. My face hit the shed door with a crack and my skin slid over it like sandpaper before I landed in a heap exactly where I'd arrived. I lay, momentarily motionless, before angrily yanking the suit off and flinging it away from me.

CHAPTER 13

Hesitantly I pried open the shed door and saw that my garden of the past was serene in the warm air of the evening. I had been expecting winter but, at a guess, this was late spring, maybe even summertime, meaning at least six months had passed since my last visit. I only hoped it was no later than 1978 — and my mother was still alive.

I went straight round the side of the house to the front door, knocked, and waited, holding my breath as I saw a light flick on behind the mottled glass panel in the door, and then movement; the rattle of a chain and the opening of the door. Two things hit me: the beautiful, sleepy-looking, smiling eyes of my mother, and the earthy green smell of marijuana. Momentarily her expression was like a question mark; then an exclamation mark. She gasped and leaned forward, bangles jangling up her arms as she reached out and gently clasped my face in her palms.

"My guardian angel," she said, and her voice was lazy like honey. "My sister from a different mister. I was wondering when I would see you again."

I felt my throat tighten, and reached up to touch my mother's hand on my cheek. Her fingers felt so seductively real, I closed my eyes, holding on to the moment.

She took my hand and led me into the house. I felt like a child, safe in the knowledge that my mother would lead the way, make sure I was in the right place and that I would come to no more harm. How I had longed to be looked after by my mother, and how easily I slipped into that vulnerable role. Maybe because I had longed for it, I knew how to be her child. I wouldn't have predicted it. I would have predicted that I would find it difficult to be the youngster I had stopped being when I lost my mother. But it seemed the child in me was only behind a closed door, not a locked one.

The living room was lit with candles, and a thin line of white smoke wound its way upward from a joint balanced in a great chunky ashtray on the large wooden coffee table that I had stubbed my toes on many times as a child.

175

"Sit down," she said, wafting a hand toward the sofa. She sat on a large cushion on the floor, crossing her legs, then leaned over, took the joint, and held it out to me. I didn't move to take it, and she made a gesture as if to say *go on*. Maybe it sounds naïve, but I didn't know my mother smoked. I mean, not even a cigarette, and here she was smoking drugs. It surprised me how shocked I was in that moment. I'm no prude, and I have friends who smoke the occasional spliff, and I already knew my mother was a bit of a hippie; but for some reason it stung me to realize she smoked, and smoked alone too. I had only ever done it at college with friends. I wouldn't even know how to roll one.

Looking at her, realizing she was an expert smoker, I saw that I was hostage to the same illusions my own children had of me, namely that I assumed my mother had never done anything naughty, and certainly not illegal.

She leaned a little closer, to urge me to take it, and I did. I took a drag.

"These are no good for you," I said.

My mother smiled and nodded. "It's been a long time since I did it, just a little treat now and then."

Jeanie sat on the carpet, perched against some pillows, knees akimbo with her bare

176

feet pressed together. Her long skirt pooled in the space created in her lap, like a big painted bowl. She stared at me, a small smile dancing over her lips. "Whenever I see you, you're all scratched up," she said. "You looked like you've been in a fight with a cat." She grinned. "And it looks like the cat won."

I took another drag on the joint, felt the smoke reach my toes from the inside, and it didn't catch in my throat or anything. It was nice. I felt calm.

"I could beat a cat in a fight," I said.

"Could you beat a dog?" she asked.

"Maybe, if it was a little one," I said, smiling.

"Ooh, I don't know, I think a little one would be all scrappy and hard to get hold of." She took a cushion and pretended to wrestle with it. "I'd do better against a big dog." She stretched forward to take the spliff from me, and leaned back, flamboyantly throwing one arm behind her head and closing her eyes as she inhaled deeply and blew a fine stream of smoke leisurely through a pout.

After a long, peaceful silence in the dim light of the room, I almost forgot what we were talking about. I was distracted by my mother's realness, the authenticity of her being here in the same room as me. Her sheer existence and tangibility. I let it wash over me; it felt good to be home.

Jeanie made a sound like a hum. She was so stoned.

"I wouldn't have to fight a bear," she said, her eyes still shut. "I could charm it into submission."

"A bear would rip you to shreds," I said.

"Nah," she said, waving her hand lazily and continuing to smoke. "I've met bears and charmed them all. Human bears." Her eyelids opened a fraction and I could see the effort it took her to focus on me. She pointed at me with the skinny joint. "Human bears are hairy on the inside, so watch out!"

I laughed, and she laughed, and after a while, she stood with unsteady effort, holding out both hands to pull me to my feet. She linked her arm through mine and we leaned against each other like old ladies helping each other across a road.

"You know, I'd never hit an animal," she said. "I'm a vegetarian."

"But you would *charm* a bear?" I said.

"Oh yes," she said, straightening up and rolling her shoulder seductively. "It's in my nature."

■ ■ ■ ■

I was too hungry to smoke, much more likely to faint, and my mouth watered as my mother hustled me into the kitchen and cut a slice from a loaf of bread. I could smell it, and when she smeared the butter thickly over it, I could almost taste the smooth coolness of it in my mouth. The refrigerator light lit up her face angelically, and she held up a jar of jam like it was the Holy Grail. "Want this?" she said.

"Henry make that?" I said, smiling.

"Best jam in town," she said.

"Give it to me. Thick!"

Bread and butter with plum jam had never tasted as good as it did sitting there eating it with my mother, our appreciation of it heightened by the smoke in our lungs We just nodded and moaned our gratitude. Jeanie threw her head back and sighed loudly, licking the jam from her lips and then from the plate.

"Pig," I said, and she snorted at me.

"Where have you been?" she said, when there were only crumbs in front of us. "I always wished I'd found out where you live, so I could drop by and see you. But when you left, I realized too late, and you were like smoke in the air. Gone." Her hand swam in the air as she said this, mimicking the smoke rising from the ashtray.

"I didn't mean to leave it so long," I said. "But you've got your lives, you and Faye, I didn't want to interfere and be a nuisance."

"Silly," my mother said, pushing herself up from the kitchen table and heading for the living room again. Her long skirt trailed on the floor and she appeared to glide from one room to the other. "You almost hurt my feelings," she said over her shoulder, and I could see she meant it, though she pretended she didn't.

Flumping down on the pillows again, she rolled another joint and I watched her in our comfortable silence.

She inhaled casually, and smoking looked so cool. My mother really knew how to do it. "Faye and me, we're on our own, we don't get that many visitors, and you're special. One: you saved Faye's life, and two: we have a connection." She pointed at me and herself. "I wasn't the only one who felt it. Right, sister? *You* are my guardian angel, ergo you cannot be a nuisance."

Her easy, wide smile displayed the confidence she had in knowing she wasn't alone in her feelings. I nodded. "We definitely have a connection. It's just been hard for me to get back here."

"I understand," she said. Although she couldn't possibly.

I must have fallen asleep because when I opened my eyes, there were a lot more candles flickering and my mother held a glass of water to my lips. I took a sip and felt every molecule of cold liquid flowing into the far corners of me, finding the flowery outcroppings of my dried-out lungs. I took the glass from her and drained it.

"When was the last time you drank?" Jeanie said.

"I can't even remember," I told her.

"You're a strange one, Faye. You were talking in your sleep." She brushed a strand of hair from my face. " 'Mother, I'm thirsty,' you were saying, and I thought, well, anyone who is thirsty in their dreams is bound to be thirsty in real life. And you look so tired. You want to stay here tonight?"

I nodded, and she took my glass, turning to set it on the low wooden table behind her, where there was a bowl of milky water. As she had done during my last visit, Jeanie tended to the scratches on my head with Dettol, but it wasn't just the last time I was here that she had done this. This was the smell of scabbed knees, the smell of a childhood spent playing outdoors, with a mother waiting at home to make everything better again.

My mother knelt on the floor in front of me. Her hair, which had been flowing around her shoulders, was now piled messily on top of her head.

"Faye." Her voice was soft and seemed to come from a long way off. My eyes slid over to her, and I felt so sleepy from the dope and, I suppose, my difficult journey, but I could see her face was serious. "Faye," she said again, holding my hand in hers. "I think you've been sent to me, I think you're my sign."

"A sign of what?" I said.

"A sign that you're meant to be a part of Faye's life, and mine. A fortune-teller told me that a woman would crash into our lives and take care of me and my daughter."

"A fortune-teller?" I said, laughing lightly.

"Don't you dare laugh at me," she said, and I stopped.

"*Yes,* a fortune-teller. She said I should look out for this woman because she was going to be important in our life. She said my daughter would grow up without a mother and that I would need your help." Her voice and eyes were earnest.

"She shouldn't have said stuff like that," I

said, in awe at the fortune-teller's accuracy.

"But she did," Jeanie insisted. "And I don't *care* if you believe in that shit or not, because, I feel it" — she pressed her hand hard against her heart — "in here. It may not be a scientific fact, but I believe it, it's my truth, *my* sign. So I'm going to need your help, okay?"

"Okay," I said, and gave her a weak smile. She took my face in both her hands and kissed me, drawing back to look at me with a warmth so full and complete that it took my feeble smile and raised it to Herculean.

"I meant what I said when I let you in."

I thought back to her first words to me, but couldn't remember them. I shook my head gently.

"You're our guardian angel."

Jeanie made tea and placed my favorite Metal Mickey mug in my hands.

"I love candlelight," I said, enjoying the coziness and closeness of the flickering on the walls.

"There's a power cut. There's always a power cut." Jeanie sat on her cushion, legs tucked underneath her; I couldn't sit like that anymore, it hurt too much when I stood up. She sipped her tea from an enormous steaming cup, then put the cup down decisively and stood up. "Follow me," she said, and I did. She led me through the kitchen and out the back door, where she told me to wait. Jeanie went round the side of the house and returned with a ladder, which she maneuvered awkwardly as though it were a huge mannequin. By the time I went to help her, she had leaned it over the fence and against a tree in the neighbor's garden and started to climb it.

"My God, what are you doing?" I said.

"Don't blaspheme. I'm climbing a ladder." She pulled herself into the crook at the top of the trunk, her foot levering her up from the top rung. I saw her reach up and pull herself higher and to one side until she was roosted on a branch that didn't look that wide. I thought I could see her smiling, but most of her was lost to me in the darkness and shadows of the tree. All I could clearly see were her feet dangling down and splayed like Mary Poppins when she descends, holding her umbrella.

"Up you come," she called down to me.

"No!" I said.

"Come on," she said.

"It's too high," I whispered loudly. "And it's not your tree."

She didn't answer and — annoyed — I put one foot on the ladder and pressed my

184

weight against it, checking to see if it would slide away. I adjusted it slightly so that the bottom of the ladder was wedged more firmly into the lawn, and less likely to slip. When I got to the top I puffed, not knowing what to do next. I could see Jeanie's face now and her teeth as she grinned at me. She looked relaxed; she could have been in a hammock.

"Afraid of heights?" she said.

"Afraid of falling," I replied, sounding more grown-up than I liked.

"Should only be afraid of landing," she said, with a tinkle of laughter in her voice. "Land well, that's my advice. Don't worry about the heights, or the falls; just land like a cat every time."

"Don't need to land well if you don't climb up trees in the first place," I said, thinking about the box and how sometimes the fall was worth it, but this wasn't.

I tried to pull myself up but couldn't get a good grip; all the branches seemed bendy. Jeanie grasped my wrist and pulled. I puffed and grappled my way into a sitting position. Jeanie was like a sparrow that looks comfortable sitting on a telephone wire, so at ease she was; I felt like an ungainly pigeon, trying to stay balanced.

"What if I fall?" I said.

"You won't."

"What if I do?" I insisted.

"I told you: *land well.*" She glanced over at me and giggled. "Come on, I bet you've done riskier things than this. I often come up here to look at the stars."

Jeanie reached into her pocket and drew out another spliff. She cupped a match, which flared and died, struggling against what had seemed like a very light breeze until we came up here where the air was more alive. After three attempts, it was lit, and somehow she seemed to lie back, there must have been a branch behind her that I couldn't see. She took a long drag, and as she exhaled we watched the smoke plume out into the night.

"Try to relax," she said, passing me the joint as though she were a doctor and this was the medicine. Gripping a branch like it was a piece of shipwreck that would save my life, I leaned forward to take it. Like her, I took a long drag, but I didn't pass it back straightaway. I found a good hold on a limb, and in my next breath inhaled a lungful; the sky spun slightly, and now I didn't care as much.

"You're reckless," I said, managing to smile as I passed the joint back to her.

"It's only a tree," she said.

186

"We're grown women," I said.

"I suppose," said Jeanie. "I'm only twenty-five. I've always felt grown-up, but maybe I've just always been a child."

She drew a breath in and blew out smoke rings that started out neat, then grew and billowed as they rose into the leaves above us, becoming less defined and disappearing into the dark foliage. We sat in silence for a while, by which I mean we didn't speak, but the sound of the leaves up there was louder than I would have imagined; they rustled and swished like a dry broom on a hard floor. The stars were bright and blinked on and off as the slimmer branches swayed and the leaves sometimes revealed, sometimes obscured the sky above. It was quiet and cool and there was a dreamlike quality amplified by the grassy taste of the smoke, and the rhythmic passing back and forth of the joint, and the gentle roll of our vessel.

"I need to be more *reck*," Jeanie said. He voice sounded slow and slurred.

"What's reck?" I said, my voice also blurring at the edges; my mouth felt gummy and made a clicking sound when I spoke.

"I don't know," said Jeanie, "I'm wondering if it's the opposite of reckless?"

"Oh, right. Yeah, if something can be reckless, then something can be full of reck," I said, pondering this word that was new to me and, for all I knew, didn't exist. "Anyway, Jeanie, you need to be more careful. You need to look after yourself, you have responsibilities. You shouldn't be climbing trees."

Jeanie tutted, and neither of us spoke for a long time. "I want Faye to climb trees," she said. And I felt the same about my own children, but my fear of being up here, being hurt, not being able to get back home because I'd fallen out of a bloody tree or something was skewing my thoughts.

"Opposite of ruthless is ruth, did you know that?" she said.

"I never thought about that before," I said.

We lay there, mostly in silence. Every now and then one of us said, "Reck," emphasizing the satisfying end of the word.

After what seemed like a long time, during which I somehow settled comfortably into the tree, I turned to Jeanie. "What did that fortune-teller say that makes you think I'm a sign?"

"That a woman would crash into our lives," she said, and smiled, turning to face me. "And that's just what you did when you came into our lives the first time. You stopped Faye being hit by that car."

I sluggishly thought of how I'd been flung

through the atmosphere, a high-speed roller-coaster ride, with no belt (and no bloody roller coaster), and how I had crashed under the Christmas tree, and crashed into the shed a little earlier that evening.

I didn't say anything for a long time; then I said, "You don't think I was just a person who happened to be in the right place at the right time?"

"Nope," she said, popping the *p* sound at the end of the word. "I know you think the fortune-telling thing is stupid — I could tell by the look on your face earlier — but I've always had the feeling that I won't make old bones, Faye. Do you know what I mean by that?"

My mouth was drier than ever and I found it hard to swallow, as if my body had forgotten what to do. I gazed at my sweet mother for a moment longer, then up into the sky, knowing with utter certainty that she only had about a year or so left to live. I nodded in reply to her question. Heat sprang to the backs of my eyes, and I let a tear roll, unseen. If a friend told me she thought she would die young, I would try to convince her otherwise. But I knew my mother was right.

She paused and struck another match.

The flame burst into life as though it were frightened it would never get the chance to be a light in the world, so much so that it almost instantly put itself out again. My mother cupped the flame and allowed it to glimmer, bringing the stubby end of the short joint to her lips and inhaling to bring it back to life.

"Why do you think you won't make old bones?" I asked, wondering about her premonition that I knew to be correct.

"I don't know, I just feel like I'm not long for this world. My parents died young, and I suppose I feel like I'm a part of that pattern. I can't imagine being older, I mean I really, really can't picture it, it's like it's not there for me. Not written. And every year I get these terrible coughs, I'm sure it'll kill me one day."

"Go to a doctor, get it checked out, stop smoking," I said, with urgency.

She shook her head. "No doctors. In my experience, doctors kill you quicker, and I don't do this very often," she said, holding up the stumpy bit of the joint. "What I'm really interested in is looking for something that makes me feel like Faye will be okay no matter what happens to me. I want to know that without me she'll be loved, be happy, live well. I always felt like it would be a good idea to surround myself with good people who could help, be a safety net for her. But somehow, that hasn't happened. The people in my life who I've trusted are nice, but hardly sensible, hardly the sort who would be good for looking after a child. Faye's never been christened, but I wish she had been, because she ought to have godparents. I've failed there. You're the kind of person I would have picked, the kind of person who could bridge what I won't be able to provide for my daughter. You're like someone I already know well."

"We've only met twice," I said, not meaning it, and I spoke so quietly I could barely hear myself, but Jeanie did.

"It doesn't matter," she said. "There are people you've known your whole life and you don't know them, can't connect, everything is superficial. And then there's people like you and me. Instant connection. Time and frequency are not relevant with matters like this."

"How did you get so wise?" I said.

I heard the smile in her voice. "Thought you said I was reckless?" I didn't say anything. She paused, as she thought about it. "Self-preservation, I guess, a lot of reading, the kind of advice and teaching you come across at festivals."

The breeze picked up then; goose bumps feathered across my arms and legs, and I wanted to get down.

"I've been thinking about you since the first time you came into my life," said Jeanie. "There's something about you, something so strong and so familiar that I can't ignore it. I just know that we'll be friends, and I know you might feel uncomfortable because we're only two meetings away from being complete strangers. But I have been dying to ask you, and promised myself that the next time you appeared in my life I would do just that. And then I worried you might think it's all a bit soon, but nevertheless I promised myself that I would ask you to help me, no matter what."

"What is it?" I said.

"If anything happens to me, I want you to look after Faye, be her godmother."

"What?" I said. "Jeanie, you hardly know me, you should pick someone you've known longer."

"But we have nobody, her and me, no family, no reliable friends. I can tell you're the right kind of person. Look at the way you were about coming up here: the kind of person who looks before she leaps, but then climbs up anyway. Me — I'm different — but we come from the same basic place, I think. You have children, you must be able to understand where I'm coming from. And we'll get to know each other better in time, so I'm just putting it out there now, knowing that I'm right about you — so if I die, will you take her?"

I felt dizzy and sick. "Can we get down from here?" I said. "I'm cold."

She reached out and put a hand over mine. "I bet you're a better mum than I am," she said, and I gasped, felt the sorrow rise up in me, louder and more intense, like the sound of those leaves higher up the tree.

"I'm only asking you to be a godparent," she went on. "Most of the people I could ask — and there aren't many — would say yes without thinking. You, on the other hand, are actually taking it seriously. It's just another thing that makes me think you're the one. You're very . . ." She paused and smiled wide. *"Reck."*

As we climbed down the ladder my thoughts turned in a slow-moving whirlpool; I was living testimony that Jeanie's daughter would be okay. It was within my power to give her something better than a promise: proof that Faye would be okay. If only I could tell her who I was. But in doing that, I would be confirming what my mother already feared to be true: that she would die, and not live to watch me grow up. I knew that telling her the incredible story that we would meet again all these years down the line, via a time-traveling box, would be no compensation for knowing that she had only a year left to live, if she believed me at all.

Part of me worried that Jeanie could so readily farm out her daughter — me — to a virtual stranger, but I couldn't help feeling flattered that she'd picked me, and I couldn't help thinking that Jeanie was completely right: I was the perfect person to look after little Faye, I was totally trustworthy, I was *me.* Jeanie's instincts were spot-on. But what I didn't like was that while *I* knew that, she didn't.

Her naïveté unnerved me. Then I thought about how she'd been passed from foster home to foster home, a child handed from one virtual stranger to another as she grew up, and, she'd implied, not a very pleasant experience. Maybe she *was* well placed to identify the most appropriate caregiver, based on her gut. Maybe she was like a child in an ice-cream shop who says *I want that one* to the first thing she likes the look of.

And in the end, what did it really matter? Despite the fact that my mother would die, in spite of everything, I *was* okay, I was happy, and I was loved. I couldn't promise my mother what she wanted from me. But perhaps I could tell her something to put her mind at ease.

This would have to be a conversation for the following day. I was overwhelmed. There is only so much the body and mind can take, and I had reached my limit. As I floated from the cool garden into the kitchen, there was a swirling sensation in my head and the room started to turn too. I swayed to the side, and the desire to sleep was so intense that I could taste it like sweet wool in my mouth. My mother held my hand, and I don't remember getting up the stairs, but that's where she took me. I have a faded memory in which I sat at the end of little Faye's bed. Jeanie picked little Faye up and carried her — still sound asleep — into her own bedroom, so that I could have little Faye's bed. I have a hazy recollection of lying down and thinking how the bed was still warm from where my younger self had lain until a few moments before; my body covering that space and creating a larger space of warmth. I think my mother returned to me — having deposited little Faye into her own bigger bed — to pull the checked eiderdown over me. And I do remember thinking that my mother was putting me to bed twice: my six-year-old self and my thirty-six-year-old self. I don't remember falling asleep, because I didn't chase it. Sleep was there waiting for me, with its soft jaws wide open. They silently shut and swallowed me whole.

CHAPTER 14

Little Faye sat like a pixie, cross-legged at the end of my bed, her head tipped to one side by a lopsided smile. She was wearing a school uniform with white patterned socks up to her knees; her messy brown hair was pulled back into a plait, stray tendrils curling round her face. I sat up and winced; I was aching all over.

"Thank you for your bed," I said.

"Mi casa es su casa," she said, smiling back at me.

"My house is your house?" I said, and she nodded. "Well, that is very kind of you." And *extremely* accurate, I thought. Her house was indeed my house.

"You going to school?" I said.

"Uh-huh."

I communicated with little Faye with the careful small talk I used with all children. I don't know if I should have been conversing differently, considering that I was talking to myself. Whether it was me or *not*, I could only do what I always do when talking to children, which was to make her feel comfortable in my company. I didn't want to interrogate myself as a child, because no matter the circumstances, I was still only a child.

"Do you remember me?" I asked.

"Of course!" she said, "You grabbed me when that car nearly hit me."

"That's right, I did. Are you completely fine now?"

"I was completely fine, even at the time. It was you who got hurt. Are *you* completely fine?"

"Actually, I injured myself again." I pointed to my scratches.

"Looks like it hurts a lot," she said.

"It doesn't."

"Will you have scars?"

"I don't think so," I said.

"Have you got *any* scars?"

"Uh, I've got a very small one on my hip, from chicken pox."

"Me too!" She pulled the waistband of her skirt down a little, to show me.

"Oh, so you have," I said. "Yeah, mine's a little bit like that. And I've got a scar on my knee from roller-skating."

"Show me," said Faye.

I pulled the cover off, and showed her the barely visible line below my knee, and the little round marks where I had fallen on stones when I was about twelve years old. "It's not easy to see," I said, peering at it closely myself.

"Will you still be here when I get home from school?"

"I'm not sure . . ." I started to say, and then my mother appeared in the doorway with a cup of tea.

"You're welcome to stay, as you know," she said, coming over and putting the mug on the bedside table. "But won't your family miss you?"

"They've gone away for a few days, to visit my husband's parents," I said.

"Well then, that's worked out well — that is, if you do want to stay."

I looked at Faye and shrugged. "It looks like I will definitely be here after school then."

She clapped her hands and jumped off the bed, shouting, "See you later!" with barely a glance back at me.

Jeanie touched my shoulder. "I'm going to walk Faye to school. I'll get you some breakfast when I get back," she said, and winked.

How I wished I could take those winks

back home with me.

While they were out of the house, I went to the shed. I knew it would take my mother about twenty minutes to get back, and I wanted to check the box and see if I needed to make any repairs. Better to do it now, in case it was dark again when I left. I needed to make sure I could get home and guard against any damage when I came back next time.

Next time: the 1970s, my regular destination. What about your past? How often would you travel there, given the chance? Often? Never? And when you got there, would you think about staying forever?

I had a proper look at the box. It was getting battered, but then the only connection I seemed to need to make with the box was getting in it. I didn't think the box itself had to stay sturdy for the journey, I didn't need to worry about the bottom dropping out while I was in between the past and the present. It was more like a portal. A door. And it didn't matter if a door was hanging off its hinges, as long as you could get through it, right? What's more, as I inspected the box, I understood that it must be a portal at both ends. I'd already noticed that the box in the past was newer than the one I'd found in my loft, and I had no doubt that there was an older version of this box sitting on my mattress at home right now, which meant things could exist at two different places in time. Plus, I knew that two of the same thing could exist at the same time, like me and little me. That was as far as my logical brain went before giving up. I stopped thinking about how it all worked; after all, I didn't need to know how the computer worked in order to use it.

But what would happen if someone threw the box away, or destroyed it? What would happen to me if the 1970s box was destroyed, but I still got in it at the other end? I didn't like to think where I could end up or what might happen to me. I pushed those thoughts away, before they ruined everything.

Even though I'd worked out that it didn't really need it, I felt happier taping up the side that had torn away, just in case the box worked better intact, and also because it was a precious item and deserved some respect. There was a roll of packing tape in the shed, and I did a quick repair job, then padded back to the house for a wash.

The bathroom was painfully familiar. The tiny things I would never have brought to mind were the most distinct. The counter-top next to the sink had a chip in it where I'd dropped a paperweight on it once, and there was a Captain Caveman sticker on the mirror that I must have put there. After a quick scrub at the sink, I borrowed my mother's face cream (roses) and her mas-cara. I was a bit nervous about handling the *will-you-look-after-Faye-if-something-happens-to-me* conversation, which I just knew she'd bring up again. I didn't want to lie to her. I could just say yes, knowing that I would end up with Em and Henry and that would all work out okay. Then again, it seemed like a big thing to lie about. And she was my mother, after all. Maybe I could simply promise that I would ensure, one way or another, that little Faye would be fine. That I would keep tabs on her. Strictly speaking, that was the truth, self-preservation and all that. But somehow I didn't think that would satisfy my mother. She wanted a solid promise, no tricks, no relying on wordplay; *not technically lying* would not count. And anyway, why add even more lies to what was already going on?

I still toyed with the idea of coming clean to my mother, telling her who I was; there was a possibility that she of all people might believe me, by virtue of her personality. But what if she didn't? It was all very well thinking that because she was a spiritual person and a bit of a hippie, with a penchant for signs and a connection with me she couldn't really account for, she would just take her time-traveling future-grown-up-daughter at her word. But I didn't think she would. If she believed me, then I would be telling her she didn't have long to live, and I didn't want to do that. And the other thing was, when all this stuff was being talked about last night, we were both stoned, especially her. Maybe when she got home, all of that would have been forgotten, and we could have a nice, simple day together.

It felt like madness, sitting in the kitchen, waiting for her. This quiet moment, the clock ticking, the sun casting a bright beam across the floor; this moment in which I did nothing other than wait, this felt the craziest. I had to repeat a mantra to myself — *yes, you are really here* — otherwise I might have started trying to convince myself I was in a hospital ward somewhere, in a coma, having a vivid dream. I was conscious of my heart beating, of the random need to scratch my leg; I touched my arm softly, felt the material so vividly under my fingertips: this time in the past was as real as the rest of my life. And what if it hadn't been? If it wasn't real, then what would I do differently? Nothing. It was like worrying; it really made no difference to the outcome.

I heard the front door open and inhaled sharply. I braced myself, so as not to appear too madly keen to see my mother enter the room. She smiled that broad, easy smile and sat down opposite me.

"Good kid," I said.

"Like a dream," she said. "I just want to protect her." She gazed into my eyes, and I knew that last night's conversation had merely been on pause. "What's your husband like?" she asked, getting up again immediately and pouring milk into a small pan on the stove.

"Eddie? He's a good man. He's got kind eyes, know what I mean?" My mother nodded, stirring the pan absentmindedly, her concentration directed at me. "He's good with numbers, always been in finance." A tiny grimace flashed over my mother's face. "I know," I said. "Sounds boring. But he's not boring, he's gorgeous, and funny, and a great dad."

"Good in bed?" she asked, grabbing a bag of oats from a cupboard.

"Yes," I said, and felt myself redden. I

don't know if I looked sheepish, but I felt embarrassed at the directness of her question, and the fact that I had never had a mother-daughter-type talk about sex with anyone, let alone my actual mother. "He's got brown hair, he lets it get too long, and I have to remind him to get it cut. He's tall, I can really lose myself in his arms."

My mother left the wooden spoon in the pan and leaned back against the counter, folding her arms. "He's starting to sound good now," she said.

"He's training to be a vicar," I said, putting a stop to my mother getting dreamy-eyed over my husband. She frowned slightly.

"Really?" She returned to the spoon.

"Yes."

"It seems a world away from finance."

"It is, but he's the same man. I'm not sure either finance or religion really suit him. But he's doing what he needs to do, what he's made for."

"The love of my life was not my usual type," she said. "Faye's father was in *law enforcement.*" She said it like it was a dirty word, but any shock I felt was nothing to do with his job description.

"I didn't know she had a dad," I said. "I mean — you know what I mean."

"He was a lovely man, but it was complicated. We loved each other, but . . ." She gazed out the window, then busied herself making porridge and tea. I watched her and waited, pressing Record on my memory button to ensure I stored this image of her moving gracefully around the kitchen, stirring, pouring, reaching up for a packet of sugar, and then putting everything on the table. Domestic perfection. She placed a jar of jam on the table.

"We get through a lot of this, good old Henry," she said, dolloping a spoonful into the middle of her bowl.

"You were saying about Faye's dad," I said, a flicker of something stirring inside me deep down. I knew *nothing* about my father. I knew I must have one — biologically — but I'd barely thought about him, never mourned his loss, and I suppose that's because you can't lose something you never feel you've possessed, never known. Vaguely, now and then as a child or a teenager, I had imagined a father coming to collect me from Em and Henry. But if I took the fantasy too far, I realized I didn't want that to happen. I had wanted my mother, always, but not a stranger. I felt safe with Em and Henry. And Henry was all the father I needed: reliable, practical, kind.

Because I had no mental image of my

father at all, I know it was a conversation I'd never had with my mother as a child, because I wouldn't have forgotten if we had spoken about it. As I got older, without giving the idea too much pointed thought, I kind of assumed I was the product of a one-night stand. Not love.

"You said he was the love of your life, but . . . ?" I said.

"But he's married, and has other children, and he's high-ranking. The sort of job that would be ruined by a scandal."

"But if you loved each other, why can't he help you?"

"I moved away to protect him, to stop him having to make choices that could ruin everything for him."

"But didn't he want to see me?" I said. She looked confused. I didn't realize my mistake at first, and then I felt the word *me* in my mouth as awkward as a marble. I tried to ignore it.

"What do you mean?" she said.

"You know, his daughter? Didn't he want to get to know her?"

"Uh, well, I moved away when I was pregnant. He didn't know. This was all years ago, obviously; I was in Ireland. He would have been thrown to the wolves if he'd been found out. He had other children, and a good wife. He was doing good things in his community, making changes, making a difference. I loved him, but I just couldn't do it to him."

"You must have broken his heart," I said.

"I'll never know," she said.

"But you do know, don't you? He loved you, and you loved him. Maybe you should have let him choose." It wasn't that I felt indignant that she'd left someone who might have loved *me,* but more that it seemed a terrible shame to not let a person know that they had a child in the world; and also I wanted my mother to feel loved — as much love as possible — she deserved that, and she'd walked away from it.

My porridge sat untouched on the table. Jeanie stirred hers slowly, and the jam made a pink swirl in it.

"Maybe I should have let him choose, but I didn't. *I* chose, and now it's in the past. And that is where it must be left." She searched my face, her eyes roaming mine. "Love is not just about taking what you want, you know. Love can certainly make you feel *justified* in taking what you want, you can *let* it make you do things, or you can make sensible choices that sometimes lead you away from love. But listen to me" — she reached out and put her hand over mine — "listen, there is always plenty of love to be found. I lost some things but gained others, I minimized the heartache of others, and I've found a special kind of love in bringing up Faye by myself. It's precious."

"Will you tell her about him?" I asked, knowing that she wouldn't.

"It's just me and her, and that's enough for now. One day, if she wants to know more, I'll tell her. I think if I tell her too much, it will just create an unnecessary longing in her. An itch that can't be scratched. An itch that doesn't need to exist for her."

My mother wasn't around when I reached the age I might have started asking questions, and she was right, I'd never had much of an itch to know my father. That longing had always been superseded — completely overshadowed — by my longing for *her*.

"Look, Jeanie, last night you were saying that you wouldn't see old bones, you were worrying what would happen to Faye if you weren't around."

"Yeah, I want you to be there for her."

"Like a godparent?" I said.

"Just a promise," she said, fluttering her fingers as though a promise is an easy thing to give away.

"Well, maybe her father would want to look after her," I said.

"No, he can't do that," she said quietly.

"Why not? Is he dead?"

"I don't know. I don't even know if he's still where I met him. But all the upset that I tried to avoid by leaving in the first place, it would all come flooding back. Why save him from drowning before, if only to drown him now?"

"Is he a good man?" I said.

"Yes, and I have no doubt he would love her, but to ask him to take care of her? That would mean his wife and family taking her in. That would be like handing a chicken to a fox. No. Where Faye goes if I die will need to be a place where she at least starts on a level playing field. Better still, a place that starts with love and open arms, not folded arms and accusations."

I felt a twinge of curiosity. I wondered if my mother was wrong, and maybe living with my father — if she could have found him — might have been a good thing for me. And then, like a trailer for a movie, I saw before me an imagined life, one that unfolded like a roll of carpet: a life without Em and Henry, a life that led me down a divergent path where perhaps I wouldn't have met Eddie and where I would have children, but they wouldn't be Esther and Evie. My mouth was suddenly dry, and I wanted to stop talking about things that might change my future; a future I was happy with, apart from my mother not being there.

"I don't want to talk about him anymore," she said, and I was glad of it.

I put a spoonful of sweet porridge in my mouth. It was delicious.

"Well, what about Em and Henry?" I said, planting a seed of what was to come.

"What? Godparents? No! They're too old," she said.

"They're safe and secure, and they live nearby. They'd do a good job," I said, in the knowledge that I was recommending them for a task they'd already done, and succeeded at.

"Oh, but they'd be *boring*," Jeanie said, pouting.

"They'd be perfect." I felt crushed and defensive of the sweet, kind people who'd taken me in, loved me, and kept me safe.

Jeanie just shrugged. "They're nice," she said, and it wasn't a compliment. I wanted to chastise her like a child who hadn't thanked someone for a gift.

"Jeanie, they care about you, *both* of you, I could see that when I met you at their place. Don't be mean, please. You know they'd do anything for you."

She shrugged again, and I dropped it.

"Anyway, about you, old bones and that. It may never happen," I said, feeling like a fraud, knowing she would be dead fairly soon and, all of a sudden finding it hard to swallow, I let my spoon just sit in the bowl.

"It will," she said.

I covered my face with my hands and sighed; my breath rebounded off my palms, warm and moist.

She concentrated on her food now, and her tea, and smiled as if to wash away the unpleasant topic of conversation.

"After this, let's go into town, okay?"

"That sounds nice," I said. I knew I shouldn't get so upset; it wasn't as though I didn't know what was going to happen to my mother. There were no surprises here.

We strolled into town; we walked and talked. It was one of the nicest times in my life, yet I can't tell you what was said. Isn't it funny that I had planned to commit everything to memory during these visits to the past, and yet I couldn't? Maybe all that mattered was that it was a lovely moment, shared with someone so special. The thing is, we weren't discussing matters of serious consequence, so I didn't feel the need to remember it. That's how most of life is, I guess.

Did you have a nice time?

Yes.

What happened?

I don't know!

I became ultra-conscious again as we walked past shops leading into town. The contents of the shop windows drew my eyes, making me smile and shake my head. Nineteen-seventies toasters, hand whisks, vacuum cleaners with the long bag at the back, very little chrome but lots of that avocado green, lemon yellow, and baby blue. Women were wearing cream slacks with sharp creases in the front, or A-line skirts, and almost everyone seemed to have a perm, except Jeanie. I was in a living museum of my own childhood. All the things I had seen in shop windows as I grew up, all the things I had noticed day after day, all the things no one ever seemed to buy that stayed in the window for years. Mannequins that always looked slightly disheveled, with hair that didn't fit, standing at jaunty angles, hands on plastic anorexic hips. I also saw the things I had always wanted, always desired, in other shops. We never had any money and I never asked for anything, not from my mother or from Em and Henry. But some objects your eyes settle on, and they don't leave your sight line until your feet carry you too far away, and then the image travels with you in your mind's eye, and into bed at night to stay with you there, gradually fading while you sleep until it is no longer there in the morning. Not reappearing until you pass the shop window again . . .

Roller skates. Shiny, metal, with red straps that go over your shoes.

I saw them, and remembered that as a child I had wanted them so badly, and vowed that if I ever got rich that was what I would buy.

I stopped and stared at the skates. My mother walked on a few paces before realizing that I had fallen behind. When she stopped and turned, I heard her laughing.

"I don't believe it!" she said. "Faye always stops and stares at those skates — you really are like two peas in a pod." She came back and stood beside me at the window.

Those were *my* skates. Not similar, but actual. I had *that* pair of skates when I was about six or seven years old, and I realized something important in that moment as I gazed at them through the glass.

I realized that I couldn't remember how I got them.

CHAPTER 15

The cold of the glass window pressed against my hot forehead as I stared at the skates. "Jeanie," I said, staring straight ahead into the shop. "Can Faye roller-skate?"

"No," she said, and I turned to look at her. "She'd love to, but skates are well out of my price range." She shrugged. "But she is *excellent* at hula-hooping."

She was right, I was. I still am.

My mother walked and talked about how she'd learned to hula, and I drifted beside her, listening, soaking her up, gathering all the jigsaw pieces of her life that she was giving me. Every piece was a clue, an important part of the whole. I walked slowly, my face raised to the sun, and sometimes it felt like my feet weren't touching the ground, and my mother's voice became a backdrop to my own curious mind. The question I couldn't shake was the one about the roller skates. How could they have come into my

216

possession? Em and Henry wouldn't have bought them for me, I don't think, and anyway, I had them *before* I lived with Em and Henry. My mother couldn't afford them, and we had no relatives. The question meandered through my mind, detouring here and there.

I would *never* have stolen them as a child. I was no thief, but then again . . . people change.

I had an epiphany, and I needed to be alone.

"Do you mind —" I said, cutting my mother off midsentence. "Sorry, do you mind if we split up for a little while? There's a couple of things I need to do."

"Of course." She touched my cheek; I loved the way she did that. And she smiled as if I was the only person in the whole world who mattered to her, which, ironically, I was.

Anyway, she told me she would get something for dinner, and asked if I would stay. I thought about the time difference between here and home; since previously twelve hours in the seventies had equated to just three in my present, two days here might mean half a day there. At that rate, with Eddie being away for a week, my absence wouldn't be noticed; I'd had the foresight to take a few days off work, just in case. I accepted her invitation, hoping to stay overnight. The excitement bubbled inside me, as if I had suddenly been told Christmas was rearranged for today. We agreed to meet in half an hour, and when she disappeared around the corner, I backtracked to the little shop that sold the roller skates.

One of the things you need to know about that shop, which was called Serendipity, is that it's a family-run store. I mean, back then all shops seemed to be like that, but this one I knew was still going, thirty years on. The lady who owned the place back in the day still owned it and, as far as I knew, still worked there a few days a week. When we visit that area, my children love it because it sells all sort of knickknacks, the sorts of treasures that little girls and boys keep forever. Small things that can be hidden in the palm of your hand. Tiny glazed animals that a child knows so intimately, because its details can only be seen when it's held very, very close to your eyes.

So when I opened the door to the shop and the little bell rang, it felt as familiar as opening my own front door. There was coolness inside like a cold drink on a hot day, and there were shelves and stacks adorned with colorful objects and large illustrated anthologies of children's poetry and stories. The bell brought footsteps from the back of the store, and a young woman, in her twenties, came to the counter like sunshine in a billowing yellow blouse with a huge collar, a brown skirt, and red sandals. She was tying an apron around her waist, and I smiled at her as though she were an old friend; she frowned for a fraction of a second before smiling back at me. In the etiquette of smiling, people are disconcerted when someone they don't know beams at them as though they've known them for years. This was a woman I knew, the owner of the shop, but younger than I'd ever known her. And what struck me is how little a person changes. As long as you can place them in context, a person is completely recognizable, whether they are seven or seventy. People who run small shops in small towns are minor celebrities, so I knew a lot about her: the man she had married, and the children they'd had, and when their shop was burgled, and when they raised money for charity; all those things and more, without ever really knowing her properly, and she not knowing me at all.

"Do you need any help?" she asked brightly.

"I'm just looking," I said, and steered into a narrow aisle, let my fingers touch items lightly, as though I were counting them. It's impossible not to touch things in that shop.

"Let me know if you can't find what you're looking for," she called.

"I will," I called back, and I heard her footsteps retreat.

The thing is, I wanted to buy the roller skates for little Faye. If I didn't buy them for her, then who would? I could leave it to chance, but that made no sense. I was here now, and I was thinking about getting the skates. So, ipso facto, I had to get them. Otherwise, who would? No one.

Perhaps my whole purpose — if there needed to be a purpose — in returning to the past was to buy roller skates for my younger self. I smiled to myself at the ridiculousness of that, and I smiled because I'd thought of the words *ipso facto,* which are words I love so much that whenever an occasion arises in which I can use them, I do. Same with *Pyrrhic victory,* although that opportunity arises less frequently.

Anyway, here I was, a woman in want of roller skates, in a shop that sold them. With no money, and nothing of value with which to barter. I was going to have to steal those roller skates, and I have to tell you, I didn't

220

feel good about that.

Apart from the fact that it was morally wrong, especially in a small shop like this, I didn't want to get caught by the police. What if I went to jail! The main thing that cleared this up for me was that I knew this shop was thriving to this very day, by which I mean thirty years later. The loss of one pair of roller skates wasn't going to ruin these people. Plus, I was pretty sure I could get away with it without being caught. I looked but saw no mirrors, and definitely no cameras.

I had a plan. I would go to the counter, and ask for something that the woman would need to go look for, out the back. Then I would just swiftly walk to the window display, pick them up, and leave. If you did these things fast enough, you could get away with it.

I walked back to the counter and called out a happy "Hello?"

The woman reappeared, wiping her hands on her apron and smiling. "Yes?"

"I was wondering if you have any of those Russian nesting dolls in a different color."

"I might, out the back, I'll go and look." She smiled again and disappeared.

That was easy enough. I walked straight over to the window and lifted the skates by their straps. I was careful, but as I extracted them from their shelf, I knocked a shiny, wooden toy policeman off his perch. He was painted with a whistle poised at his lips and had a rounded bottom that made him rock accusingly. I felt he wanted to blow that whistle for real and alert the shopkeeper. Well, let me tell you, he might as well have done, because as I put my hand on the handle of the door, I heard her voice.

"Do you want to buy those?" she asked, not unkindly, but not unknowingly either.

I deflated. The breath I'd been holding came out long and rushed, and I returned guiltily to the counter and placed the skates upon it.

"I do. More than anything, I do," I said.

"Would you like to pay for them?" she said.

"I want to, if you'll believe that. I have money, but not here, and I need these skates before I am able to give you the money for them."

She frowned at me. "You're not my usual shoplifter."

"I'm not. Not a shoplifter."

"But you were going to steal these." She pointed at the skates without taking her eyes off mine.

"Yes, I was," I said. "If I had anything to

222

give you for them, I would. If I had anything I could swap them for, then I would do that, but I don't."

"We don't take that kind of payment here anyway, I'm afraid."

Then I realized I did have something for this woman — whose name I knew as Elizabeth — something that might be more valuable to her than anything I could physically give her. I had information. I knew things about her. I suddenly felt elated and a bit breathless.

"Do you believe in fortune-tellers?" I asked her.

Her eyes crinkled, and she laughed. "What, those old ladies with the crystal balls at the seaside? Of course not."

"Okay, me neither," I said. "But if I could tell you about your life, your future, and you like what you hear, will you let me have these skates?"

She was curious, I could see that, but she was not taken in for a second. She thought I was a chancer, and she was no fool; but there was something in her eyes, and enough hesitation for me to have some hope. She walked past me and turned the open sign to closed on the door.

"Come out the back," she said, and then turning to look at me cynically over her shoulder, she added, "I'm only doing this because you're making a very quiet Tuesday morning more interesting than usual." She led me to the back of the shop, pointed at a stool, and sat on one herself. "You've got five minutes," she said.

And then I told her.

I told her the name of the man she would marry, and the names of the children they would have. I told her that her shop would be successful and loved by many for more than thirty years. I told her that she would win some money when she was older and her family would go on a foreign holiday for two weeks, and while they were away, their shop would be burgled, but not to worry, because everything would be all right anyway. And then I told her the thing I thought would make all the difference. One day, I said, her son would go missing, and he would be missing for three days. But he would be found safe and well, so when it happened, she must not worry too much, she must know that all would be well.

Her cynical face didn't change during all of this. She looked amused, as opposed to amazed. After a minute or so I stopped talking and leaned back. "So, what do you think?" I said.

"I think this is the craziest thing I've ever heard."

"Oh," I said, deflated. It was all true, and although I knew she had no reason to believe me, her disbelief was frustrating.

"Andrew Keel?" she said.

"Yes, you're going to marry him and be very happy. He's a lovely man."

"I don't know anyone called Andrew Keel," she said, pausing and looking at me with frank dismay, as though I were a magician who hadn't done a very good trick.

"You haven't met him yet, but you will."

"Elizabeth Keel," she said under her breath, whispering her future married name, even though she didn't believe it would ever be true.

"Elizabeth and Andrew Keel, and your children, Adam, Connie, and Zara."

"I do like those names," she said ponderously, but the distrust in her eyes only increased.

"Well, you would," I said. "You will choose them for your children."

"Well, maybe I won't now that you've told me I will," she said. "And you say that my son, Adam, will go missing?" She leaned forward, elbows on knees.

"Yes," I said, more keenly than ever, because she was showing an interest. "And

I can't remember the circumstances exactly, but he turns up, unhurt."

"What do you mean, you *can't remember*? I thought this was stuff from the future."

"Well, it feels like remembering, the way I do it," I said. "But as a mother, I know that it would kill me if one of my children went missing. I want to save you some future anguish. Adam will be fine, so try not to worry. Elizabeth, you are going to have a long and lovely life, with a good husband and three happy, successful children and a thriving business."

Elizabeth pushed against her knees and stood up. "Well, it's been fun, but your five minutes are up," she said, her voice as sunny as her clothes. "Time to reopen the shop and time for you to go."

"Can I have the skates?" I asked coyly.

"No," she said, guiding me out from the storeroom.

"I really need them," I said.

"I like your ingenuity. I like the lovely tale you told. Imagine if it were true," she said wistfully. "Imagine if I could actually believe in it." She laughed, and it sounded just like the bell when the shop door opened.

"You can live your life without any fear. Elizabeth." I turned to her, imploring. "You don't need to worry about your health, or your children. You're free to enjoy your life, knowing that all will be well. I guarantee it."

"All this for a pair of roller skates," she said. "Listen, I like you. I can't help it. But you're crazy. In a nice . . . unusual way." We were at the front of the shop again, and she was ushering me toward the exit. "But there's no way I can give you those skates in exchange for a bit of fairground whimsy."

I started to protest, but she showed me the palm of her hand, as though she were stopping traffic, so I shut up.

"However, I did notice you're wearing rings," she said. I offered my hand to her, and she took it, gently running her thumb over my wedding and engagement rings. "If you're desperate, give me one of your rings and you can take the skates today. When you come back with the money, I'll give it back to you."

I looked at her. She looked so young — she *was* so young — and pretty and practical, and she was doing this out of kindness, and that kindness was perfectly balanced with an astute sense of business. No wonder she had done so well.

"I have to be honest with you," I said. "It could be a very long time before I come back for it."

"Well, according to you, in a very long time I'll still be right here, so that's okay, isn't it?"

"You have to promise me you'll keep it safe," I said, feeling nauseated even as I was twisting the engagement ring from my finger.

"Funny, isn't it," she said, taking the ring in her palm and holding it tightly. She looked at me with a most serene and amused expression. "You tried to steal my roller skates, and now you're asking me to make the promises."

"Please," I said.

"I promise," she replied, closing her eyes and nodding once.

CHAPTER 16

When I visit people, I'm accustomed to bringing a gift, a bottle of wine or something. But I couldn't buy anything for my mother, obviously. Even if I'd brought some with me, my money was no good here — the future was as foreign as Mars when it came to currency — and I was finished with trying to steal. Anyway, my mother didn't seem to mind. She loved having me around, and that was a wonderful feeling.

We spent the day hanging out at her house and in the garden. After we got back from town, I took my brown paper bag with the skates inside up to little Faye's room and put it under the bed. When I came downstairs, my mother was standing in the kitchen, thumbing through her recipe book. She looked up and threw me an apron.

"Put this on, we're making sticky toffee pudding. I don't know why I'm looking at this," she said, holding the little book aloft.

229

"I should know the recipe off by heart by now." She put it facedown on the kitchen table.

I picked it up and turned it over, smiling at this little book in which I'd found the photograph of myself under the Christmas tree; a book that linked me to my mother, and her to her mother, like a private joke.

"Come on, put it down — it might be full of magic, but I can do it without looking. The brown sugar is in that cupboard, can you find it for me?"

Of course I could find it, and we worked together, laughing and weighing out ingredients, getting flour all over the place. I chopped the dates, and when one of them shot across the counter and onto the floor like an escaped cockroach, we giggled like drunkards. While the pudding was in the oven, we sat in the back garden with cold lemonade, ice clinking in the glasses.

"It's too hot for sticky toffee pudding," she said, leaning back, her eyes closed to the sun. "I've got ice cream to go with it, though."

"Sticky toffee pudding is perfect whatever the weather," I said, copying my mother and shutting my eyes.

"It's Faye's favorite," she said.

"Mine too," I said.

230

"Well, it would be," she murmured.

I stop breathing for a moment. I didn't say anything, and the silence wasn't uncomfortable, but for me it was full of the echo of her words. Why had she said that? What did she mean? I turned my head and opened one eye to look at her; hers were still closed, her lids soaking up the sunshine.

I suppose the best way to describe the feeling is like this: You know when you like a boy, or you like a girl, and you know they like you, and you want to ask them out, take it to the next level? But you know that if you read the signals wrong, when you ask them out you will ruin *everything.* They might not even want to be your friend anymore. So your friendship remains in limbo for months, maybe years, maybe forever, because the risk of losing them, by admitting how you feel, is too high. That's how I felt. It was enough for me to be with my mother, loving her, and spending time with her. And learning about her: not just the facts, but the way she was as a person, her kindnesses and her flaws, her values, her perspectives, her love of Faye, of me. It was enough for me to have this time that I never should have had, that nobody else who loses a loved one gets. This was the very best Christmas present I could possibly have: being with the mother I lost as a child.

To want more would be greedy.

More would mean telling her who I really was, at the risk of her kicking me out.

The thing is, it didn't feel like it was *me* who was fishing for more. It wasn't me who was trying to give out little clues to indicate that there was something otherworldly about what was going on here. It felt like my mother was doing it. *She* was the one fishing. She was the one who wanted to say, *I know this is crazy, but are you my future daughter, come back in time to meet me?*

At least, that's how it seemed.

I may have been projecting, but she had been asking all the questions I would expect her to ask if she knew who I was, about what life was like for me, about my children and my husband, my friends, my hopes and aspirations. She'd asked what life had been like growing up, and I'd done my best not to give myself away, without lying too much.

And then she said, "Everyone loves sticky toffee pudding; only the die-hards eat it in the summer."

The smell of baking drifted into the garden and she left me for a few minutes while she got the pudding out and plated it and covered it to protect it from flies. I could really smell the sweet, thick warmth of it and it made my mouth water, but we'd wait till little Faye got home before we ate it.

When she returned, she brought a tray of cheese and crackers, and we ate and drank cold Panda Pops. I was conscious of time tapping like an impatient foot somewhere far away in the back of my mind, and yet I found that *simultaneously* I was enjoying the time indulgently, like honey oozing over the edge of a spoon.

When my mother left to go get Faye from school, I pondered this dual speed of time: the years that sometimes seem to stretch impossibly ahead of us, especially when we're young. When we're children, the time for us to learn to drive, get a job, marry, and have children of our own seems unfathomably far away. And yet inevitably comes the time when we say we may as well have clicked our fingers, it happened that fast. The feeling that things are over when they haven't even started yet was the one I couldn't shake, and I had never been able to.

And I thought about this: if time in the past with my mother was roughly four times that experienced in the present, then it was possible for me to stay here for a couple of years and only be away from home for about six months.

It would mean I could see my mother through her illness, but I would have to sacrifice that time with my daughters. And what if something happened to them because I wasn't there? There was no way I could explain an absence of six months (with no contact, no telephone) to Eddie. I pushed the idea to one side as I heard the happy voices of Jeanie and Faye returning to the house. The little girl dropped her schoolbag on the grass and carried on walking toward me, flopping down at my feet like a puppet whose strings had just been cut. She had the biggest grin on her face, and I mirrored it.

"Good day?" I asked.

"School's not the best. I'm hoping my day will improve," she said, plucking a daisy out of the ground.

"I guarantee it will," I said.

"I guarantee it too," she said, mimicking me.

"No, but I *really* guarantee it. Go and look under your bed and bring down the bag that's there. But don't look inside, just bring it back here." She jumped up and ran toward the house. "Promise you won't look," I shouted.

234

"I promise," she shouted back, not turning to look at me.

My mother and I sat in the garden chairs with little Faye back on the grass in front of us, the big brown bag clutched on her lap.

"What is it?" Faye asked.

"Open it," I said, and she carefully unrolled the scrunched-over top of the bag. She peeked inside and gasped, looking up at me in shock and then at our mother. Jeanie looked at me, a little crease of anticipation between her eyebrows.

"What is it, darling, show me," Jeanie said, leaning forward.

Faye lifted the roller skates out of the bag as though they were made of something fragile, and Jeanie cried out in surprise and clapped her hands.

"Oh, you lucky girl," she said, kneeling on the grass beside Faye and hugging her. "Let me help you put them on." Faye was awestruck and didn't move at first; then Jeanie coaxed her legs out from her, and started to align the skates under Faye's T-bar shoes, carefully pulling the straps over the tops of her shoes, making sure they didn't twist, and securing them in place. She looked up at me as she worked and held my gaze.

"You know how to make someone happy,

don't you," she said, tipping her head toward Faye, who was touching the skates and spinning the wheels.

"Well, you said she always admired them in the shop window. And you've been so kind, it's just my way of saying thank you."

Jeanie stood and held out her hands to help Faye to her feet. She couldn't skate on the grass, and Jeanie helped her walk awkwardly over it, until she got to the concrete path that led along the side of the house. Faye wobbled in that way only people on skates or ice do, like a poorly coordinated marionette: righting herself with her arms, and clinging to everything within reach — the wall, the fence, a thin branch on a tree that bent with her weight and made her double over. But gradually she started to get the hang of it, and my mother and I talked while the sound of metal wheels on concrete faded in and out of earshot as little Faye skated down the path and along the pavement in front of the house and back again, for what seemed hours, only stopping — reluctantly — for dinner. She said she would rather skate than have a second helping of sticky toffee pudding, to which we adults feigned shock and pretended to have heart attacks. My mother brought out a bottle of crème de menthe and two little glasses.

"Remember this?" she said.

The sound of the wheels kept us confident of Faye's whereabouts while Jeanie and I talked in the garden, grimacing whenever we sipped our minty concoction. And we three all spent our time like this until the sun went down.

It had been a warm day, which only made the night seem colder, and when Jeanie brought Faye in and took her up for a bath, I gathered all the things from outside and shut the garden up for the night.

I lit candles in the living room, even though there wasn't a power cut, wrapped a blanket around myself, and got cozy on the couch.

"Faye said thank you again for the skates," my mother said, walking wearily into the room.

"She already said it a hundred times."

"Well, she said it again. That was a nice thing for you to do. Do you want one of these?" Jeanie was carrying two small bottles of cold Babycham and two glasses. "Courtesy of Em and Henry. They bought me a six-pack at Christmas and I still haven't had any! We can pretend it's Champagne."

"Please," I said. "Better than the green stuff!"

Jeanie flopped down at the other end of the sofa and tucked her knees up to her chest. I passed her a folded blanket and she pulled it up to her chin.

"How long can you stay?" she asked.

"I better go tomorrow. I don't want to overstay my welcome."

"You couldn't do that. You have an open invitation. I'd like you to stay longer if you can."

"I'd love to, but I better get back," I said, wishing I could stay but really feeling the pull of my other life, the fear of never being able to return, the screaming urge in my DNA to be nearer my daughters, which I had muffled until now but was starting to get louder.

"I understand," she said. "Will we see you again?"

"Yes," I said.

"Promise?"

"Yes. I promise," I said.

"When?"

"Soon."

Jeanie leaned awkwardly to open a drawer next to the sofa, and took out a ready-rolled joint and some matches. "Shall we?" she said, and I shrugged.

238

She lit the end and it crackled. She squinted one eye against the smoke that darted there, then blew out a long, straight stream of smoke.

"Do you believe in God?" she said. "I suppose you do, if hubby's going to be a vicar."

"I struggle with the notion," I confessed.

"I pray," she said, and inhaled deeply before handing me the spliff. "Do you pray?"

I nodded and told her that my praying was indiscriminate, that I prayed to anything or anyone to help me when I felt desperate.

"I pray in quiet moments," she said.

"Is it . . ." I hesitated. "Do you pray because you're worried you'll die?"

She shook her head and removed a piece of marijuana from her lip. "I'm not worried I'll die, I *know* I'll die. I worry about Faye, about missing out, about not knowing what will happen to her without me. More than *anything*, I have prayed, with all my heart, that when this life is over for me, I will get to see her again. And I believe that I will."

I felt dizzy. I wasn't used to smoking pot — last night was the first time I'd done it in years. But what made me really dizzy was the prayer that my mother had offered up to God. Had he answered it? Was *I* his response to her heartfelt request? But how could that be? My mother wasn't seeing me after she was dead; I was seeing *her* after she'd died. Was that the same thing? Maybe it didn't matter whether she was dead yet in her time; the point was that the essence of her prayer was to know that her daughter would be okay without her. That's what God had answered, surely? My thoughts were like a bag of beetles, clambering over each other to get to the surface.

"Are you talking about heaven?" I said.

"Oh, I don't know what I'm talking about," she said. "But something has been preying on my mind. If I see my daughter after I die, will she recognize me?"

"How could she not?" I said, thinking of Elizabeth Keel in her little shop, and how she looked the same at twenty-five as she did at fifty-five, more or less. "People don't change so much that you can't recognize them, unless — you know — under extreme circumstances."

"Maybe she wouldn't recognize me because she's just a child, and if she hadn't seen me for years . . . if she saw me, if we met, would I be a ghost? Would I scare her? Would she think she'd gone mad?" Jeanie's eyes searched my face as though I were an expert.

I hesitated. My mother looked sad, forlorn, and I wanted to take that away from her.

"I don't think you'd be like a ghost," I said. "But even if you were, I don't think you'd scare her. I think you'd be more like a guardian angel. A person who would show up in her life, and somehow, deep down, she'd know. She'd know it was you."

"You don't struggle with believing in guardian angels, then," she said.

"Not as much as I struggle with God."

I averted my gaze. My mother leaned forward, coming closer to me on her knees, and held my face in both her hands. Her eyes darted over my face as though she were looking for a microscopic diamond. I looked at her and willed her to know me.

"You look so much like her," she said.

241

CHAPTER 17

For a fraction of a second after she said those words, I pictured us both laughing, slapping our thighs theatrically at the fact that I was her daughter, visiting from the future to tell her all was well, that her daughter would survive and, even better, be happy. I visualized us looking at each other in enthusiastic awe, saying things like *When did you first realize that it was me!*

But much as I wanted that, and as much as you might want to hear that, it's not what happened. My mother slumped back into her corner of the couch, looking like a beautifully disheveled elf, messy hair falling around her face.

"I don't know what's wrong with me," she said in a charmingly petulant voice. "Too much of this." She waved the spliff, then relit it, taking a long, therapeutic drag.

"What did you mean? Who do I look like?" I had to ask.

Jeanie sighed. "Well, I'm not sure, because the photo I had wasn't that clear." She blew a smoke ring and we both watched it rise to the ceiling, becoming blurred at the edges, until it was nothing. "But the thing is, you look like my mother."

My expectations stumbled over her unexpected words. I had assumed Jeanie would see little Faye in me, but it made more sense that she would liken me to an older version of myself, rather than a younger one. I had never known it, never even thought about it, but I must look like my grandmother. And this explained a lot. Maybe this was the reason Jeanie had warmed to me so readily, seemed idealistically keen to form a connection, perhaps even why she saw me as a good choice to look after Faye should anything happen to her.

Jeanie wrapped her arms round her legs. "I was very young when I lost my parents. My memories of them are so faint, I can't remember what my dad looked like at all, and I only have the image of him from a photograph, although I do remember being held by him. My mother, I don't know if I can remember her outside of the photograph, but you make me think of her. You're just like my image of her, though she would have been younger than you are now when

243

she died." Jeanie stared into the middle distance as though trying to see something that wasn't there. "There's a physical similarity, I think." And Jeanie touched her hair and nose, while looking at mine. "But there's also such a familiarity about you, which I can't explain. But when I'm with you, I sometimes pretend I'm with her."

She stubbed out the smoking joint, as though it were to blame for her wistfulness. "I'm sorry, I really can't remember anything about her. I'm being silly. You must think I'm nuts."

I held her hand. "No, you're not." Then, "Can I see that photo?"

"I'm not sure where it is, I put it inside one of my books, and I don't know which one, I've looked for it a few times, but . . . I'll search it out for you." She slapped her hands on her legs and grinned. "I don't know how you came into our lives, or why, but I'm glad you did. I like having you around," she said. She watched me watching her. I was stoned, I was happy, and I felt a surge of belonging to think I looked like my mother's mother.

"Do you really know nothing else about your parents?"

She shook her head for ages. "No. Nothing. There's just me and Faye. I suppose

244

that's why I worry about her so much. I worry about what would happen to her, if something happens to me. There is no one else."

"Why are you so sure you'll die young, apart from the fortuneteller?"

"I *feel* it," she said, putting her hand over her heart. "And I believe what that woman told me at the fair, she was telling me the truth."

"Surely you know they're all frauds," I said, feeling like one myself after my stunt with Elizabeth.

"Yeah, well, I could see it in her face, that something was wrong, and she tried to dress it up, but I made her tell me what she could see, she didn't just joyfully tell me I was going to die."

I just nodded, topping up our glasses with Babycham.

"I guess it's made me a bit desperate," she said, sipping. "For hope."

"Would it make you feel better if I did a bit of fortune-telling myself?" I said.

She stopped midsip. "You can't do it, you're a nonbeliever!" She smiled at me. "And you are not qualified."

"You don't have to be bloody qualified," I said, "you don't study it at university."

"But you need to know how to do it, you

need to know stuff," she argued, laughing.

"I am completely qualified," I said with a confident nod. "I absolutely know my stuff. I know I've laughed at you, and it *is* all bunkum, in the nicest possible way. Nevertheless, I can actually read your palm."

"Then I would like that very much." She wriggled into her end of the couch, like a child getting ready to hear her favorite story. "But please" — she reached out her hand — "only the truth. The good and the bad."

"I guarantee it," I said solemnly. "Ready?" And she nodded.

"Okay, here goes. Jeanie, I think you're right," I said, looking very closely at her palm and tracing the lines that ran all over it. "I think you're a precious soul who will not be on this earth as long as she ought to be. But your light will never go out because it will live on in your daughter. If you die . . ." I swallowed; I didn't want to cry, but those words were like a valve on a tap; my voice trembled. "If you die, then your daughter will never forget you. She will miss you, and she will miss out, because nobody will love her as much as you do. And you will miss out, because you won't see her grow up. But know this, because this is important, this is what you want to know: your daughter will grow up and be happy, she will have good friends and marry a good husband, and she will have children and they will be healthy and happy and good at hula-hooping, just because you are." My voice cracked and I stopped talking for a moment, because I couldn't trust my words to stay steady. "Your daughter will pass that on to them. She will pass on so many good things to them that come directly from you."

I breathed deeply; it felt like I had been holding my breath.

"Will she believe in heaven?" My mother's voice was small.

I hesitated. "Yes. Probably."

"And if she doesn't believe in heaven, then to her I will simply be gone. Is that right?"

"No, you won't be gone, you'll live in her, and through her, and your genes will be passed on to her children," I said.

"But if she believed in heaven, then she would know that I was watching over her, that I will never really leave her. And she could believe that one day, a long, long time from now, she will see me again."

"If you believe in heaven, Jeanie, then you know that you'll see her again. Why do you need her to believe in it too?"

"Because it would bring her comfort," she said.

"Listen to me, Jeanie, you will see your

daughter again. You know that. And I know that. In the meantime, glimpses of heaven are available on earth."

Tears ran down my mother's face, and tears ran down mine too.

"Will you be there for her?" she said, almost inaudibly.

"I will always be around, and she will be okay. I promise. I absolutely guarantee it," I said.

She leaned forward and kissed my cheek. "You're good at fortune-telling, you should consider giving up journalism." She stood and slowly gathered all the smoking paraphernalia and put it away so little Faye didn't see it in the morning. "I'm going to bed, are you?"

"Yes," I said, unfolding myself. "Come here." I held out my arms, and my mother put the things she was holding down on the table. We held on to each other, her damp cheek resting against my own, and I guessed she was imagining I was her mother, and that was close enough for me in that moment. She rocked me slightly and we swayed on the spot in our embrace and I didn't ever want to let go. But all embraces come to an end, and then we stand alone once more. We climbed the stairs, and Jeanie got into her own bed with my younger self, and I returned to my old bedroom.

As I was undressing in little Faye's bedroom, I saw a photograph on the bookcase: the one of me in the Space Hopper box. I took it and crept downstairs, tucking it inside the little cookbook that was still on the counter in the kitchen because I didn't think anyone else would do it.

And in a funny way, I suppose that was the beginning.

When I said good-bye, I wanted to say *See you soon.* I intended to come back, but I couldn't say when, because it might be a few weeks for me but months and months for them. I knew Jeanie would expect to see me within days, and of course that's what I wanted, but I couldn't promise that — and I knew it was even possible that the next time I came back, my mother would already be dead.

So when we hugged and kissed good-bye, for me it was like losing my mother all over again. The potentially final good-bye.

Little Faye hugged me hard and thanked me once more for the roller skates, made me promise I'd come back soon. I nodded.

"Do you guarantee it?" she asked, grinning like a wolf cub.

"I guarantee it," I said, because in that

moment it felt true that a broken promise to myself was better than no promise at all.

They left for school, and I left for the shed. I dreaded getting into the box. I was tired of being hurt. I looked around the small space, and considered staying; my heart was impossibly torn. But much as I didn't want to leave, I had to get home. I wouldn't be in the same country as my children, but I would be in the same time, and my longing to be nearer to them now outweighed my urge to stay in the past.

I made sure the area where the box sat would be clear of everything, and not too close to the door. I wanted more skidding room next time, and I double-checked that the shed door was firmly shut; it seemed a bit loose because it had taken such a bashing. I hoped I wouldn't at any point crash completely through it; I didn't want to appear flying out of the shed in a storm of splintered wood.

I'd borrowed my mother's clothes the day before, but now I was back in the clothes I'd arrived in. I pulled on the ski suit, drawing the cords of the hood tight, as before. I fastened the Velcro of the gloves, and as I stepped into the box I tried to picture myself beyond the journey and at my destination. I would be landing on a mattress, and I was going to be okay. I breathed deeply and braced myself, and realized in a very small but distinct epiphany that all journeys are a process — often a painful one, with difficult decisions — to which there is always a beginning, a middle, and an end. Even if the beginning is not the beginning in every sense of the word. Even if the end is not the end as we know it.

As I now expected, the journey was like a fairground ride I badly wanted to get off. I just had to brace against the fear, the sickness, the inability to breathe, the terror of maybe never getting home. Lost in space, disoriented, and speeding into nothingness at what must be more than a hundred miles an hour, with no certainty that the ride would let you off in the same place you got on; no assurances that it would even stop at all.

And then it did. It felt like I'd run at a door with my shoulder to get it open, but it wasn't a door, it was my bedroom wall and I actually made an impression: literally a crack in the plaster. Exhaustion was the overwhelming sensation, and I rearranged my limbs on the mattress to look less like a discarded rag doll, lay on my back, and shut my eyes. I wanted to sleep — time travel drained me — but as my eyes insisted on closing, my mind wouldn't let me go under. There was something I needed to do. I just couldn't remember what it was.

I opened my eyes slowly, and one stayed shut for a moment longer than the other, like a broken doll's. What had I forgotten to do? It was dark, so it was definitely later in the day than when I'd left. But I needed to know how late it was, and whether or not it was the same day. I needed to check the time, and the date. It was important to gauge the pattern of time between the past and the present. I rolled over, feeling fat and ungainly in the ski suit. I was like a drunk who had fallen on the pavement and decided to sleep there, and then been asked to move on. I got onto all fours and then to my feet, and waddled to the other side of the bed, where a bedside clock was turned slightly away. The time was eleven thirty, but I forced myself to go downstairs and switch on the television to find out the day.

I was surprised; I don't know what I was expecting, but not this. I wasn't sure what to make of it: three hours had passed. No more, no less, not a whole day, just the same amount of time as had passed during my first visit to my mother, even though I'd stayed so much longer this time. I had plenty of time now, before Eddie and the girls came back. I turned the television off and sat in the darkness; the effort of climbing the stairs again seemed too much. I could hear the far-off sounds of neighbors who had had dinner and drinks in their gardens and were still out there now, the faint sounds of laughter and clinking glasses — I love nighttime in the summer — and I wished I were one of them, with a simpler life and simpler dilemmas. I made myself climb the stairs, unzipping my ski suit as I went, stepping out of it as I stood by the bed and flopping onto the mattress facedown. Nothing crossed my mind. I slept soundly.

A crack of light through the curtains hurt my eyes, rousing me. It was nearly midday, so almost three times as long had passed while I slept as when I was in the seventies with my mother.

This fact gently spun the web of an idea as beautiful as a spider's creation on dewy grass. If three hours was the amount of time that passed here in the present, *no matter how long I spent in the past,* then what was stopping me from staying in the past for a lot longer?

I mean, a *lot* longer. Like Lucy and the others in Narnia, could I live my entire life twice over? Even in my groggy state it didn't seem like a good idea. But if it were possible, then I'd have to make a list of pros and cons; the potential of the idea invigorated me. Before I pursued my options, I needed to get the basics done: call Eddie, shower, dress, and eat. Then I'd make the bed, and then . . . then I'd set my mind to everything I needed to do, and everything I *could* do. But before I even put pen to paper, I knew that the task at the top of my list was to get my engagement ring back, as soon as possible.

But I wasn't going alone. I wanted Louis to come with me to Elizabeth's.

CHAPTER 18

I drove to Louis's place and parked in the drive. I'd never been to his house before, and I'm not sure what I expected, but it was spotless; I guess I thought it would be messy, because blind people can't see dust, and therefore can't see the need to clean and tidy up. He led me into a lounge that was soothingly pale: soft, light-gray sofas and a cream carpet, with a large vase of white roses atop a white, glazed coffee table, around which he stepped with practiced dance moves — side, side, forward — before he sat down.

"Your place is not what I expected, Louis," I said, shuffling my cardigan off and backtracking to hang it on a peg in the hallway.

"What did you expect?" he said.

"I don't know." I plonked down into a wing chair beautifully upholstered in a gray-and-mustard geometric pattern. "I thought, man living alone, it would be more of a bachelor pad: sagging sofa and empty beer cans thrown in the corner, that sort of thing."

"I can't have clutter, I'd just be tripping over it all the time. My sister's an interior decorator and she ordered the furniture and everything; we designed the layout together. She says it's quite a clinical look."

"It's very clean-looking, very peaceful. I love it."

"See the flowers," he said, pointing slightly left of them.

"Beautiful. Who are they from?"

"When I know I've got a visitor, I call the lady next door, and she cuts me some flowers from her garden, puts them in a vase, brings them round, to take the edge off that clinical look. She's my cleaner too."

"Well, she does a great job, I can confirm that," I said.

We went into the kitchen, also very white and shiny, and Louis put the kettle on.

"Your kettle's red," I said.

"Whatever that is," he said.

"It's a nice spot of color in here."

When he poured the tea, he put his finger over the edge of the cup, so he could stop pouring when the water touched it.

"My hands are clean," he said, as if I was worried he might contaminate my drink. "I hope you don't mind, it's just the most practical way to do it."

I didn't mind, of course. We sat at the kitchen table, which — unlike everything else I'd seen in the house so far — was old and wooden, worn pale from being scrubbed daily for years and years. I ran my hand over it; it was impossibly smooth.

"This was my mother's," he said, in response to the whooshing sound my hand made on the surface, and he smoothed his hands over the tabletop too. "I think of her whenever I sit here. She was always in the kitchen, so it's fitting."

"I went back again," I said. Louis stopped what he was doing, which wasn't much, but there was a sudden extra stillness to him, as though he'd detected a faint scent in the air.

"You mean, back in time?" he said, and then made a faint snorting sound, which surprised me.

"Yes, I visited my mother again, and my younger self."

"When?"

"The day before yesterday. I stayed a couple of days. But get this." I leaned forward conspiratorially. "When I got back to the present, the *same* amount of time had passed as when I went back in time for less than a day. Just three hours."

Louis shoved his chair back and fetched a packet of chocolate cookies; he fumbled for the little strip that opened it at one end, and took one, pushing the packet toward me.

"Okay," he said, hesitating. "How come we're doing this here and not at work?"

His question threw me, but only for a second. "I've taken a couple of days off, because I didn't know how long I'd be gone this time, but it's turned out to be almost no time at all. And I couldn't wait to see you and tell you what happened, so that's why I called."

Louis frowned and tipped his head to one side.

"Plus," I said, "I'm really glad I did, because I love your place, and now I'll be able to picture you at home."

"Okay," he said, leaning back in his chair with a sigh. "Let's hear it. What happened?"

I launched breathlessly into the whole thing: getting stoned with my mother, and how I'd thought about stealing the roller skates but ended up exchanging my engagement ring for them; the sticky toffee pudding and my mother's premonition that she would die young; her request that I look after Faye if that happened, and the nugget

258

of information about my father.

Louis methodically ate cookies with the air of a bored judge while I talked, and when I stopped, he wiped crumbs from around his mouth.

"So," I said. "What do you think?"

He exhaled deeply. "Wow, well, you've given me a lot of information there, Faye, I'm not sure where to start. I'm impressed at the detail."

"What's that supposed to mean?" I said.

His eyebrows arched and I momentarily wondered why, before my stomach sank like a ship.

"You don't believe me, do you?" I said, my voice suddenly small. I put a half-eaten cookie on the table and my hands in my lap, like a chastened child. I wanted to cry.

"Faye," he said. "What's going on here? You don't expect me to believe all this is *actually* true?"

I looked up at him, my eyes full of tears, but they were wasted on him; as far as he knew, I was stony-faced. "You think I'm lying to you? Why? Why would I do that? Do you think I'm nuts?" The tears were clearly audible in my voice.

"No, I . . ." He stumbled over his words. Looking truly confused, he reached out his hand, searching for mine. I put my hand onto the table so he could find it, and let him hold it.

"You're my friend," he said. "But I assumed this story was part of one of those experiments you do."

"What?" I said, lost.

"I don't know, it was fun and interesting when you first told me about it, and I've been thinking about it since then, and we've talked . . . I mean, I had to come up with a reason why you would tell me something like this."

"How could it be an experiment?" I said, my voice sharp. "What are you talking about?"

"You're always doing experiments, comparing blind and sighted people. I've been trying to work out what all this is about, and the best I could come up with is that you have designed a scenario to test for differences in the logic and problem-solving skills between blinkies and nonblinkies. You have done vaguely similar studies before, not quite as unusual as this, but still. I thought I was doing quite well, I came up with some good ideas — you know, regarding time travel and so on."

"Yes, you did," I said, very quietly. "You came up with some very useful ideas."

"And so I'm wondering why you would

come here and talk about it on private time, rather than at work, where we get paid for having conversations like this."

"I thought you believed in me, Louis," I said. "I was kind of relying on it." I let go of his hand and bunched my fists under the table.

"So you're saying to me that all this stuff is really happening to you?"

"Well, either it is, or I'm crazy," I said. There was a long silence.

"It could be both," he said. "It could be happening *and* you're crazy."

"True," I said, and sniffed.

I chuckled, half laughing, half crying. And he laughed gently too; his laugh was one-third apology and one-third disbelief, and I couldn't give a name to the last third of his laugh.

But this was not really a laughing matter. Not to me. This was life or death. Or more accurately, life *and* death. And it felt like I'd just lost the only person in the universe I could talk to.

Despair hit me like a punch in the stomach, and loneliness, like treading water in a deep, dark well, knowing that no one could hear my cries and I wasn't going to see Lassie peering over the top to reassure me help was on its way. A howl surged up from

261

deep inside me. Primal. Feral. Desperate. I called out no words, but the sound that forced its way into the room and filled it said everything about the way it felt to not be believed, to not belong, to have no way of proving your innocence, your story, your truth. For the only time in my life, I felt like a kind of god who wanted to demand faith.

"I'm telling the truth," I wailed, and Louis shifted back in his seat, bolt upright, looking horrified.

"It's all real," I said, but this time my voice was broken and small.

In the silence that followed my outburst I heard a distant lawn mower and wondered what it would be like to feel normal again.

"Listen to me," Louis said, his voice heavy with sincerity. And then he said nothing, although his mouth opened and closed a few times in aborted attempts to respond.

"What?" I said, my voice a croak. My shout had scratched my throat.

"I don't think you'd lie to me. So either you're telling the truth, or you really are . . ."

". . . crazy?" I finished his sentence. "I know."

"Yeah. It's one or the other, definitely not both. But in fact, despite the madness of it all, Faye, my dear friend, I don't believe you *are* crazy. It's just hard. You know? Hard for me to believe without some bit of proof. I'm a scientist. Faith is not something I'm that good with. But I'm going to try, okay? I'll try to totally believe you."

The temperature behind my eyes rose and tears slipped down my face. Louis didn't know, so I told him. "I'm crying," I said.

"You okay?"

"I think so." I was emotionally exhausted and hadn't realized how very alone I would be if I didn't have Louis. "I need you, Louis."

"Look, let's have some more tea," he said. "Or how about a beer? Have a couple, leave your car here, take a cab home. You can have a bite to eat if you want, as Eddie and the girls are away."

"Can you cook?" I said, sniffing.

"Not really, but I'm an excellent microwaver," he said, with a comical gesture in roughly the direction of the microwave. I noticed it was the only thing in the kitchen that had a smudge on it.

"Sounds good, a beer would be great," I said. "Thank you."

We got comfy in the lounge; the beers popped open with a hiss, and when we talked it felt like we were starting again. Louis asked me questions and we took it more slowly. He said the way I had told him what happened was like a trailer from a film, all the highlights; he said he wanted to know *everything.*

And what we got talking about most was philosophy. In particular, by going back and changing things, would I have changed the present? In fact, Louis very carefully asked me if I had spoken to Eddie and the girls since I'd returned, and he breathed a huge sigh of relief when I said I had.

"Oh God," I said. "I didn't even think about that. You were worried that Eddie and the girls might not even exist anymore?"

"I wouldn't know what to expect. Look, the first time you went back, it was an accident, so if things had changed when you returned, you couldn't really blame yourself. But the second time you went back, you chose to do it, and you did a lot of stuff, you spoke to people about the future, you gave your younger self a present. You gave away your ring, Faye."

I looked down at my wedding ring, and the pale mark where my other ring had been.

"I can't get my head around that ring," he went on. "If you gave away your engagement ring in the nineteen-seventies, then how would Eddie have been able to buy it and give it to you when he proposed? If that woman, Elizabeth, has had it all this time, how would it have been available to Eddie?"

"I didn't think of that." I drained my beer, and Louis, recognizing the sound of a bottle being emptied, got up.

"Another?"

"Thanks," I said. While he was in the kitchen, I called out, "So do you think I might have changed things in the present that I don't know about yet?"

"I'm not sure," he said, coming back into the living room with a couple of cold beers, dripping with condensation. "I mean, who knows which theories are true? If any. There's the butterfly effect, which is where tiny changes have large consequences, the flapping of a butterfly's wings can change the course of a tornado. That kind of thing."

"I read a book to Esther about a year ago, where this child goes back in time to the dinosaurs and accidentally steps on a bug, and then when the kid comes back, everything's different, the world is not a very nice place. The kid has to go back again and make sure to not step on the bug, so that things in the present can go back to normal."

"Wow, that's kind of sinister for a kid's book," Louis said.

"All the good ones are."

"True. Well, you seem to have done a lot more than step on a bug, and in fact you may have literally stepped on several, but so far you haven't noticed any changes?"

"No," I said. "The thing is, I actually feel like some of my actions were required in order to ensure that the present is the one I'm familiar with. Like the roller skates. I don't think I would have had roller skates and got so into it as a teenager if I hadn't been given them as a child — but who would have given me those exact roller skates, if not myself?"

"There's another time-travel theory I heard about, might be relevant," Louis said, getting up and walking out of the room. "Come on." I followed him upstairs to a study. This room was also pristine (the filing was to die for), but the decor was darker, the walls and carpet were dark gray, and there was a very comfy-looking black leather office chair, which Louis sat in.

"Do we need a light on? What's the time?" He fumbled under his cuff for his watch. "Nine thirty, still light?"

"It's fine," I said, pulling a chair from the corner in order to sit next to him at the computer. He tilted the screen in my general direction; there were images of a variety of guys, looking for love. Louis started tapping away, and another window opened up.

"I've got a screen reader on, and it's fast, so just ignore it if you can."

Louis, like most blind staff at RNIB, had a screen reader at home too, a computer program that reads the text off the screen. Now, I'm not going to suggest that blind people have better hearing than sighted people, but when they get used to those screen readers, blind people have the program set to such a high speed that it's pretty much impossible for the uninitiated to understand it. So when Louis pulled up a web page and the screen reader kicked in, it sounded like gobbledegook, a loud electronic rattling purr, and I jumped.

"Hang on, I'll just turn it down a bit," Louis said. "I'm looking for something in particular, something I was reading a few weeks ago, bear with me."

I waited while he pulled up web pages and typed in search words. He was looking up theories of time travel, and images flashed up on the screen of the DeLorean from *Back to the Future* and the sled-shaped machine with the red-velvet seat and the round contraption on the back from the original *Time Machine* from 1960. Then Louis paused on a screen that looked a little more scientific and scrolled down — I couldn't understand the garbled speech that he was skipping through — then he stopped.

"This is it," he said, and he slowed the screen reader right down. It was a bit like listening to a lecture by Stephen Hawking, not only because of the voice but because of the subject matter too. At first I could understand, but then there was a lot of stuff about paradoxes and I got lost in the jargon. When the screen reader finished, Louis turned to me.

"I think that last bit seems the most reasonable explanation," he said. "Especially seeing as you're still here, and nothing major, or even *minor,* seems to have changed as a result of you going back and forward in time, even though you were messing about quite a lot back there."

"What's the bottom line?" I said.

"Bottom line: you can't change what's happened, because it's already happened. You wouldn't be able to go back and kill your parents before they had you, because you exist. Simple."

"So the fact that I grew up with that pair of metal roller skates . . ." I said.

". . . happened precisely because you went back in time and gave yourself those roller skates. It's basically a self-fulfilling time-travel theory where anything you do to try to change the past ultimately *only* causes the events that happened, meaning that time travel can never change the future, or the present."

We watched a couple of online videos about wormholes and traveling faster than the speed of light, and pretty soon my mind was swimming. I couldn't take any more, and I told Louis so.

"Come on, I'll call you a taxi," he said, switching the computer off and pushing back his chair. I got up and moved toward the hallway, then cringed as he stubbed a toe on the chair I'd been sitting in; I hadn't moved it back to its original position.

"Fuck," he said.

"Sorry, Louis," I said, and winced.

"That's why the place is so fucking tidy," he said, replacing the chair.

As we went down the stairs, I remembered something. "What's the opposite of reckless, do you know?"

"Reckful," he said, without missing a beat.

"How do you know that?" I said, impressed.

"I play a lot of Scrabble," he said. And even as I thought it must surely be impossible for him to play, he tutted and said, "You know there's braille Scrabble, right? You work at the bloody RNIB, woman."

"Do you have a board?"

"Yeah, you want a game sometime?"

"Yeah, but you'd thrash me," I said.

"Ya think?" he said, with a touch of sarcasm that bordered on rude. We both paused at the bottom of the stairs. "What are you doing tomorrow? You've got tomorrow off, haven't you?"

"Uh-huh," I said. "I'm not sure what I'm doing yet, maybe potter about, think about my dual life. Maybe I should start writing a journal about it, make sure I remember all those details and everything my mother said to me. Yeah, I think I'll do that."

Louis rang a cab firm, and I shrugged back into my cardigan and put my shoes on.

"That's not what you're doing," he said. "Not tomorrow."

"Go on then, Einstein, what am I doing? Playing Scrabble?"

"We," he said, "are going to get that proof I want. Not that I don't believe you, honey, because I do. You're going to get a cab back here in the morning and you're going to drive us to Elizabeth Keel's shop. We're going to get your engagement ring back."

"Funny," I said. "I came here to ask you to do just that."

CHAPTER 19

On my way home in the cab, the world outside the windows that flashed before my eyes went unnoticed, as another world unfolded in front of my mind's eye. I replayed my time with my mother in her garden, and her holding my face in her hands; I could hear the thrum of little Faye's roller skates, and that rhythmic sound blended with the sound of the car's wheels on the road, and I must have nodded off, waking as the taxi drew to a stop in front of my house.

I wanted to talk to Eddie and the girls, needed them to ground me. My heart ached, and I didn't know if it was because I had been away from them longer than they had been away from me, or because they couldn't join me in this lonely journey into the past that I was making, but I needed them so much that it felt entirely physical. My heart was hurting.

There is something about the way the ring tone sounds when you call another country that makes me feel like I'm calling another planet, and when Eddie answered the phone I felt like he'd died and gone to heaven, and I was able to speak to him anyway. He said hello, and my voice shook as I answered.

"Hi," I said.

"What's wrong?" he asked, my single syllable giving me away.

"I hate it when you're so far away from me. I'm just missing you." I was whisper-crying.

"We talked yesterday, you seemed fine," he said, worry in his voice.

"I am fine, I just wish you were here, that's all." I wiped my nose on my sleeve and sniffed unattractively.

"Have you had a drink?" I could hear his sympathetic smile down the line.

"Yes, detective, I had a couple of beers with Louis," I said, managing a smile myself now. "But it's not that. I just wanted to hear your voice. I miss you."

"Don't worry, you and me, we're like John Donne's pair of compasses — when one of us needs to leave for a while, the other stands firm in place. We never really let go of each other."

"Compasses?" I said (although I do know

what they are).

"Yes, remember at school those metal things with a nasty point on one of the arms; you stick that bit in the page, and then you can draw a perfect circle with the other arm."

"I know, but you mean there's a poem about it?"

"Yes, John Donne. It's called 'A Valediction: Forbidding Mourning.' I'm looking at the spine of one of his poetry books in a bookcase as we speak. Mum's a fan."

" 'Forbidding Mourning.' I like the sound of that. Will you read it to me," I said quietly.

"You won't like it, it's got a lot of *doths* in it, and that kind of thing."

"Read it to me," I said again, ignoring his sarcastic and absolutely accurate knowledge of my likes and dislikes.

"Okay," he said, and I heard him move about and rustle some pages as he got the book from the shelf and found the right page. "I'm not reading the whole thing. But here goes. . . .

"If they be two, they are two so
As stiff twin compasses are two;
Thy soul, the fixed foot, makes no show
To move, but doth, if the other do.

273

"And though it in the center sit,
Yet when the other far doth roam,
It leans and hearkens after it,
And grows erect, as that comes home.

"Such wilt thou be to me, who must,
Like th' other foot, obliquely run;
Thy firmness makes my circle just,
And makes me end where I begun."

He stopped and there was silence down the line. I listened to his breath. "Read it again," I said. "Slowly this time." He did, and when he'd finished there was more silence on the line, filled with love.

"I'm proud of you, Faye," Eddie said after a while.

"Are you?"

"Yes, for not laughing at the words *erect* and *firmness.* Well done."

"It wasn't easy, but sometimes I can be very mature. There was also the word *stiff,*" I said, grinning and tasting my own tears.

"You like the poem?"

"I do," I said, and with those words, like a trigger, our wedding day popped into my head, then time rewound from that image to another, and I saw Eddie on one knee, proposing to me. I looked down at where my engagement ring should be, and felt a hot rush of fear.

"I like the idea that when I need to leave you, you are there at home, a steady presence, waiting for me to come back," Eddie said.

"Like a good little woman?"

"No, you know I don't mean that."

"What happens when we're both roaming about and there's no one at home to come back to?" I asked, feeling tearful again.

"What are you talking about? What does that mean?"

"Nothing," I said.

"What do you mean by 'we're both roaming about'?" Eddie said, sounding a little darker now.

"I didn't mean that, I just meant, oh, I don't know what I meant. I just want you home, okay?" I said.

"All right, look, I'm just in France, you're at home, we'll be back soon." He hesitated. "Or should we come back early?"

"No," I said. "I'm fine, really, it's just the beer talking, and I'm being stupid. I can't wait to see you all."

"I love you. I'll see you soon. And Faye, please, keep yourself safe; I need you. Let's speak earlier tomorrow, before the girls go to bed."

■ ■ ■ ■

In the night I woke from dreams of my mother; in one, I was a child, and we were holding hands, spinning in the garden. "There's only you and me," she said. "Think about who needs who more." I jolted awake, sweating. I needed my mother, but more important perhaps, she needed me. I had been a happy child, and she was torn away from me, unfair on both of us. I thought of Eddie, Esther, and Evie, and in my hazy mind's eye I saw them holding hands and spinning, while I stood outside the ring. They had each other, they had Eddie's parents and our friends. Maybe I was more useful in the past, taking up the slack, making up the numbers.

At some point I fell asleep again, and slept deeply, dreamlessly. The next morning, surprisingly, I felt better.

I got a cab back to Louis's the next morning about eight. Finding Elizabeth Keel meant getting my ring back, and I wouldn't feel right until it was back on my hand. And perhaps even more important, I wanted to convince Louis, help him believe my story. If we couldn't find Elizabeth, or if she'd died, then I guessed — though he might not say it — that would add to the list of evidence suggesting this was all in my imagination. And then there was the worry that she might deny me or not remember me; I couldn't know what to expect.

The town where I grew up is about an hour's easy drive north, up the motorway from London. I hadn't been there for a couple of years but, like a lot of English towns, it had expanded and improved and had an infrastructure that spread continuously and gradually outward like a piece of butter melting in the sun. I hoped the shop, Serendipity, was still there. Elizabeth Keel would be in her midfifties now, and I thought she had been working in the shop when I went in with the girls the last time we visited. I was increasingly nervous. What if I couldn't get my ring back? How would I explain that to Eddie?

We parked and found a place for coffee and breakfast. The waitress asked me what Louis wanted, instead of asking him directly, and she did it repeatedly, even though I kept throwing the ball back in his court. He was seething, but I managed to distract him.

"I hope the shop's still there," I said.

"You could have googled it," he said.

"I'm not sure they'd be online."

"Everything's online," he said sharply. "Is there a fucking sweetener on this table?" He patted about, searching for some. I put a packet in his hand. "Thanks," he said. "Sorry. That fucking waitress."

"I know," I said. "She thinks she's being kind, but it's just patronizing."

"I was only going to have some toast, but she annoyed me so much I went for a full English," he said. "I blame condescending do-gooders for my waistline."

Actually, I was glad to spend some time having a proper breakfast; it was a delay tactic. I wasn't in a hurry to go to the shop — in fact, I felt a bit sick at the thought of what might happen. I know it's all real, what's happening to me: the time travel, the conversations with my mother, it's real. But I'll tell you what it's like, it's like being accused of a crime, and being offered a lie-detector test. If you're guilty, you might as well take it, because it's going to be wrong sometimes, and you might get lucky. But if you're innocent, and you get *un*lucky, you're screwed. No one's ever going to believe you then. Elizabeth Keel was my lie-detector test. If we couldn't find her, or the shop, or if she didn't know what the hell I was talking about when I asked for my ring back, what would that mean?

I still had to accept that I might be insane.

It wasn't just Louis who was in need of a little proof. I think I needed it too; something concrete that reassured me: *You're not crazy.*

The route we took to get to Serendipity meant that I saw the shopfront face-on, because it was situated opposite a little passageway that led from the huge, new library. The cut-through was new, because the library had been built since I was last here, on a site that had previously been obscured by the row of little buildings across the street from Serendipity. As fortune would have it, my shop, the one I was interested in, was on the untouched side of the road; otherwise, who knew what I would have done.

I stopped when I saw it. In the past, I had always approached it from the side, the contents of the windows being the first thing to catch my eye. But from this angle I could see it in a new way: the place stood before me like an image on a postcard, and I was struck by the large, cursive, colorful name. There was something about the shop that made me think of gypsy caravans, and underneath, in smaller, curly painted letters, were words I had never even noticed before.

"Huh. . . ."

"What?" Louis said. He was holding my elbow and simply waited while I stood there.

I pulled Louis to one side so we could stand in the shade instead of sweating in the sun. "It says: *Serendipity, the discovery of things you were not in quest of . . .*"

"Quaint," said Louis, and I checked his expression for sarcasm, but found sincerity. "It's still here, then. Is it open?"

At that moment a woman emerged from the shop and the little bell rang, like a talisman from the past. She held the door with her hand high up the doorframe as her young son walked out under her arm, looking at the contents of the bag he was holding.

"Yes," I said, but I didn't move.

"Let's just go inside and see what happens," Louis said kindly. He must have known how nervous I was. "We don't actually have to talk to anyone, or do anything." As we crossed the road my legs felt like lead, just like they do when I dream I'm running away from something but can't move properly.

The tinkle of the bell and the coolness inside the shop were identical to when I was there the other day, thirty years ago. The layout was different, and of course the contents were more up-to-date, although there were some very traditional little trinkets that were hard not to touch. Louis squeezed my elbow tight and drew closer, keen not to knock anything.

"How many people are in here?" he whispered.

"Uh, there's us," I said, and leaned around to see into another aisle. "There's a woman looking around, and someone working the till."

"Who's at the till? Is it her?"

"No, too young, and it's a guy," I said, just as the man looked over at us and smiled. "It's her son, Adam," I whispered to Louis.

"Can I help you?" Adam said.

"Just browsing, thanks," I said, looking pointedly at what was on the shelf in front of me.

"Ask him if Elizabeth is here," Louis whispered too loudly.

"I thought you said we could come in and do nothing," I whispered back irritably.

"Yeah, well, I say a lot of things."

I looked over at the guy again, and smiled; he smiled back at me. "Are you sure I can't help?" he said pleasantly.

I walked over to him, taking Louis with me. "Well, actually, I was hoping to speak to Mrs. Keel," I said.

"My mother, Elizabeth?"

"Yes?" I said, as though I wasn't sure if she really existed at all.

"She's gone out to get some shopping, but she's coming back." He lifted the phone as he spoke. "I'll let her know someone's here to see her, who shall I say it is?"

"My name's Faye, I think she might have something of mine." He dialed a number and smiled up at me and Louis as he waited for the call to be answered; but just then the door opened, the bell rang again, and the sound of a ringing mobile phone entered the shop. I turned to see Elizabeth Keel, with a bag of shopping in each hand, fumbling to get her phone out of a handbag, trying not to drop anything.

The young man clicked the phone back into place and shot from behind the counter to take the bags from her. "It's me calling you," he said, as her phone stopped ringing, and he kissed her on the cheek. "I thought you were just going to get a couple of things? You've got like a week's shopping here."

"This is *not* a week's shopping, darling, but I did get more than I intended," she said, tucking a strand of hair behind her ear. She had smiled at us briefly, but otherwise ignored Louis and me. The man took the shopping, deposited it out the back, and quickly reappeared.

"Mum, this lady says she wants to talk to you, says you have something of hers?" He said this looking at me, as if to check he'd got it right, and I nodded at them both. Elizabeth Keel's smiling face welcomed me. She was a little heavier than when I'd seen her a few days ago, by about fifteen pounds, and more buxom. She had lines around her eyes, and her jawline looked a little slacker; she was clearly thirty years older, but I would say, apart from those minor things, she was exactly the same. The biggest difference was that although she had seemed perfectly nice when I met her as a young woman, she had definitely carried a touch of cynicism back then, had been less trusting. Now her face was wide open, the face of someone who only expected good things.

Louis elbowed me gently.

"Hi," I said. "I gave you something a long time ago, you said you'd look after it. I was hoping you still had it." I grimaced at how cryptic I'd made myself sound.

Elizabeth looked puzzled and tilted her head, still smiling. "Really? What was it?"

I felt sick. She didn't know what I was talking about. Louis bent his head roughly to my ear. "I think you need to be more specific," he said, in another embarrassing stage whisper. I smiled apologetically at Elizabeth for Louis's indiscretion, but it wasn't really an apology.

"It was my engagement ring, in exchange for some roller skates," I said, feeling like I was making the whole thing up. "Like I say, it was a long time ago."

Elizabeth stepped closer to me, closer than etiquette permits a stranger. She looked into my eyes, then stood back slightly, taking in my whole face. She touched my hairline.

"What's happening?" Louis whispered.

"Louis, stop whispering, it's not a library, and she can hear you. She's looking at me," I said, not letting my gaze leave hers.

"Mum?" the young man said. He stepped around the counter, clearly confused by his mother's reaction to me.

"Oh my God," Elizabeth said under her breath, to herself, or perhaps even to God.

"Who is it, Mum?" Adam asked.

"I'm not sure," Elizabeth said. "I think it's my guardian angel."

With those words, I knew that she remembered me. My chin creased upward, and my eyes stung with tears of relief. I gasped, on the edge of a sob, and she put her arms around me.

"My God," said Elizabeth, her teary eyes mirroring mine. "All these years, I've been expecting someone older."

CHAPTER 20

Elizabeth asked her son to close the shop, go get us some takeaway coffees, and then take the rest of the day off. You could see he was reluctant to leave her, but she said everything was fine, and she'd explain later. Although I'd bet she wouldn't.

She led us up a very narrow staircase to a couple of rooms above the shop: a little kitchenette area painted bright blue, and another room with a single bed and a chair in it. A sweater and some socks were strewn across the messy bedspread. Elizabeth straightened the cover a little, and she and I sat on the edge of the bed; Louis took the chair.

"My son is studying and helps out in the shop now and then," she said, balling the socks and throwing them toward a laundry basket. "When he goes out with friends in town he sometimes stays here rather than drive back to ours, and then he'll open up the shop in the morning. It's a great help." She leaned over the bed to open up the little window, her speech explaining the tinge of testosterone in the air.

There was a pause after she spoke, born of the fact that not one of us wanted to talk about such trivia. But trivial conversation was simply a habit, and there was nothing wrong with it. After all, I'd had many trivial conversations with my mother, and treasured every one.

Louis was blessedly silent, but smiling a bit too much. He'd told me once that children born blind are told to smile a lot, because that's what friendly sighted people do. I explained that sometimes he looks like a grinning buffoon because he smiles too much, and sometimes it feels like he's either looking overfriendly or telling people to fuck off in the pub; one extreme or the other. So we have a deal, that if he's smiling unnecessarily in company, I clear my throat, and hope he gets the message. I cleared my throat now, and his face dropped to normality. Elizabeth thought I was gearing up to say something and looked expectantly at me, with relief, I think, that I was planning to start this conversation.

"You remember me, then?" I said.

"Remember you?!" she said, as though I

were out of my mind. "You have lived with me for years, in here." She put her hand to her chest. "I spent a long, long time wondering if you were real or if I had imagined you." She reached out and touched my cheek as if to double-check I was really there in the room. "I thought you might have been a vivid dream. More vivid than any actual dream I'd ever had, I had your ring, after all. And then I began to come to terms with the fact that it didn't matter whether I had made you up or not, because my belief in you — real *or* imagined — has made my life so wonderful."

"It has?" I said, surprised.

"Yes," said Elizabeth, as though I had missed something obvious. "As soon as I met Andrew, I recognized his name, because you had told me it. And I knew we would be married and that I could trust him. I was amazed when he first told me his name, and for a moment I wondered whether you and he could have somehow tricked me. But Andrew isn't wily enough to engage in any deception, and in the end I accepted that fortune-tellers sometimes get things right.

"I loved Andrew, and knew that we would be together, because of what you'd said. So I opened myself up to him like I'd never done before. And I had a confidence that stemmed directly from you, the confidence to make the business a success. I was happy because you told me I would always be okay."

Elizabeth welled up, and I didn't know what to say. Maybe this is how surgeons feel when they save a life and the family tries to thank them, *just doing my job.* She blew her nose, and I took out my purse, counting off five twenty-pound notes.

"One hundred pounds," I said, holding it out to her. "For the skates, with interest, and for looking after my ring."

She scoffed, smiled, and shook her head. "No, child, no money. You took my skates, and in return you gave me a better life than I could ever have hoped for." She leaned toward me. "You gave me the gift of a life without fear." Her voice was hushed and intense. "A whole *life* without fear," she repeated. "But the one thing you told me that I valued above all others was what you said about Adam."

"Your son?" Louis said.

"Yes, the one you met, the one who stays up here sometimes," she said, directing her conversation toward Louis. "When Faye first came to me all those years ago and told me what my life would be like, she said my son would go missing, but that he would be all right. She told me he would be found after three days, and he would be absolutely fine." She hesitated. "Do you have children, Louis?"

"No," he said.

Elizabeth looked at her hands, and her breathing became ragged as is often the case when people relive difficult times. "Well, when he was nine years old, he did go missing. He went out to play and it got late, and he didn't come home. At some point I looked at Andrew and I just knew he was feeling the same as me. I was putting the girls to bed, so he pulled his coat on and said 'I'll find him,' but he came back an hour later, alone, and called the police."

Louis leaned forward on his knees. "But you were okay, because of what Faye had told you. You weren't so worried, is that right?"

Elizabeth shook her head. "It wasn't as simple as that. All the other things Faye had told me about — who I would marry, how many kids I'd have, the business, the burglary — when it came down to it, those things didn't really matter. But this time it did. I prayed like I'd never prayed before." Elizabeth looked at me, her eyes shining. "But I didn't pray to God," she said. "I prayed to *you*." She slid her hand forward on the wrinkled bedspread and touched the tips of my fingers with hers. "I prayed for you to be real, and that what you'd told me was the truth. I allowed myself to have faith that everything would be all right, but just for three days, because you told me that's how long he would be missing for. When I was out looking for Adam, I was looking out for you too, but I was looking for a woman about fifteen years older than me — and yet here you are, and you're younger. . . ." She paused, looked at me in bewilderment, not for the first time.

"I was looking out for you, because when Adam was lost, I told Andrew about you, and what you'd told me. He thought I was talking gibberish, and then he wondered if maybe you had something to do with his disappearance, and started to make me doubt you. Your mind plays tricks on you when you're frightened, you get desperate. It can be hard to believe, even when belief is all you've got," she said, with an apologetic expression. "I remember being on my knees beside my bed, putting all my belief in you, all my trust. And deep down, I knew that if Adam wasn't found after three days, I wouldn't know how to cope, I wouldn't know how to breathe in and out. I survived for three days because you told me he would come back safely." Her head was in her hands now, slowly trying to shake off the memory of it all.

"But you did find him, obviously," said Louis, not unkindly. "What had happened to him?"

Elizabeth sighed. "He just roamed off, exploring. He'd read *Huckleberry Finn,* and he got a tea towel and wrapped some food in it, and actually tied it to a stick." She smiled at the thought of it. "Then he went off into the woods and walked and walked for hours. He slipped down a hill and broke his ankle. He was miles away, because when he thought he was headed for home, he was still walking the other way.

"After that . . ." she continued, looking at me again, ". . . believing in you has been tantamount to believing in God. You *are* my God, because my faith in you made me stronger, a better, more fulfilled person. The type of person we could all be if we really had faith that someone was looking out for us."

"Stop," I said, holding my hand up. "I'm not God, Elizabeth, I'm just an ordinary woman." I saw Louis raise his eyebrows.

"Not to me, you're not," said Elizabeth. "To me, you are far more than that: you have shaped my life, made it happier."

"But that doesn't make me God," I said. "Other people do things like that. I was just a person in need of roller skates, and I gave you some information about your life that I just happened to know." I was faltering a bit in my explanation.

"But how did you 'happen to know' this information?" she asked. "And why haven't you aged? How can you *not* be some sort of god or angel?"

"To me, all this happened just a few days ago," I said. "Saturday, to be precise. I had the conversation you're talking about, with you, on Saturday. That's why I haven't aged."

"Well, you're about three days older," Louis said.

"Thanks, Louis," I said, looking at Elizabeth as if to say *typical.*

There's an animallike quality to a person when they tip their head to one side — waiting for information, or an explanation, or a doggy cookie — that is quite charming, and Elizabeth was doing this now.

"It's hard for me to explain, because it's preposterous," I said.

"Are you serious?" Elizabeth said. "Look at what I've believed most of my life. Do you think I'll find anything you have to say unbelievable? If I can trust anyone to tell

293

me the truth, no matter how farfetched, then it's you."

"Blind faith," said Louis, very quietly.

"Exactly," said Elizabeth. "I have blind faith in you."

I felt dizzy with the responsibility I'd had over Elizabeth's life. What if I'd got it wrong, the number of days Adam had been missing? What if it had been five days, or a week? It didn't matter that I wasn't God, or an angel. It didn't matter that I was just a woman with a family, a job, friends, and ordinary dilemmas. To Elizabeth, I was more important than that, whether I agreed with her or not. And that gave me responsibility. So I told her about traveling back in time, how I'd done it, the meetings with my mother and my younger self. I told her why I'd felt the need to steal the roller skates, and why I was glad now that she'd caught me. I talked for ages, and she listened without interruption, captivated.

"It's like a fairy tale," she said at last, in a soft, reverent tone.

"And now that I'm back again, I'm thinking about my return, thinking about what I can do for my mother, to help her," I said.

Elizabeth suddenly sat up a little straighter. "Oh, you mustn't go back again," she said, concern lining her face.

294

"Why not?" I said, glancing at Louis, his expression impenetrable.

"Well, because you might get hurt, and you might mess things up." Elizabeth also glanced at Louis in vain. Sometimes a third party in the room is most useful for their reaction-expressions, like a flight attendant on an airplane. But Louis was not the right person for this job.

"You went back a few days ago, and what happened between you and me made my life wonderful, without you even intending to." Her voice was kind, but there was an urgency to it. "So surely it would be just as easy for you to go back and make things go terribly wrong, with no intention of doing so whatsoever."

"I wouldn't come near you, I promise," I said, leaning toward her.

"Faye can't change what's already happened," Louis said. "Whatever's already happened has already happened; it can't be amended one way or the other."

"How do you know that?" she asked.

"I, um, I googled it," he said.

"You *googled* it?" She laughed. "You know that doesn't make you an expert, don't you."

"Yeah, I realize," said Louis. "Sorry."

"These are real *lives* we're talking about, and changes that could generate a whole

295

thread of different consequences," Elizabeth said. She looked faintly terrified.

"We're pretty certain that I can't change anything that's already happened," I said, completely sure of that conviction with no real evidence, except that it did seem to be that way.

"Faye, you're talking as if you are an expert in time travel, but you're not. You've traveled in time, but that doesn't mean you understand how it works. That would be like someone saying they know how a television works just because they watch it all the time. It might be that you'll never understand the rules of what you're doing. You can't play with this, it's not a game," she insisted.

"I know that," I said. "I don't play games that nearly kill me without putting a lot of thought into it." But how much thought *had* I really given it? My desire to see my mother did seem to stop me looking, as closely as perhaps I should, at the worst-case scenarios, the possible unpleasant outcomes of my journeys back and forth.

"When there is a big catastrophe and lots of innocent people die, people use it as a reason to suggest that God doesn't exist." Elizabeth's voice was softer now, and she held my hand. "Because if there were a

God, how could he let that happen? But the thing is, we don't know what God's rules are; there may be things that are out of his control." Her voice dropped to almost a whisper. "You don't know the rules, Faye, you're playing with fire. You said only three hours or so pass when you're away, but what if that's not the case next time? What if next time fifty years have passed, and you've missed it all? What if you cannot be there for your children? You can't live in the past."

"I'm not living in the past," I said. "I'm just visiting." My voice shuddered with a veiled sob.

"But what if next time it's not a visit, what if you get stuck there?" She looked at me the way a mother does when she is telling her child why she mustn't put her fingers in the socket, even when she really, really wants to. "You have to choose between the past and the present, and there really is no choice, Faye, it's a no-brainer. You can't live in both, and if you don't choose between the past and the present, then one day that choice may be made for you, and you might not like the way it goes." Tears rolled silently down my face, and she wiped them away with her thumb. "You were there for me with some information that has undoubtedly given me a better life than I would have had otherwise," she said. "Now let me return the favor. My advice to you is to leave the past where it is, and stay in the present. You have your memories; that's what they're for. They will be tinged with sadness, that's just life, a sadness to make you appreciate the good things you have. Don't lose sight of your purpose. You're a mother."

"My mother will be expecting me," I said, tasting my tears.

"She wouldn't expect you to do this, would she? To risk everything, risk yourself. Would you want one of *your* daughters to risk her life or her health just so she could sit with you in the garden for an afternoon?"

I wept, and she held her hand to my cheek and I leaned into it, her hand taking the weight of my head.

"Don't let your children lose you. You lost your mum, and you have hurt all your life because of it. Why would you risk doing that to your own children?"

"I hear what you're saying," I said. "I'm taking a risk, but wouldn't you do it?"

"I think I'd be too scared, to be honest," she said.

"But so far, there's nothing to suggest that anything has changed as a result of what I've done. In fact, quite the opposite. It feels like going back in time made lots of good things happen just as they should. Nothing's changed."

Elizabeth gently lifted my left hand. She ran her thumb over the indent in my fourth finger above my wedding band, and we both stared at the skin that was whiter where it hadn't seen the sun for years.

"My ring," I said, wiping my nose with the back of my other hand. "Have you got it?"

Elizabeth hesitated. "Something *has* changed," she said, and she lifted her eyes from my fingers to meet my gaze with steady unease. "I don't have it anymore. I haven't had it for years. Your ring was stolen in the burglary."

I looked at Louis, and in a flash his expression, which had started to be a bit too smiley, was suddenly alarmed.

We stayed a little longer, but when we were back down in the shop and about to leave, Elizabeth asked us to wait a minute. She disappeared, to the storeroom I guess, and came back lifting the lid of a box and folding back layers of white tissue paper as she walked.

"I have something I'd like to give you, Louis," she said, putting the box on the counter and lifting out a heavy-looking roundish object.

"What is it?" he said.

"Here." She put it in his hands.

"It's a big egg, or egg-shaped," he said.

"That's right, an enameled egg, and it's so beautiful. The colors on the outside are like jewels: sapphire blue and emerald green," she said, coming closer and touching it as he rotated it in his hands.

"I don't know colors," Louis said.

"They're as crisp as an ice-cold drink on a hot day," she said to him, and he smiled. "Feel the clip?" And he rested the egg in one hand, skimming the surface with the other, until he felt the tiny hook. He lifted it, and helped the top of the egg flip back slowly on a strong hinge. Inside, the bottom half was a smooth, white enameled surface, with a raised bump in the middle, painted gold, like an egg yolk. She described it, and he explored it with his hands. While she spoke, a grin broke on his face, not just a polite smile.

"This is wasted on me, surely?" he said.

"Whether or not you can see it, it's beautiful, and beauty isn't wasted on anyone," she said. "You can appreciate that, can't you? And you can display it in your house for others to enjoy as well." Then she looked at me and said, "You don't need to see a thing in order to know it's there. You can still love and enjoy it."

"Thank you so much, Elizabeth," Louis said. "No one ever gave me a gift just because it was beautiful to look at. This is a first for me." She took the egg from him, wrapped it again, and bagged it up.

It was hard to leave and hard to say good-bye. I told Elizabeth I'd like to come back one day, and then she hugged me as if she'd never see me again. Which is something I guess we sometimes just have to do.

CHAPTER 21

After the trip to see Elizabeth I felt oddly bereft. Before I went to see her, I'd eagerly contemplated another visit to Jeanie while Eddie was away: because I'd convinced myself that I would never be away for more than three hours, I knew I'd be able to go, and stay a few days, at least. But Elizabeth had made me hesitate, doubt myself. She was right, I conceded, up to a point; I needed to give time travel and its potential consequences more thought.

And while I was giving it more thought, I cleaned my house, which is how I came to realize that my fear of spiders had diminished, or changed. We have a nice house, but it's a family home, *lived in.* I'm only really completely at ease when the place is tidy, but if I'm honest, it doesn't have to be impeccably clean for me to have peace of mind. Which means I spend a lot of time picking up socks and things, putting books back on shelves, filing paperwork, and throwing out leaflets, and less time actually vacuuming and polishing.

It was Wednesday when I started the spring clean (technically it was nearly the end of summer). I put on an old T-shirt and jersey shorts and I snapped on yellow gloves. I did the job one room at a time: put all the knickknacks, frames, bowls, and anything on a surface that could be moved into a big plastic container, then pushed all the furniture into the middle of the room and vacuumed underneath. The spiders I encountered made me jump, but still, I encouraged them onto a duster, held it at arm's length, and then flapped it against the windowsill until they fell outside. I cleaned the windows, the furniture, and the curtains, and every ornament was gleaming before I put it back in its place. Anything that could be chucked out, I chucked. Then I opened the windows to let in air, and moved on to the next room. I left the kitchen till last, because it was a bigger job. I emptied the fridge and the cupboards and cleaned them, before putting all the tins and boxes back, with the labels all facing forward, like someone with OCD. It took me all of Wednesday and Thursday. My back and shoulders ached, but it was a good, hard-work ache. The whole house smelled of lemons, which made me think of gin and tonic, so I took a long bath, then poured a large drink and sat in the garden.

I listened to the birds still chirping at 9 p.m. and I hardly moved as they got quieter and dusk deepened toward night. I saw a bat swoop through the garden and over the shed, and there might have been another one, or it might have been the same little bat. When I say I saw it, I mean barely; it actually looked like a small black envelope whisking though the air. I guessed it was having fun whipping at high speed through our long back garden, until its sonar picked up the shed at the bottom about twenty yards away. I closed my eyes and remembered a time at school when people used to say that earwigs laid eggs in your ears when you slept at night, and how bats would get tangled in your hair if they got too close. But now I know that bats would only ever keep their distance.

The peace of the garden felt almost spiritual, like when everyone prays in church. I thought of my mother. My memories of her used to be blurred and I couldn't be sure of them because they were the memories of an eight-year-old and overshadowed by her death, as if death were a high brick wall that plunged everything near it into darkness. But now I have these wonderful crystal-clear memories of her, a thousand or more mental photographs taken over my two recent visits. I could see her smiling eyes and smell her hair when she hugged me, hear her voice, her choice of words and her laughter. A cool breeze washed over me, and in it I was sure I could smell sticky toffee pudding, and I saw my mother jump up to get it out of the oven. I felt happy to have these new images of her, but tears leaked from the edges of my eyes. I missed her so much. I went inside to pour myself another drink, but the house was so lovely that I stayed indoors, climbed the stairs, and fell asleep on my bed fully clothed.

I was supposed to be at work on Friday, but called in sick. I wanted to hang out in the house. Eddie and the girls would be back in the afternoon and I was keen to see them as soon as they got home. Despite the impression I may have given, I don't normally take much time off work, and the boss was fine about it.

I made myself fried eggs on toast and a pot of coffee and had breakfast in the garden in my dressing gown about 10 a.m. Luckily I heard the knock at the front door and took delivery of a small parcel, addressed to me, which I had to sign for. As I walked through the house back to the garden, I tried to think what it could be; I couldn't remember ordering anything, and I braced myself for something dull. The excitement of an unexpected delivery is directly proportional to how boring it turns out to be, I can usually guarantee it. But it was far from boring.

The parcel was a puffy brown envelope, sealed up with brown masking tape like it was never meant to be opened. I tried to get into it, but soon gave up and got the scissors. Inside were layers of bubble wrap with something small and hard inside, and a letter. I snipped open the taped-up plastic and extracted a ring: an eternity ring, about a quarter of an inch wide, with what looked like diamonds all the way round it. I didn't think they could be real — the diamonds — although they glinted with tiny colors, which someone told me once was a sign they're genuine. I put the ring on, because I was scared I would drop it, and it fitted my fourth finger perfectly. I held my hand up to the sky and turned it this way and that to watch it catch the light. It was a thing of beauty.

I pulled the letter out, blue paper, two

sheets, written on both sides in old-fashioned cursive handwriting that I didn't recognize. I sniffed the paper, don't ask me why, and it smelled of nothing. I turned the pages over to the end and saw it was from Elizabeth. This is what it said:

Dear Faye,

Words cannot fully express how I feel about finally seeing you again after all these years. To me you have been an angel that I thought I might have dreamed. To see you in the flesh, so real, so lovely, has come as a shock. But a very welcome shock. I have been waiting for you for years, so that I could have a chance to thank you for the kind of life you have given me. In many respects I have lived an ordinary life, but I have lived with peace of mind and contentment, and I attribute much of that to our meeting thirty years ago, (or "just the other day," as you put it). You have lightened my burden.

To have someone tell you that everything will be okay, not just because they hope it will or because it's an easy — if unfounded — reassurance, is one thing. Quite a different thing it is to have someone tell you that everything will be okay, and to know that it's the truth.

The fact has not escaped me that I cannot be sure that my life from now on will be fine. Presumably you only had knowledge of my life up until now, at most. And anything could be waiting for me round the next bend. But I'm so accustomed to living with faith in the future that it is a habit for me. I'm not scared. All will be well.

I hope that you too can live your life this way, because ultimately none of us knows what's in store. Stop worrying about the future, and leave the past behind — live for now, enjoy what you have. Try not to hanker for things that are beyond reach.

I have been mulling over our recent conversation and fear that I may have seemed selfish, worrying about my life and not wanting you to do anything that might disrupt it. I can only apologize and say that I suppose it is selfishness: I love my family, and what I have, and cannot bear the thought of anyone taking it away. I wonder if I would even have this life if it weren't for you. If it has been given to me, then it can be taken away, perhaps. I know that you can understand how terrible that would be.

You also seem to have a lovely life, and I worry that you will put that at risk too.

You gave me peace of mind, and I hope that in some way I have helped you too, because I vouch for you: I bear witness to your extraordinary journey and want you to always know that if you ever doubt yourself, or what has happened to you, remember that you are not alone. I was there with you.

One last thing. I have enclosed a gift. I gave Louis a present, and I wanted to give you something too; I just needed a little time to find the right thing. I feel bad about your ring, so it seemed appropriate that I send you something to replace it. And a diamond eternity ring seemed appropriate.

At your service, and with gratitude.

Forever,
Elizabeth Keel

I reread it a few times. The words *you are not alone* made my heart swell.

I lay on the sofa and watched a movie, closing the curtains and pulling a blanket over me. Now and then I was lost in the film; now and then I gazed at my new ring, twisting it on my finger and rubbing the back of it with my thumb, feeling it snug and comfortable against my wedding ring. Elizabeth had given me so much to think about. She was right: I was risking everything to visit my mother. If I had to choose between my life with Eddie and the girls, and living back in the past, then of course I would choose Eddie and my children. But did I *have* to choose? That was my dilemma. Until very recently I hadn't thought of the past as being out of reach, as Elizabeth put it. I had thought I could have both.

Before I met with Elizabeth, I'd believed I could visit my mother as many times as I wanted, until she died, so that she wouldn't be alone. I wanted to do that for her, for me. Knowing that only a few hours passed while I was away made me think it was doable. That, and the fact that my expeditions to the past didn't seem to have any real impact on my life in the present. Since Elizabeth had told me my ring had been stolen in the burglary, I felt differently. If that could change, then she was right, wasn't she? Anything could happen. And she was certainly right when she argued that I didn't know the rules of time travel and its consequences; I was still a novice.

The physical damage I was doing to myself, well, I could handle that, but Eddie wouldn't be able to. Since I kept hurting myself I knew that I couldn't talk to Eddie about my time travel. Even if he believed me, he would definitely try to stop me, if only for my own safety. As far as I was concerned, a little hurt was a small price to pay, and if I was wearing the right clothes and didn't land too awkwardly, I could minimize the damage. Surely it wasn't much different from what someone with a dangerous hobby would put themselves through.

Doubts had been awakened in me. But I didn't have long to decide what to do. I had left it only a few weeks between visits last time, yet six months had passed for my mother when I saw her again. If I left it too long, it might be too late. And there was this nagging desire for just a little bit more. I had been back twice, and it had been beautiful, important, emotional. But if I had known that my second visit was the last time I would see my mother, maybe I would have done things differently.

I sighed. No matter what we do, we seem to leave the conversations we should be having till too late. I bet that when Eddie returned, he would say the same: that even though he'd spent the week with his own mother, with the intention of avoiding that mistake, there would still be things left unsaid, unknown. Maybe a few locked doors are inevitable in life; maybe there are questions we all have that will never be answered, and that is something we simply have to accept. I closed my eyes and laid my head back. The voices on the TV were saying words important enough to make the script, but I wasn't listening, and the velvet darkness behind my eyelids was so inviting. I was sleeping a lot lately. My inner voice whispered to me: *One more visit, one more time; one more chance to get it right. I'll tell my mother who I really am.* And I drifted off to sleep to the hum of the dialogue on the TV.

The voices of my children and the sound of Eddie shepherding them, grunting as he hefted cases from the car to the house, woke me. Familiar sounds are as comforting as a pair of perfectly fitting shoes. I raised myself up on one elbow, remembering to slip the eternity ring off and push it into my pocket.

"You're home!" Eddie said, his lovely face beaming at me. "I didn't think you'd be back from work." He hesitated, looking at the blanket I'd just shoved to one side. "Are you sick? You been sleeping?"

"I took the day off, wanted to be here for you when you got home." I was still sleepy

312

as I stood and wrapped my arms round his waist. I breathed in his smell, and there were layers of it, like an aromatic Russian doll. On the outside he smelled of campfire, then vaguely of washing powder, and his deodorant, and as I nestled my head into his armpit I smelled the most human of smells, sweat, and my body responded instantly, positively. "I've missed you so much," I said, still with my nose tucked under his arm.

"You must really love me, to want to sniff me there," he said. "I've been driving for hours, I've got dirt in my hair and on my face from having the windows wide open all the way." He rubbed his face hard with the heel of his hand.

"Take a shower and I'll get you a drink, we can sit in the garden."

"Place looks nice," he said, breaking away from me and heading for the stairs.

"Well, I had to keep myself occupied somehow while you were away," I said. The girls barreled into me then and I couldn't get enough of their little bodies, their skinny arms and legs with the finest down appearing on them, the smell of their hair. "Let me look at you," I said. I knew and loved every little bit of them: the crooked tooth, the curl of hair, the freckle northeast of an eyebrow, the dark eyelashes, the pale ones, the perfect, dirty toes. We fell back onto the couch as one wriggling mass, cuddling and tickling, and in overlapping voices erupting with giggles and childish sincerity, they told me about ants' nests, and swimming and being stung by a bee, and a ghost they could hear in Grandma's house, and stinky cheese they didn't want to eat, and Grandma getting drunk one night, and a hundred other stories, badly told, confusing, disjointed, and all the more beautiful because of it. I felt myself falling into place; my body and mind were exactly the right shape for this, and I slipped easily into the carved outline of my life with my children. I had a sense of belonging that was unavailable elsewhere.

In the back garden, the girls ran barefoot through the grass, and I followed them. We plucked buttercups and they taught me a French clapping song I'd never remember, and that was okay.

And when I saw Eddie come into the garden from the kitchen, he took my breath away; I couldn't wait to hold him and be held again. He was barefoot too, and wore jogging bottoms with no top. "We didn't really do clothes and footwear at Mum's," he said, by way of explanation. "The girls went a bit feral, actually, they started peeing in the bushes at one point."

I laughed. "It's good for them," I said, handing him a cold beer, the glass bottle beaded with condensation. He took a sip, and sighed. "You have a good week?" I asked.

"We did, it was fantastic. The only thing missing was you, you should have come."

"Well, I did get some things done, and loads of rest," I said.

"Nothing interesting happen?" he asked.

"No," I said. But my lie came out an octave higher than my normal voice, and I laughed a tight little laugh, like self-sabotage. Eddie looked at me in silence. There was love in his expression. And mistrust.

"Who wants an ice cream?" I shouted down the garden.

"Me!" shouted the girls, and there was my excuse to throw myself into the bustle of normality.

CHAPTER 22

I didn't look at the clock, and the girls went to bed late. We carried them upstairs, one each, and they smelled of warm, dry dirt and straw. Evie was asleep in my arms before we got to the top of the stairs and Esther had put her thumb in her mouth, which she only ever did when she was dog-tired.

"Don't put your fingers in your mouth, they're dirty," Eddie whispered, nudging her forehead with his.

"I ate a daisy," she replied sleepily, mumbling around her wet thumb, and as he laid her in her bed, she curled into a ball like a wood louse and turned her back to us.

I sat on their beds and spoke into their ears, my words a little damp against their hair, "You are good, you are kind, you are clever, you are funny," and I felt a pang of sorrow that it was me who had said this to myself all those years ago, and my mother never got the chance to whisper good things to me beyond the age of eight. And if I didn't take proper care of myself, keep myself safe, then I wouldn't be able to do it for my children either.

When I came back downstairs, Eddie had already poured a couple of glasses of red wine and was out on the deck, so I grabbed a blanket, wrapping it round my shoulders.

"Tell me how it went with your mum," I said.

He sighed and then smiled; it was easy to get him back. "It was good. I'm very glad I went. It was a good idea."

"You're welcome," I said, and he tutted.

"I told her why I'd decided to visit: to ask all the things I might one day regret not asking," he said. "We talked a lot, and I asked her loads of questions. For most of them, she'd just assumed I already knew the answers."

"Like what?"

"Like how she felt about certain things. I asked her what she'd thought of me as a child, and she asked me what I thought she thought. I made a rough guess, and I was pretty much correct." He took a long sip of wine, and I just waited for him to go on.

"She said she understood my need to clarify certain things, but when it came to how she felt about me and the things I'd done, she said that if, in the future, I wondered how she felt and it was too late to ask, I was to always assume that her over-riding feelings were of pride, love, and joy." Eddie's voice cracked on the word *joy*.

"What is it?" I said. "Emotional?" He nod-ded, pinching his nose between his eyes to stop the tears. "Oh, Eddie," I said, laying my hand on his.

"But it made me realize something else," he said, sniffing but composed again. "We never talk about your mum. I know it's a great sadness to you, losing her so young."

I sat up straighter, wanting to tell him. My nostrils flared and I inhaled deeply, the oxygen squashing my secrets down inside.

"Why do you never talk about her?" he said.

"There's nothing to say. I don't remember enough, just a child's memories. Unreli-able."

"Aren't all memories unreliable?"

"Maybe." I stared into the bottom of my glass. "But whether they're reliable or not, even if they're unreliable, there's not many of them." I had almost lost track of the little I knew before, the tiny collection of snip-pets I had of my mother pre–time travel. As I lied to Eddie, I could see all the new memories I had made in the past couple of months, and longed to share them with him.

"Well, what *do* you remember?" he prompted.

I could only tell Eddie what I remembered from early childhood, the ones that had now been superseded by my newer memories.

"Working backward, I remember missing her when she died, she got a cold, a chest infection, she used to get those, I think, every winter. The way I remember it, she got a cold and then, well, then she . . . died." I tried to picture it, and it was like a blank page in a photo album; I couldn't make the images appear. I could remember the facts, insubstantial as they were, but I couldn't see them the way I could the new images.

"That's vague," said Eddie, not unkindly.

"If I'm honest, I can't really remember that time clearly. I went to live with Henry and Em, down the street, and at some point they adopted me." Eddie knew this part. "They were in their late fifties when I went to them, and I guess at first I thought it was temporary. I think *they* thought it was temporary, that was how it felt, but maybe it became permanent when we all got along. They were sweet. I remember when they decorated my bedroom, and some of my old things were given back to me." I paused, picturing the Space Hopper in the corner of my old room.

"I remember asking them what had happened to my mother, and they sat me down. They kept looking at each other as though they would prefer it if the other explained it. I honestly think that if I'd never asked them, they would have pretended nothing had ever happened, and that one day I would forget all about her, for my sake."

"They were trying to be kind," Eddie said.

"I know," I said. I stared into the middle distance, seeing Em and Henry as if on an old film recording, black and white, silently moving about, laying things on the table for a roast dinner and smiling into the lens from the past; then seeing them in Technicolor, the newer memories more vibrant and accessible.

"They said she'd got a cold, fell ill, and died. I never saw her again. I guess they thought that was best for everyone involved. I don't remember her body being taken out of the house. I was protected from it all."

"If two animals live together and one of them dies . . ." Eddie glanced at me, checking that I was okay; I nodded a fraction. ". . . you're supposed to put the body of the dead one near the one that's still living for a few hours, so they realize their partner is gone. If you just remove the body, the other one will wait and wait for the other one to come home. They can pine, get depressed; they will always wonder where their buddy is. It's the same with humans, I think."

"Do you think I've been waiting for my mother all these years?" I said.

"I don't know, I suppose it's different. Not waiting exactly, but maybe pining. Did you ever ask Em and Henry about her when you grew up?"

"No," I said. "I didn't want to upset them, or rock the boat. I don't think I ever asked them any questions, they didn't seem to like me doing that. And what could I ask? I thought I knew her better than they did, I didn't even tell them how much I missed her. They took me to her grave when I was young, but only twice, maybe three times, I took flowers from their garden and laid them there. Then that all stopped. I remember asking if we could go to the grave again, but there was always some reason we couldn't go, and eventually I stopped asking, because I got the feeling they didn't like it. I really think they thought I would forget about her, at least for the most part."

"How do you think she died? It's strange, isn't it, you not knowing any more than that."

"I think adults just protected children from stuff they thought they couldn't understand back then. But what they gave me was a lot of unknowns, and that's worse. I guess she died of cancer or something. Maybe, I don't know. She wasn't much of a drinker, but she smoked."

"Did she?" Eddie said. "I wonder why you remember that. Perhaps the smell."

Of course, I hadn't known or remembered that she smoked before my visits through the Space Hopper box — this was new information; I was being careless.

"Have you thought about speaking to Henry again, and asking him more about your mother?" Eddie asked. "Before it's too late."

Em had died more than ten years ago and Henry, who was nearly ninety, lived in assisted living. I don't visit very often, I'm ashamed to admit, but now and then I do.

"I don't know, Eddie."

"It's pretty much now or never, you know that," he said. I looked at my husband, his eagerness to make sure I live with as little regret as possible, now that he had got into the idea of it himself. "If you don't speak to him before he dies, you'll think of something you wished you'd asked. Maybe he can tell you more about your mum now that you're all grown-up. You won't know unless you try."

"I'll think about it," I said.

We sipped our drinks in the darkening garden, and Eddie lit a lemon-scented candle to keep the midges away; the flame danced, ducking and rising, searching for air and then retreating from it. It was mesmerizing, and I stared into its blue center.

"My mum was right," Eddie said after a while. "A lot of the questions I asked her, I knew the answers already. And I think it's a good idea if you adopt that sentiment in terms of your own mother." I didn't say anything. "What I mean is," he went on, "your mum loved you, she cared about you. She'd be so proud of you, and the girls."

"I know," I whispered.

"But do you?" he said, intent on making sure I believed in what he was saying. "You don't need to remember your mother or the things she said to you in order to know that she loved you as deeply as we love our own sleeping beauties."

"I'm starting to get there, starting to understand that," I said. Obviously I hadn't gotten to that understanding in the way Eddie would imagine. I had real confirmation, proof, and that felt good. But Eddie was correct; the truth was this: even if I had not returned to speak to my mother, I could have depended on her love. I could have trusted in that.

For a while we both just looked out into the garden; our own little pocket of the world felt safe and complete. It was comforting — misleading though it was — to imagine for a moment that this was all there was to the universe.

"To be able to trust in someone's love is a wonderful thing," he said, breaking the peace. "I've always tried to trust in you and the way you feel about me. But sometimes I worry, Faye. Recently you seem so far away. I've never felt like that with you before. You've always been right here." He held his palm to his heart. "But lately — I don't know — am I losing you?"

I set my drink, half-full, on the table and got up so I could snuggle into his lap. I wrapped my blanket around him too. "I have been distant," I said. "I know that, but you're not losing me."

"I know you're not telling me everything, and I can't work out why. I don't want to ask, but I have to. Is there someone else?"

There was someone else. There was my dead mother. But I knew what Eddie meant, and I kissed him long and deep, to reassure him that there was no other man in my life.

He pulled away gently. "Am I putting you under too much pressure by going into the clergy? Mum says it must be really hard on you, and I think I've been trying to ignore that."

"I'm coming to terms with it," I said, pressing my lips to his cheek and letting them linger. "I think there's more to God than the big beardy feller in the sky. I know that God is on earth, in people, in good deeds. God is in the big things and the small things. He's under the fingernails of our daughters, and he's in all the kindnesses we show people. I know that what people call 'God's work' can be called 'lightening the burden' for another human being. My kind of God might be a bit different from yours, maybe that's all."

Eddie pushed me away so that he could look me in the eyes. "You've been giving this a lot of thought."

"I have, and I'm on board."

Eddie nuzzled into my neck, and when I felt the heat from his breath against my skin I knew he would carry me upstairs and we would make love quietly, so as not to wake the girls. I sensed — as I had many times before — that everything I really needed was well within physical reach. His arm hooked round my waist and I closed my eyes as he moaned softly, and I weaved my fingers into his. Then he stopped. He held his breath, and so did I, knowing in that instant the mistake I had made. His fingers in mine moved almost imperceptibly while the rest of our functions — even our heartbeats, it seemed — paused. He pulled away, his lips still slightly parted from our kiss, and held my hand in his, looking at it momentarily before fixing me with a quizzical stare.

"Where is your engagement ring?" he asked.

I shifted in his lap, wishing I were farther away, in my own seat. I would have preferred to deliver my explanation from a slight distance. They say weapons are easier to administer the more remote they are; when this grenade went off, we were both going to explode.

"I, uh, lost it," I said.

He leaned back, squinting as if to make sure I was in focus.

"What do you mean, you *lost it*? Where is it?"

"If I knew that, I'd have it," I said. A logical response that he didn't appreciate.

"Where do you *think* you lost it?" he said, irritation making him more specific.

"In the house, I think. When I was cleaning." But I hated this excuse, because I made a point of not taking my rings off, not for anything. Eddie shoved me off his lap and stood.

"You lost it? I don't believe you!"

I peered up at him, barely daring to make eye contact. "Do you mean you don't believe me as in you can't believe I'd do something so stupid?"

"I mean," he said, "I actually *do not* believe that you lost it cleaning. I *mean,* I think that you're lying. Is that clear enough?" His pointed glare could have pinned me to a cross like a nail. "You've been lying to me about a lot of things, for a long time. I've been patient, but that's enough. I want to know the truth. Who is he?"

I understood, of course I did, and yet I felt indignant. Why couldn't my husband just believe me? I know I was lying, but his implication was what? That I'd taken my rings off to go and meet someone for sex and lost one of them? For him this was the simple worry that I was having an affair. Well, I wasn't. It wasn't my fault that I couldn't tell him the truth.

"I think I'd be a little more clever if I were having an affair, don't you?" I said.

327

"All I know is that you're lying, and the simplest explanations are often the right ones."

"And yet you won't accept that I just lost it when I was cleaning."

"When I say 'simple,' I don't mean 'stupid.' No wonder you wanted us to go to France," he said.

I looked at the table with our wine and the candles, the discarded blanket on the floor, and how this evening had been spoiled. Tears of frustration filled my eyes, and I flicked away one that fell down my cheek.

"What would you say," I said quietly, feeling brave and looking straight at him, "if I told you I'd swapped my engagement ring for a handful of magic beans?"

Eddie stepped toward me and leaned down, his beautiful face inches from mine.

"I'd say 'Fuck you,' " he said. Then he turned and looked out at the dark garden. He walked forward a pace or two and leaned on the railing of the deck; his head hung down, and he shook it like a captain who knew he'd sailed in the wrong direction and was looking out at an ocean that held no answers, or at least none he wanted to hear.

"Eddie —" I said, but he held up his hand

328

and I stopped.

"Unless it's the absolute truth, I don't want to hear a single word," he said. And I respected him enough to say nothing.

After what felt like minutes, but was probably seconds, he turned to look at me over his shoulder. His eyes were glistening. I held the blanket up to myself like a child with a make-believe shield, and I anticipated his forgiveness for whatever it was he thought I'd done. I predicted his trust that he would know that I loved him and would never betray him. I believed that he would know me well enough to trust that whatever I was hiding, it wasn't this sordid, ordinary type of betrayal. I looked at him with all the love and loyalty that I felt for him in my very bones.

"Eddie," I said again.

He held up his hand as if he were about to do a magic trick, and put his ring finger in his mouth, all the way, and took it out. Then he slowly slid the platinum band down his finger, looking for all the world like a magician who wanted to make sure my attention was just where he wanted it. Then he held it above his head and turned, throwing it into the garden. I gasped. For one moment I imagined I saw moonlight glint on its silvery surface as it spun through the air; then it disappeared, landing silently in the black grass.

Eddie looked in the direction of his missile. "If that turns into a beanstalk," he said, "feel free to fuck off up it."

Then he took the blanket, grabbed his half-empty glass of wine, and went in to sleep on the couch.

The girls slept late and I was up before them. The bed, too big without Eddie, seemed to drive me out, and I crept downstairs. The double doors that led into the living room from the kitchen had glass panels in the top, and I peered through them. But instead of my sleeping husband, I saw neatly folded blankets, and cushions arranged along the sofa as if it had never been slept on. My throat tightened at the thought that he'd already left the house. I was scared something would happen to him before we had a chance to make things right between us.

I padded through to the kitchen and flicked on the kettle. I leaned on the counter, inspecting the shiny bits in the marble surface, self-pity bearing so heavy on my shoulders that it was hard to stand up straight. When I found the strength to lift my gaze to the window, I saw him. Eddie was on his hands and knees, face close to the dewy grass. I could see he'd thrown off his jogging bottoms, which looked soaked through from the wet lawn, and there he was in his boxer shorts, like a dog looking for a ladybug. He sat back on his haunches dolefully, and pressed his hands to his eyes. When he dragged them down his face, our eyes met, and though I'd barely been moving, I was arrested; I didn't breathe or blink. I slowly straightened up, but not for one moment did I break my line of sight with him.

He stood and walked wearily toward me, grass all stuck to his knees, which were red and engraved with lines from kneeling for so long. I opened the kitchen door, and when he got to it, he put his arms around me as though he were just very, very tired.

"I'm sorry," I said.

"Me too," he said, his voice gruff, just holding me tight against his body, his hands in my hair.

"I'm not having an affair," I said, though I assumed he believed that already, so tender were his looks and actions.

"I *miss* you," he said, looking into my eyes so intently I could feel the heat of his gaze in the back of my skull.

"I'm right here," I said. "I'm not going

anywhere." And in that moment, I promise, it was the truth.

CHAPTER 23

I could have wallowed in obsessing over Jeanie and my recent trip to see her, and meeting Elizabeth, but I tried to get myself back to normal. After all, after traumatic events — life-changing trials — people still drink tea, take showers, go to bed, go to work, eat chunks of cheese while standing in front of the open fridge door. And I did all those things. Looking after my family was easy, I'd been doing it for years.

After a week or so I could watch a whole movie, prepare and eat an entire meal, wash my hair and get into my pajamas, without thinking about the fact that I was a time traveler. But it was there, just below the surface: I could take a coin and scratch very lightly over my everyday life, and there, revealing itself piece by piece, was my time with my darling mother. When I looked in the mirror I saw her face, so different and younger than mine. When I lay in bed and closed my eyes, I remembered watching her while she slept, breathing her in, and my pillow would sometimes be wet with silent tears.

I tried to concentrate at work: did my experiments, wrote reports, ran focus groups, attended meetings. It was hard, because all I wanted to do was get to lunchtime and sit with Louis and talk. We'd become closer since Elizabeth. His true belief in me had taken us to another level; sharing a secret will do that to people. I think, for a while, Louis felt a bit jealous of Elizabeth, because she'd actually been in the past with me. I started to get a sense of that after I read him the letter she sent and described the diamond eternity ring. I'm not saying Louis was out-and-out envious, I just mean he wanted to be the bigger part of this. It felt like I was the captain, and he was my first mate, wary of new crew. And as far as I was concerned, he was my main man. I needed Louis, and I knew him. I didn't know Elizabeth; I'd only had two proper conversations with her in my whole life. However, I knew that to Elizabeth I was something very much more than an acquaintance.

Mild jealousy aside, Louis was a big fan of Elizabeth, and we talked about her a lot.

He loved that she'd given him the enameled egg; it was a thing of beauty, and he knew that whether or not he could see it. He was so proud to have this beautiful egg on the mantelpiece in his house for everyone to see.

"It just shows how far I've come," he said one lunchtime at a café.

"Meaning?" I said, biting into a sandwich.

"Well, when I was a kid I didn't even know the shape of an egg, and now I've got a very expensive, beautiful, breakable one in my house. It is like a *fuck you* to the withholders of eggs."

"You don't know it's expensive," I said, my mouth full.

"Don't ruin it, it probably is. And your ring is bloody expensive."

"And fits me perfectly." I twisted it on my finger, which was a habit now. I had told Eddie it was a bit of costume jewelry to wear, as my finger felt naked without my engagement ring.

"Maybe it's worth losing the other one?" he said, not really meaning it.

"Oh God, no, but it was a sweet and generous gesture. She didn't have to do it." I paused. " 'Withholders of eggs'?" I said.

"You know what I mean."

We sat and ate in companionable silence.

The café was busy with people ordering takeaway lunches; one or two of them smiled at me in an admiring way, as if they thought I was doing a good deed taking the blind guy for lunch. I hated that. We were tucked away in a back corner, farthest from the entrance and the cold wind that whooshed in every time someone entered; it had been a warm October so far, but a cooler autumn was knocking at the door.

"Would you go back again, if it were you?" I asked him.

Louis wiped his mouth with a napkin. "I would. But that doesn't mean you should," he said. "I don't have kids, I don't have a husband. I don't have anyone who relies on me or would miss me if something went wrong."

"That's not true, Louis, I would miss you," I said. "*I* would."

"It's not the same," he said. "I'm just not that important in the lives of the people who I know. I'm replaceable."

"You're *not* replaceable," I said. "Louis, you are not replaceable."

"So if I had a box and wanted to go back in time to visit my dad or something, would you be encouraging me to do it?"

"Well, if it's what you really wanted to do, then yes."

"That's because if I got lost or injured or killed, it wouldn't have that much impact on the world. One day I'd go off in the box and then, when I didn't come back, after a while someone would say *Hey where's that blind guy who was always kicking over my wastepaper basket?* And after a bit longer everyone would stop asking where I was, and I would be just missing. My sister would be upset, probably presume I'd jumped in a lake because I was pissed off being blind, then she'd sell the house, and get on with her life."

"Not true," I said in a fierce whisper.

"True," he said calmly, confidently.

"It's not *my* truth," I countered. He just shrugged and bit his sandwich. "Don't you *ever* go jumping in a fucking lake." And then, in a pathetic little voice, I said, "You've really upset me, Louis. You're incredibly important to me. I need you."

"I need you too, and so do lots of people, but you keep threatening to get in a box and disappear forever."

"You didn't used to think like that, before Elizabeth."

"I know," he said. "But that stuff she said about not really knowing how this time-travel thing works worried me."

"Me too," I said. "I keep thinking that if

337

something as solid as a ring can go missing, what else could go wrong? Maybe something catastrophic. It's weird, because before it felt like going back was actually making the present as we know it."

"Oh, well, that hasn't really changed," he said. Louis sipped his drink.

"What do you mean? I thought that because I've always had my engagement ring, the fact that it was stolen from Elizabeth means the timeline has changed."

"No." He shook his head. "That's not the case. I've been thinking, and the timeline of your life and when you had your ring hasn't really changed, has it? You had it all your married life until the other day, and now you don't have it. I'm thinking nothing's actually changed as a result of your journey or the burglary."

"I'm confused," I said. "You mean there's still no evidence to say I would change anything if I go back again?"

"Well, except that I am starting to think you've only been back twice, and we can't be certain of the rules." Then he thoughtfully held a finger in the air.

"What?" I said.

"If you do go back again, you could take some money and pay Elizabeth for the skates and bring your ring back, before it gets stolen. At least that way you'll have it again and not piss Eddie off too much. When was the burglary?"

"Years after I first met her," I said. "That could work. But my money would be no good in the seventies."

"You can probably buy it on eBay," he said.

"Buy nineteen-seventies money?"

"Hmm," he said. Then he shook his head. "No, it won't work."

"Why?" I asked.

"Because the ring's already stolen. You can't undo stuff, you can only make things as we know them to be, *not* change what's already happened. And on second thought, you absolutely mustn't pay for those skates."

"Why?"

"I don't know. Because Elizabeth said you never did that, so that would be changing things."

"Oh God, stop." I clutched the sides of my head as if my brains might fall out.

"Don't go back, it won't help, and it's too dangerous," he said.

"Make up your mind." I put my napkin over my plate. "The downside of *that* is I never get to see my mother again. That's all. Thanks."

The argument for going back was going

in circles: I wanted to go back, but the risks could be too high. If it weren't for the ring, I probably wouldn't have thought twice about it, despite the physical risk and all that I had to lose. It was blasé not to take more seriously all that I had to lose, including my life, I knew that; and knowing that, I had to engage my head, turn down the volume on my heart a few notches. I had to come to terms with the fact that I'd lost my mother again before I'd had the chance to say everything I needed to say to her. I felt I was losing her for the second time in my life, or maybe the third. Every time I left her, I was bereft. But wasn't that going to be true no matter how many times or how brilliantly I managed to say good-bye? Now here was Louis, explaining once more that in fact I hadn't changed anything — the stolen ring meant nothing — and my life as I knew it would remain untouched regardless of what I did in the past. I'd considered myself a naturally cautious person, so why was I risking everything I had? My expeditions to the past were always tinged with the fear of not being able to get back, yet the compulsion to return was physical, emotional, consuming.

I got us some coffees and returned to the table, lifting Louis's hand and touching his cup with it. "Did you know I was adopted after my mother died?" I asked him.

"I guessed you were, or fostered. We've never talked about it."

"An old couple took me in, I called them Aunt Em and Uncle Henry. They were nice people, like cozy grandparents. It always felt like I was just visiting, even when I lived there permanently."

"How did it work out?" Louis asked.

"Good. They were kind, I didn't cause them any trouble. They had their lives, they went bowling, played darts. They had a gentle routine, and I guess it was good for me. It was like one day my mother was there and the next she wasn't, Em and Henry took me in, and then I just stayed. I can remember Sunday evenings: we would watch *Bullseye* on the television and eat pâté on toast and cup-a-soup out of actual red-and-white Batchelors cup-a-soup mugs. Then *Bergerac.* And the *Bergerac* theme tune just feels like Sunday night to me; it meant school the next day. My mother was really a hippie, I suppose, and there was lots of love and care, but I guess not always a lot of routine. Em and Henry probably saved me, stopped me going mad after she died. They really looked after me. They filed for adoption after a couple of years."

"They still around?"

"Uncle Henry's nearly ninety. They were nearly sixty when they took me in, can you imagine? Em died a decade ago." I sipped my coffee and smiled fondly because Louis had a frothy top lip and it looked like a tiny French mustache. I didn't bother telling him.

"Eddie thinks I should visit Henry and ask more questions about my mother, before it's too late."

"What could he possibly know about your mum that you don't know better since you visited her?" Louis said.

"Well, they never told me exactly how she died, so the story I know is she got a cold, and that was it. Well, that's not right, is it? It must have been something else, a heart attack, cancer, asthma. I don't know. They were protecting me, I understand that, and child psychology was not what it is today. They took me to her grave a couple of times, and maybe that was their idea of closure. But honestly, I wouldn't even know where that grave is now."

"Then talk to Henry, ask him about it, what harm can it do?"

"I don't know, it feels like a potential can of worms."

"Just visit him and don't ask him, then,

just see where the conversation goes."

"That's what you said when we went to Elizabeth's shop," I pointed out.

"Do you want me to come with you?"

"Not this time. I think I should go with Eddie and the girls. I'll update you afterward though," I said, squeezing his hand.

"This is good," Louis said, his voice reassuring, strong. He held my hand tight. "This is progress. This is what *normal* people do when they want to find out about the past: they speak to living people who were actually there, rather than getting in a time machine. This is a step in the right direction."

CHAPTER 24

Uncle Henry is jowly — always has been — and reminds me of Droopy, an American cartoon dog. Droopy had to hold up a sign saying I AM HAPPY because just by looking at his face, it was impossible to tell. It was much the same with Uncle Henry, but he was a far from miserable man. If I had only two adjectives to describe him, they would be *solid* and *content;* he made you feel safe by doing nothing at all except being present. Even now, his firm hold of my hand as I perched on the edge of a sofa next to his wheelchair was the grip of a man who knew no different than to give heart; reassurance was in his fingertips.

When I think about the first night I stayed with Em and Henry, the image I remember is a plate of cookies laid out in a pattern: caramel wafers in their shiny red and gold wrappers fanned out in a circle like sunrays, the gaps in between them filled with chocolate tea cakes in silver foil, and then pink wafers, naked in comparison. Too many cookies to eat, but just the right amount to make the pattern work. It wasn't weird, it was nice. They treated me like a very special guest, and were lovely to me.

Now that he was very old, Henry was getting jowlier; it was the only thing about him that changed — there was nothing wrong with his mind. When we arrived at the home, he chatted to Esther and Evie, asked them about school, and their trip to France, and what the worst thing was about each. He always asked what the worst thing was about your day, your holiday, your weekend because, he said, everyone always asks what the best thing is and it's good to be different. Evie climbed into his lap and he put his arm around her. She gingerly held the loose skin of his droopy cheek and lifted it slightly.

"What's under here?" she asked conversationally.

"Sweets!" he said, and pulled a bag out from a pocket, like a pannier, on the side of his wheelchair. "I got some out for you earlier, from under my cheeks, and bagged them up."

This was a routine we always went through when we visited. The first time Evie had come with me to see Henry, the first time she could speak, that is, she'd crawled all over him, and I was mortified when she lifted his face and inquired what lay beneath. But he laughed and told her a family of tiny birds lived under there. And the next time he said it was sweets, and was prepared with the real thing.

He and I now sat next to a floor-to-ceiling window overlooking the gardens and watched Eddie and the girls playing hide-and-seek outside.

"You had many visitors recently, Uncle Henry?" I asked.

"Most days, love. But when you get to my age, and your visitors are made up of the bowling team and their wives, gradually their numbers diminish," he said, matter-of-fact. "It's a terrible part of getting old, when you outlive everyone; you're basically condemned to see your friends die."

I squeezed his hand. "I was hoping I could ask you some questions, Henry, about my mother. Things I never asked before."

He closed his eyes. "I know," he said. "Before it's too late."

"I didn't want to say that."

Henry held my hand a little tighter and stroked the top of it with his thumb.

"Your Aunt Em and I, we loved you, I still

love you, of course. I hope you know that you brought us a lot of joy," Henry said. "Em, my darling Em couldn't have children, and it was a great sadness in our life, but we loved each other and we surrounded ourselves with friends and activities. It was harder in those days if you couldn't have children." Henry's voice went scratchy, and it made me want to clear my throat. "It's always hard for a woman who can't have children, if she wants them. But what I mean is, in those days, it could be harder to find another purpose to fill the time, distract from the sadness. When you lost your mum and came to us, we had already come to terms with the child-shaped hole in our life. The hole never closed, we just got used to it being there." He stared out of the window, unblinking. "You probably don't remember, but you used to drop in with your mother now and then, and Em would make such a fuss of you. She adored children.

"You were more like a grandchild to us, because of our age, but Em — and I — we loved you like you were our own. And you were such a good girl, you really brought us happiness."

"You were good to me, Uncle Henry. I'm glad you were both there for me."

We sat in silence for a while. I was agitated

because Henry must have known I wanted to know more about what had happened to my mother, and he wasn't volunteering anything.

"When I was little," I said, "when I came to live with you, I don't remember what happened to my mother. You said she got sick, had a cold, right? And then she died? But it's all so ambiguous, surely you know more."

Henry looked at me. His lips were pressed tightly together, and I worried that he would not pry them open to let any words out.

"Uncle Henry," I said, scooching closer, keeping my voice low. "I would never judge you. I know you and Aunt Em wanted to protect me from the details of my mother's death. You didn't want me hurting, and you wanted me to forget, because I was a child, and nobody wants to see a child in pain. I understand. But now, as I get older and my connections to the past are threatened" — I grimaced in faint apology — "I need to know, Uncle Henry, otherwise I will wonder for the rest of my life. The hurt of losing her is compounded now by not knowing the truth."

I implored Henry with my eyes. "Losing her hurts *anyway*," I said, "but I can't do anything about that. The truth of why I lost her, the details, are something I need. It will help me. Please."

Henry nodded, and patted my hand, as if to stop me trying to persuade him. "Get me a glass of water, love," he said.

He sipped, and we both looked out of the window. From this angle I could see Esther hiding behind a tree with her hand over her mouth, trying not to giggle and give herself away, and Evie hiding in a bush, clearly visible.

"There are no details," Henry said, and I closed my eyes. He wasn't going to tell me anything. "In fact, we told you more than we knew."

I turned to look at him, and he continued to gaze unblinking out of the window as he spoke. "I didn't even know she had a cold, *you* told *us* that. You said your mother got colds and bad coughs, and that she'd had one at that time. But I don't know how she died."

"Did you go to the funeral?" I asked.

"There was no funeral," he said, turning to look at me, and I thought I saw something in his face, I thought I saw an apology. A high-pitched scream made me jump, and I looked out to see that Eddie had sneaked up on Esther from behind and grabbed her. They were both laughing now.

"Why wasn't there a funeral? What did they do with her body?"

Henry sighed, a long sigh, and I smelled mints on his breath. "There was no body," he said. "Nobody knows what happened to your mother — well, nobody knows for sure. There was speculation, and we protected you from all that. But there was never a body. She was missing, presumed dead."

"*Presumed?*" I said, and it was suddenly hard to breathe.

"We think she committed suicide," Henry said, trying to move closer to me in his chair, but not actually moving at all.

"No, she wouldn't. Why?" My voice was nothing but a husk. "Why would she kill herself? She was happy."

"You were a child, darling, it's hard to know if adults are happy when you're a child. There's always so much more going on in life than children ever know, you know that now, don't you? Your children assume you're happy, don't they? Even when you're not."

"But I know she was happy, she loved me and she didn't want to leave me. She wouldn't have chosen to leave me."

"She took drugs," he said. "That was common knowledge." He held up his hands in surrender before I had a chance to protest.

"I'm not judging her, I'm just saying that maybe it contributed to her state of mind. Some people said at the time that she was troubled, and was saying strange things."

"Like what?" I said, utterly confused. I had met my mother as a grown-up and she was perfectly normal, in a bohemian kind of way; she didn't seem at all suicidal and she hadn't said anything that strange to me, and we'd had lots of conversations. Yes, she was spiritual, yes, she smoked dope, but surely . . . Maybe that was strange enough for the more conventional types in the seventies. What I know for sure is she would never have chosen to leave me on my own.

Henry sighed deeply and leaned back in his chair, closing his eyes. "Apparently she was waiting for a guardian angel — or searching for one — something like that. Somebody said as much, and it became a rumor. Em and I thought maybe she'd gone on a trip of some kind, looking for something, whether it was a guardian angel or not I don't know. Whatever, it didn't matter; the fact remained: she was gone. But we assumed she'd come back for you. So when you came to us, it was like a visit, and then it became obvious to us that if she was able to come back, she would have done so already. Rumors went round that she had committed suicide, and we didn't want you to hear about that."

"What about the police? Didn't they look for her?"

"I don't know what happened with the police, they came round and asked some questions, that's all. But like us, they knew it was hard to be a single mother, hard now, even harder then. And what with her habit of taking drugs, I think people just made their own minds up about what had happened; suicide seemed the most likely explanation." He paused. "Shall I stop?"

"No." I sniffed, and rummaged in my bag for tissues.

"I think the signs were that she'd just walked off willingly, and never came back. Some people wondered if, in her own way, she had done what she thought was best for you. There didn't seem to be anything suspicious, or anyone else involved, and the police had no idea where she'd gone. You can trace people these days with mobile phones and CCTV, but not then."

I couldn't take it in. The hazy image of my mother passing away in bed following a chest infection, which I had imagined, or which had been implanted (or both),was replaced by a vision of her walking barefoot through woodland in a long flowing dress, with flowers in her hair, hands heavy, dangling by her sides, until she disappeared completely from view.

"The grave!" I said, suddenly and stupidly. "You took me to her grave."

Uncle Henry shook his head. "I'm sorry about that, I really am. Em and I decided at the time it was a good idea, but we weren't sure."

"What was it, a stone put there for her, because she was missing?"

"It wasn't hers, it was someone else's gravestone; it had no name on it, just said *Beloved and missed, one day to be reunited.* We thought it might somehow be better for you if you'd seen a grave, something real, so that you could move on with your life."

I was mute. Dumbfounded.

"Everything we did, we did to try to help you, to do what we thought was best for you. I know we got some things wrong, and I am so very, very sorry about the grave, it seems terrible now that we took you there."

Leaning over, I held Henry's hand and rested my face in his palm. He stroked my hair with his other hand, tucking stray tendrils behind my ear. "I understand," I said, finally. "I don't blame you for anything. I was very lucky to have you. And I'm upset, but not angry with you."

"Thank you," he said, his voice low and croaky again.

"Why didn't you tell me before?" I whispered after some time.

"There was never a good time. You always seemed so happy, and we didn't want to spoil it. We talked, Em and I, and we were frightened that if we told you, you might abandon your happy life and try to find her. People spend their whole lives searching for people, you know?"

"I know."

"My worry," he continued, "is that you may go searching for her even now. A body is so important, gruesome as that may sound. If she happened to be alive somewhere, she'd be in her fifties. You won't go looking, will you?"

"Where would I even start?" I said.

Henry held both my hands within his own, slowly rubbing them.

"What do you think happened to her, Uncle Henry? Really? Honestly."

He sighed again, a sigh heavy with the weight of his unspoken words. "Honestly," he said, "I always imagined her walking into water. I imagined her drowning."

I leaned back on the sofa and tried to compose myself when the girls came back inside. Eddie could tell I was shaken, but the girls were too bustling to notice any-thing. "Let's have our picnic!" they shouted, and I wheeled Henry into the garden and spread a blanket on the ground.

Eddie kept looking over at me, silently checking if I was okay. I nodded at him, and I managed to pass round strawberries and flapjack and slices of pork pie, I man-aged to pour tea out of a flask into old-fashioned china cups that the children insisted on bringing to picnics, and all the time I felt the burden of my actions press-ing heavier and heavier on my shoulders.

My mother hadn't died: she'd disappeared and ended up God-knows-where going mad in search of me. She had embarked on a futile search in the belief that I was a guard-ian angel who could help her with her child if something awful happened to her. And I had brought all that about by visiting her in the first place. I could understand why she'd gone off searching, but why hadn't she come back? Had she fallen off a cliff into the sea? Had she met a bunch of hippies and got lost in some heady, half-conscious world? I didn't believe that. If my mother could have come back to me, she would have. She'd gone looking for me — the grown-up me she'd met when I went to visit her — and while she was away something had happened to her that meant she couldn't get home.

My time traveling had resulted in Jeanie being missing from my life. But there was no proof of her death one way or another. And so, only one simple thought occupied my head: my mother could be alive.

CHAPTER 25

The following day was Sunday, the last day of October school break, and we had done that blessed thing: made no plans. Our no-plans days with the girls actually involved a kind of plan: late breakfast, watch a movie in our pajamas, a walk, and a takeaway as a special treat before going back to school. Come to think of it, our no-plans days were stricter in their itinerary than some of our organized days out. Even the walk we took on days like this tended to involve a route, which led across an old bridge over a motorway. Eddie had taught the girls and me how to get trucks to honk their horns by putting an arm straight up in the air, making a fist, and pulling down as if yanking the cord on an old-fashioned bus. At first we'd thought Eddie was teasing us, but the first truck that thundered toward us blaring its horn had us leaping around in disbelief and delight as if our team had just scored in the World Cup.

But I was desperate to talk to Louis, so I sent him a furtive little text asking him to call me and say he was really upset about something and beg me to come over, so I could make my excuses convincingly. If I just announced I was going out to see Louis, or anyone, Eddie would be suspicious. I felt like a teenager lying to my parents to get out of the house, but I absolutely couldn't wait.

"Really? Today? Won't it wait till work tomorrow?" Eddie said as I pulled my coat and boots on.

"He's really upset, Eddie," I said. "And when you're a vicar, all our Sundays will be ruined. This is just good practice." He frowned as I kissed him on the lips, and he didn't kiss back. "Just kidding," I said. "I won't be long, couple of hours, and we'll . . ." I pulled an imaginary chain in the air as I walked backward down the driveway, smiling at him.

"Honk-honk," he said, without smiling back.

When Louis opened the door, I pushed past him, hung my hat on the neat row of hooks, and pulled my boots off with a grunt.

"Come in, why don't you?" he said.

"I went to see Uncle Henry yesterday," I said.

"Tea?"

"Please."

"What did he say?" Louis headed for the kitchen and the kettle.

I told Louis everything, and as I finished, I felt this wild sensation, as though I had told my story on a windy day at the top of a mountain. I was breathless. I had feelings of despair, it's true, a sort of nagging misery that everything was my fault. But during the night I'd been increasingly imbued with these powerful feelings of hope that were like shining gold threads through my gloom. Hope that my beautiful mother was in this world, here and now, with me. At the same time as me.

"Your mum, if she's alive, would be about fifty-six, right?" Louis said.

"Yes," I said, still breathless.

"Sit down, for God's sake, I can feel you looming over me."

I sat, but on the edge of the seat, desperate for action, movement, discovery.

"This is actually interesting," Louis said.

"And the rest of it hasn't been? You're a tough audience, Louis."

"So if she's alive, she's potentially findable," he said, resting his chin on a fist.

"But . . ."

"But what?" I said.

"She had to know where you were — you didn't move away, you just lived up the road. For years. You were findable for a long time."

I knew where Louis was going with this logic, of course, I'd thought of it myself; but hearing it from him, I started to deflate like an old balloon.

"I realize she could have tried to find me," I said.

"Hand," Louis said, and I gave him my hand to hold across the table. "Don't take this too hard," he said. "But from what you've told me about your mother, I can't imagine her just wandering off and never coming home." He put his other hand to my face, his thumb on my puckered chin. "It's okay to cry."

"Again."

"As many times as it takes," he said patiently.

A clock ticked and the sound seemed loud, though I'd not noticed it before.

"If she's alive and well, then she really doesn't want me," I said.

"Well, you're right in that you can't possibly know what happened to her, Faye. Maybe she *is* alive, it's a possibility now.

But maybe she's not well. Or . . . God. Who knows what happened."

My thoughts tripped over themselves, slapstick-style. I couldn't mentally order the various options of what might have happened to my mother, couldn't keep track of my speculation. Too much was happening to me at once. Louis helped me lay the theories out like playing cards. Unfortunately there was no real ace in the pack. My mother could be dead. Suicide, as Henry had thought, or maybe another kind of death. Or she could be alive and well, living right now in the present: an older woman somewhere at the end of a telephone, a flight, a car journey, a woman who had chosen not to come back to me. She could be alive in the present, but *not* well, something so wrong that she was unable to find or contact me. Or maybe there was some other reason that she hadn't gotten in touch.

"What do you think, Faye, what's your gut reaction? You've met the woman."

"The woman I met wouldn't leave her daughter behind willingly," I said.

"So you don't think it's possible she's alive and well?"

"Not likely."

"You think she's more likely to be alive and totally unable to contact you for whatever reason? Maybe sick, or lost her mind, or . . ." He paused. "Sorry."

I shook my head.

"Faye?"

"Oh, Louis," I said, barely audible even to my own ears. "You've got me thinking that the most logical conclusion to all this is that my mother is dead after all. I was just clinging to some fragment of hope that I could see her again without having to risk everything by going back in the box."

"But there's still a chance she might not be dead, and if we can find her, we should try," Louis said. "Worth a google, at least. Come on." He pulled me to my feet and led me up the stairs, and I wondered what I should wish for as Louis's computer screen blinked and woke up.

"What's her surname?" Louis said, his fingers poised over the keypad.

"Jones," I said. And Louis turned to look at me, as though he could see me. "Oh dear, I was hoping for something a little less common."

"Sorry."

We trawled the Net. Louis is a good researcher, but we couldn't find any lead or any information. We had no other names by which to find her in a more indirect way, and after a while we gave up.

"I'm going to go back," I said. "Make things right. Save her."

"What's the point?" Louis said. "You can't change anything, Faye, because you've already lived your whole life without your mother. Whatever happened to her, it *already* happened, you can't change anything. We've discussed this."

"I have to try," I said. "If I go back and tell her who I really am, if I explain everything, she won't go looking for me. She won't wander off and she won't disappear."

"But she *will* disappear, won't she?" Louis said, as though frustrated with an intelligent child who couldn't understand a simple equation. "Because she already has."

"We can't be sure it works like that. Like Elizabeth says, we don't really know the rules."

Louis took a massive intake of breath and then puffed his cheeks and let it out slowly. "You can't change things," he said again, sounding resigned.

"Well, maybe I can." I watched as Louis shook his head, and felt annoyed. I was being unfair, but what I really wanted was for him to just support me, whatever I decided to do. I didn't need him to tell me this was a bad idea; I just needed a cheerleader.

"The easy option didn't work," I said. "We

looked for her online, from the comfort of your study, a nice safe space between us and the real world, and it didn't help. So I'm going to have to do something, something . . . practical. I'm going to have to get my hands dirty."

"I'd go back for you, if I could, if it would make any difference," he said.

"Bullshit," I shouted.

"I'm only trying to help, Faye. I understand how frustrated you are, and maybe you're feeling guilty about what happened to your mum, but you shouldn't. You didn't know the consequences, it's not your fault. But I think you need to stop for a moment and look at what you've got to lose. I think going back is too risky. I think you know that."

"Do you know what I *think,* Louis? I think you're jealous, I *guarantee* you're jealous, and I think you're worried, like Elizabeth, that my actions will spoil your status quo, and frankly that surprises me a little." He looked up and managed to stare straight at me, in that unnerving way. But I was annoyed; that was the fact of the matter. He didn't say anything, didn't apply the hand brake to the conversation, and that's my feeble excuse for what I said next. "Maybe if I go back and change things, then when I get back, maybe you won't be blind anymore."

"Don't do me any favors," he said, and the silence between us weighed a ton. He got up and headed downstairs at speed. I trotted behind him.

"I'm sorry, Louis, I didn't mean that."

"Didn't you?" he said. "Well, I would prefer not to be blind, as it happens."

"It was a stupid thing to say. I'm sorry," I said. "I'm sorry. You know, I've assumed my whole life that my mother was dead. I've been lied to, and I know why they did it, but still . . ." My words petered away. "She was wronged, and I was wronged. But the bottom line is, it *is* my fault. So if I can do something to fix it, then I need to try. Can you understand that?"

"Yes, I can understand that, but please listen to me for a moment. Please?"

"Okay," I said, forcing myself to shut up.

"Sit," he said, and we both took our places at the wooden table again.

"People lie," Louis said, and then he was quiet for ages, and I felt like he was testing me to see if I would resist interrupting him. I didn't say a word, and after a few long beats, he spoke again. "People lie, and they do it for all sorts of reasons, sometimes they do it to protect you, and sometimes they do it to protect themselves. But lies are like wasps in the grass, waiting for a bare foot to find them. A lie is like a living thing, surviving until it's discovered."

"Skip to the end," I said in a singsong voice; a private joke between us, when the other is going off on one.

"Okay, my point is this. I had a visitor yesterday too." He paused for dramatic effect.

"Who?" I said.

"Elizabeth."

"Why?" I said, feeling lost.

Louis stood up and opened a shallow kitchen drawer and took out a slim puffy envelope, which he pushed across the table toward me.

I opened it, and out dropped my engagement ring. It sat on the table like an old friend I thought I would never see again. Its familiarity stunned me.

"How?" I said.

"Elizabeth lied about it being stolen."

"She what? So what made her tell you?" I asked, bewildered.

"Because I guessed that she'd lied, and I wrote to her, and then we spoke on the phone, and then she brought it to me. She feels bad about it, felt bad all the time about it. But she wanted to say something that

366

might stop you going back to the past."

I played with the ring, getting to know it again before putting it back on, swapping the eternity ring to my other hand.

"She wants you to keep the ring she sent you," he said, as I was sliding it up my finger. "She's very sorry, Faye, don't be too hard on her."

"How did you guess she'd lied?" I said.

"It was the fact that the eternity ring she sent you fitted your fourth finger perfectly. Either it was a coincidence, or she took the measurement of the ring she already had in order to get the right size for you. It's my understanding that finger size is not an easy thing to guess, so I decided it probably wasn't a coincidence."

"Sherlock, I'm impressed," I said. "And pleased to have my ring back."

"Elizabeth didn't want you to go back, that's why she lied. She thought your ring being lost might give you pause enough to stop rushing back in time, make you think you could change things, perhaps for the worse. Even though that logic doesn't work, as we know. We don't know the rules for sure, Faye, and yet I *am* sure there's no point in going back to change what happened to your mother, because you can't. And I am terrified you'll hurt yourself, and never come home."

"I still think I can stop her wandering off, stop her disappearing," I said.

"For goodness' sake Faye. You can't. I don't want to sound like a broken record, but it's already happened. There's no point. At best —" He stopped.

"At best, what?" I said.

"At best, I think whatever you do, she'll die anyway. You can't have her. Because you never did."

The funny thing is, I didn't feel the slightest bit deterred by his words. Maybe I just needed the slightest of excuses. Maybe Elizabeth had been absolutely right to stop me rushing back to the past. But now I'd had time to think about things, and the hesitation I'd had seemed to evaporate in the certainty that I couldn't hurt Esther, Evie, or Eddie by visiting Jeanie one last time; my mind was made up.

"Nothing is going to stop me seeing her again," I said, pushing my chair away from the table and heading for the door. "And I know I can't change anything. But maybe I can do something to atone."

The idea that being the wife of a vicar was too difficult to bear because I don't believe in God had started to seem trivial; it was no longer the terrible dilemma it had so recently seemed, compared to everything else. Louis's words regarding a return trip — there's no point — replayed in my head, and I felt indignant, as if changing what had happened to my mother or warning her not to go off in search of a guardian angel were the only things worth going back for. He had *missed* the point, which was that I could go back at all. I was going to see my mother again, I was quite decided.

Was I angry with Elizabeth? Not really. I understood her, and understanding can take the anger out of a thing. She had clearly begun to worry, as we talked that day above her shop, that my going back could do a lot of damage, if not to her, then very likely to me. I think her intent was damage control. According to Louis, Elizabeth had never really intended to keep the ring, but felt that I needed something to stop me scampering into the past and back again as though it required as little thought, and had as few consequences, as a trip to the seaside. She had a point. I could admit that now.

My dilemma had changed. I no longer questioned the wisdom of going back. I knew there were risks, and I was willing to take them. My dilemma now was, well, not technically a dilemma, but a concern.

Although I was mad at Louis, I had to concede that he was right in that I could do nothing to prevent my mother from going missing. So I couldn't change that fact, but maybe I could change the *reason* she went missing. I was going to return, there was no doubt in my mind. I would tell Jeanie who I was, and then whether she believed me or not, at least I wouldn't be the reason for her disappearance. She wouldn't go in search of me — her guardian angel — it wouldn't be my fault anymore.

Just as I was about to go through my own front door, my phone pinged: a text from Louis. If it were me, I would go back too, it said. I smiled, eased my engagement ring off before I got in the house, and then hid it in the bedroom, to be "found" a bit later. Otherwise, what would Eddie say if I'd miraculously found my ring again after a visit to Louis's place?

I didn't want to leave it much longer before getting in the box. But I needed to be prepared this time. You're probably wondering why I was so sure that my mother would be there when I returned. I wasn't. I couldn't be certain how much time would have passed when I got back, as there seemed to be no particular reason why six months had gone by last time I went. It had been a couple of months since my last visit, and it crossed my mind that maybe I was too late. Maybe my mother was already gone. There was only one way to find out. I realize you must think this was a stupid thing to do, but once a friend is decided, you might as well be on their side, right? You can't abandon me now, just because you think I'm an idiot.

This was my plan: a weekend would be best, and I thought it would be a good idea to take the box to Louis's house and "transport" from there. That way we could put the box on a mattress and surround it with pillows like I did last time. Obviously I couldn't do that in my own house with Eddie there. I would wear the ski suit again, and the gloves and boots too. I would take a small first aid kit and painkillers, and tuck a newspaper inside my clothes; it seemed like a good prop for convincing someone I was from the future.

Then Louis came up trumps. He came to the research department at work on Monday and hugged me in the corridor. We don't do a lot of hugging, but this was a good one. I abandoned my desk without bothering to tell the boss, and Louis and I sat in the staff cafeteria (another thing we rarely do), which was empty as it was so early, and I got us tea. He liked my plan and said he would absolutely help. I hadn't doubted it for a second, even if there had been tension between us the day before.

The weekend coming up was the one closest to November 5, Guy Fawkes Day, one of our favorite celebrations, and as usual Eddie and I were having friends over for our traditional bonfire and fireworks in the back garden, and a ready supply of burgers and drinks. I asked Louis if he'd come — it would be nice to have him there anyway, but then when he got a taxi home he'd take the box with him to his place (I'd fold it up so it was easier to maneuver). He promised me he'd guard it with his life. Literally, if necessary, he said. I had total faith in him, but didn't want the box to be out of my sight until the last minute. Louis said he'd stay sober too, just because that seemed like a good idea.

I decided not to drink much either. "We'll get pissed another day," I said.

Friday night, fireworks party; then I'd go to him on Saturday, making my excuses to Eddie, didn't matter what. Louis would then stay home, with the box in its padded surroundings, and wait for me to come back. Three hours. If I came back hurt, he would be there to help me. We were trying to be sensible and organized, but there was such a buzz of excitement between us, like children planning a midnight feast.

"I ordered something for you last night, online," he said. "To take to your mother. It's going to take a few days to arrive, but should be here in time."

"What is it?" I asked, intrigued.

"Old money," he said with a smug grin.

"Old money?" I let the implications sink in. "Oh my God, that's such a good idea. How much?"

"I've got about five hundred pounds' worth, it's all I could get. I thought it might make quite a big difference to your mother, and to you as a child."

"How much would five hundred pounds feel like back then?" I said.

"About four thousand pounds," he said.

"That would make *such* a difference to us, Louis."

"Well, as I've said, I honestly don't think it will actually make any difference, because you don't seem to have ever got that money. But in the spirit of not truly knowing what the fuck will make a difference, I thought money would be a good thing to take."

"Brilliant thinking," I said, shaking my head in admiration. It was good being

373

friends with a nerd, they have such great ideas. But I saw him grimace.

"What is it?" I asked.

"I do have a reservation about this money," he said. "A request."

"Go on."

"Just in case you can change things, Faye, just in case this does make a difference to the outcome of things, please don't be tempted to visit Elizabeth when you go back this time. Please don't go and see her, please don't pay her for the roller skates." He paused. "I know that you've thought about the risks, the consequences, and I know that you've weighed it all up and decided to go anyway, for better or for worse. But I think you'd find it hard to live with the guilt if your actions have a detrimental effect on Elizabeth's life." He sighed. "I think I'd find that hard to live with too."

"I promise — I give you my absolute guarantee — I will stay away from Elizabeth. As we know, she never needed the money in order to be okay. It would be pointless to interfere with her," I said.

"And one other thing," he said, with a sadness on his face that spoke of pain yet to be experienced. "I think you should write a letter to Eddie. I'll look after it, and if I need to . . ." I saw his Adam's apple bob as he swallowed hard. ". . . I'll deliver it to him."

CHAPTER 26

It wasn't a suicide note, because I wasn't
planning to kill myself, but then I suppose
I'm mincing words. The letter affected me
in three main ways. The first was plain relief
in writing everything down for Eddie,
however mad it sounded; it brought home
with sharp clarity how keen I was for him
to know the truth of my extraordinary life.
Second, it was a chance to say everything I
would want him to know if I never saw him
again. In fact, I came to realize that this was
a letter I should have written anyway: a letter for a loved one to find in the event of
death, or some other kind of loss, such as
mental illness; to bring comfort and closure,
to answer all the questions we didn't know
we needed to ask. And the third thing was
that in writing this potential good-bye note,
I was acutely aware of what I was leaving
behind, if my fate was to never return. While
I pondered what to write, I touched my

engagement ring to my lips, and could see in my mind's eye the relief and surprise on Eddie's face as I remembered the moment I told him I'd found it. And once or twice, as I wrote, a tear plopped onto the page and I would look at those briny domes, to see if they magnified the words beneath them.

If a week seemed too long to wait to see my mother again, I needed it to write that letter. I wrote about when Eddie and I first met and how my hopes had grown fast and strong like garden mint after the first time he kissed me. I reminded him of conversations we'd had and some of the words he'd said in passing — things he would likely have forgotten — but that had meant so much to me that I thought of them almost every day. I told him my wishes for the future and how much I wanted to work with him to follow his calling, the impact I felt he would have on people's lives and how I wanted to play my part in that.

And then, the task I'd been evading: I wrote a letter for my daughters.

Dear Esther and Evie,
  I didn't think I could love anyone in this world as much as I love your dad, until you two came along. Imagine that! I didn't even know I was capable of that

much love. You have brought me joy every single moment. You are the best things in my life, and not by a little, but by a lot. I love you both from the bottom of my heart, or, as Daddy once said, "I love you from the bottom of my bottom, because that's bigger than my heart."

Although I'm not there for you, I want to be part of your lives, and because I can't share my advice or wisdom with you in person when you need it, there are a few things I want to tell you, which I think are important and might be of some help.

Always be yourselves, because you are perfect, even when you're not.

As you grow older you will do wonderful things and people will say, "Your mother would have been proud of you." And I want you to understand how true that is. I am proud of you, and not just when you do wonderful things, but when you do good things, and everyday things, and even when you do nothing at all. But sometimes you'll make mistakes, and do things that you're not proud of. When you do, make it better, and I will be proud when you do what you can to make things right.

Esther and Evie, be kind. Now, I know that you are both naturally very kind, but remember to be conscious of your kindness. By which I mean, sometimes you should go out of your way to be kind, even if it's in a small way. When I was a grown-up, I met a man I knew as a boy at school. Everyone used to tease him and call him names. And when I was older I told him I felt sorry for that, and he told me I shouldn't worry because I was one of the good ones; he said I had only ignored him. And that upsets me so much. I wish I had done more, wish I had at least smiled. I learned from him, and now I smile more at people, because you never know, it might just be the kindest thing that happened to them all day. Be wise, though. Be polite to strangers, but remember to keep yourself safe.

There are a lot of trees out there, make sure you climb a few of them. Climb all the trees you want. You might break a bone or two, but sometimes it's better to break a bone than to leave the tree unclimbed.

Experiment with your hair. If you don't like it, it will grow back.

Read lots and love it. Reading is so

good for you, for so many reasons. Always carry a book with you, because then you will never be bored. And although you should marry whoever you want as long as they love you and you love them, I would really prefer it if you fall in love with readers.

I think that's enough from me, although reading this back I wonder if you'll worry that I love you more than your daddy. But you mustn't worry. Since you came along, I love him even more, partly because he made you possible, but also because he loves you and keeps you safe, which makes him more precious than he ever was before.

I know this letter will be hard for you to read, and bring you as much sadness as happiness, because I know what it's like to lose a mother. I lost mine too. So my last piece of advice is this: don't dwell too much on the past. Life is ahead of you, and if you keep looking back you won't be able to see where you're going.

Know that you are loved by me, always, and I am in your hearts forever.

Mummy Xxx

It was not an easy letter to write, and gave

me pause, I admit; especially the last part. To know that I was ignoring the advice I gave my daughters — and presumably the advice my mother would give me — made me think, even if it didn't make me change my mind. Never ignore for yourself the advice you give to others. Especially if you know you're right.

And now there's you and me, we are nearly up-to-date, and just in case you don't hear from me again, there are a few words I need to say to you, my friend:

In your life you're a god, and I'll try to explain it like Eddie did once. When you're asleep and you're dreaming, you are God, because you are everything and everyone. If you dream that you're one of the passengers on a plane that crashes, remember that you are also the pilot, and you're not one but *all* of the passengers, you are even the plane, because this dream is in your head, and you made everything happen. In dreams you're like a god. It's not quite the same in real life, but there can be touches of God in everything that you do — how you care, what you say and do — that influences others. God is in a baby's smile, but it's still just a baby's smile, and you can call it whatever you like. Call God what you will, and belief will follow.

I know that I'm here, and you're there, not much distance between us, just the distance between my words on this page and your eyes; I estimate about twelve inches. But that distance can be recalculated, depending on your point of view. We could be on different planets, and we may exist in different times — it doesn't matter, it's still just you and me. And I want you to understand that I believe in you with all my heart. Never doubt it. And when you're ready, when the time is right, you will believe in me.

So there we are, letters written, and in your case, read. Plans made, ski suit and other clothes ready at Louis's with the newspaper and first aid kit, old money on its way. Oh, and of course, I have given some thought to what I'd like to say to my mother when I reach her. Between you and me, this is a funny sort of good-bye, because you are able to see if anything comes after this page . . . but at the time of writing, I have no idea whether or not the pages ahead are blank. If they are, you can assume I never made it back.

CHAPTER 27

Well, it turns out I'm still here, and I suppose you're not surprised. But I may surprise you yet. I'd go so far as to guarantee it.

The last time I updated you was the week I wrote my good-bye letter to Eddie. Inevitably I was never completely happy that I'd said enough, but hoped with all my heart he would not need to read it, or at least not for a long time. And it was better than nothing. Much better.

We planned for friends to come over on the Friday evening for Bonfire Night, and it was fun on Thursday evening, because the four of us went to the supermarket to get all the food and drink. We bought burgers and hot dogs and potatoes for baking, and I got beans, pineapple chunks, and barbecue sauce to make my famous sweet barbecue beans. If you think it sounds disgusting, think again. I bought zucchini and eggplant to make a vegetarian chili, and big tubs of sour cream and jalapeños; avocados, mayonnaise, and lemons to make guacamole. Eddie got the beers and wine, gin and tonic, and the girls asked if they could be in charge of a sweetie table like one they'd seen at a wedding reception last year. To their surprise, Eddie and I said yes, and they went wild in the sweet aisle.

I remembered the time we'd been to a theme park for the day, and couldn't recall that we were any happier or had any more fun than we did in the supermarket that night, as we prepared for our fireworks party. Or maybe I'm seeing that night through rose-tinted glasses, in light of what occurred soon after. Eddie and I both had to go to work the next day, and the girls had school, so we stayed up late doing most of the preparations on Thursday, and Eddie and I drank wine and laughed and we made love that night too. I can remember the lust I felt, and the feeling of total devastation as I imagined it being the last time. I went to sleep with my mind riding a wave of hope and fear.

We already had our fireworks. Eddie had bought them the week before, and safely stored them high up in our shed. Trash cans and fireworks are Eddie's domain. I mean, he does other things, but those two tasks are very definitely his responsibility. Eddie took the firework ritual very seriously, and had talked solemnly about coming home a little earlier on Friday in order to nail the Catherine wheels securely to the fence and prepare buckets of sand for standing the rockets in, while he still had enough light to do it. Clem's husband, Dave, was also coming over early "to help," which also meant "to drink." It's fair to say we loved Bonfire Night, as we loved Halloween and Easter — because they were fun, but involved very little pressure and not too much buildup compared to Christmas. Easter would become a very different experience when Eddie became a vicar. But that no longer worried me. I planned to relish it all, but the church would never get in the way of our Bonfire Night.

Eddie was pleased, I think, to hear I'd invited Louis. Our usual guests were Clem and Cassie, their husbands and children. A couple of Eddie's mates at his financial company usually came with their wives and kids, and this time Eddie had also invited a man he'd met through his training, who was a little further ahead and had been ordained as a deacon, and his wife. Louis and I decided to get a taxi to my place after work rather than take the train, and in the days leading up to Friday we couldn't stop talking about what was going to happen when I went to his place the next day and then back in time.

"It's easier for me," he said, "because when you get in the box, I only have to wait three hours to find out how it went. But for you, depending on how long you stay there, it could be days before you get back and tell me what happened. It could be weeks."

"But I'll know what's happening sooner than you, because I'll be there, stupid," I said, giving him a friendly dig with an elbow.

"Yes, but you won't know what's going to happen on your second day there, for example, until you've been there twenty-four hours. Whereas I'll know the whole story in less than four."

"Oh yeah," I said. "You're right."

We'd had to stay late at work, which we really didn't want to do, because the courier with the old money Louis had ordered was on his way. Originally it was supposed to arrive on Thursday, then on Friday morning. Now they promised it would be at the RNIB reception desk by 6 p.m., so we waited at the front desk — me smiling apologetically at the receptionist, who wanted to leave and lock up; Louis constantly feeling his watch for the time, and tutting.

The reception area at RNIB is gaudy: bright yellows and deep purples divided by sharp lines that juxtapose in a seemingly random geometric pattern. There's nothing random about it at all, it's for the benefit of partially sighted people and helps them navigate the building independently.

The receptionist snapped her gum as if to say *How much longer?* and thankfully just then a leather-clad courier in a motorbike helmet strode in with a box. I grimaced, wondering how I was going to carry something that big into the past. We signed, then left and got a taxi straight away; there's always loads round there on a Friday night, picking up suits who are blind and drunk.

"How the hell am I going to take this to my mother's?" I asked Louis in the back of the cab. "I can't carry a box, there's no way, and I can't zip this into the ski suit."

"Once you've got the ski suit on, we'll stuff as many loose notes as we can down the legs and into the arms and around your middle. When you take it off, all the money will just fall out, but as you're planning to explain everything to your mother anyway, I don't think the weirdness of that will matter. Plus, it'll be extra padding for you."

"All right," I said. "And maybe there's a lot of packaging here." I rotated the box in my hands. "We'll leave it sealed; you can take it home with the Space Hopper box later tonight."

"I won't stay late," Louis said. "I'm keen to get the box and this money safely home. I'm looking forward to the party, but it's not the highest priority right now."

"I know what you mean, but it's strange," I said. "Because for me, this party feels like a very high priority." I put my hand on his and squeezed it. "I know I'm going to come back, but I have to be realistic. Maybe I won't. This could be the last time I see my friends and family."

"The last supper," said Louis.

"Oh God, don't say that," I said, pinching him behind the top of his arm, which he hates (which everybody hates). "I know you're a doubting Thomas, or at least you were. You're not Judas, are you? Are there thirty pieces of silver in here?" I said, shaking the box, which made no noise at all, and laughing.

"Don't even joke about it. I don't want to think about you not coming home. I need you to know something, Faye: you're my best friend. Even if I'm not yours, and I don't for a moment think I am. But you're

388

mine, and I can't bear the thought of losing you."

I laid my head on his shoulder, and shut my eyes. "You're my best friend too," I said. "You know so much about me. Who else would help me with all this stuff? Anyone else would have called the men in white coats."

We sat in silence for the rest of the journey, my head still on his shoulder, and I felt a tear, one of Louis's, drop onto the top of my head.

As soon as we got through my front door, I whispered, "Wait here," to Louis and left him in the brightly lit hallway while I dashed upstairs to hide the box of money. As I took his arm and led him to the back of the house, we heard voices coming from the kitchen and farther away too. People were mingling in the garden. It was cold, and we kept our coats, hats, and gloves on, in anticipation of standing outside.

Cassie and Clem were in the kitchen, their wineglasses full.

"Andy's driving," Cassie said, raising her glass with glee. "I'm going to get so pissed!"

"And we're getting a cab, so I'm getting pissed too," Clem said. "Who's your friend?"

"This is Louis, we work together," I said. Louis held his hand out steady, and the girls stepped forward to take it.

"Nice to meet you," everyone said, and I felt a bit sorry for Louis; it's hard to go to a party where you only know the host. And I wondered if being blind made it easier or worse. Maybe it was easier, like a child who covers his eyes, he could pretend nobody was here at all.

"Where is everyone?" I asked. I heard the sound of laughter and low male voices, and the odd squeal of children's laughter.

"Men are in the garden, beating their chests and discussing manly things, like fire and meat," Clem said. "The children are gorging themselves at the sweets table in your living room, so they're vacillating between vomiting and running round like Tasmanian devils."

"Nice one," I said, pouring myself a G&T, heavy on the T. "Isn't there a deacon here with his wife?" I added.

"They're in the garden too, with Eddie," said Cassie.

"He's like a hairy dog, and his wife looks like a mouse," Clem said. "It's sweet, it's like you've invited pets to the party."

"I'm taking Louis out to meet Eddie, and get him a beer," I said, offering Louis my elbow and leading him out the glass doors onto the deck. We always kept the beers in a huge bucket of icy water at parties, and when Eddie saw me he came straight over, dipping down midstride to take a beer from the bucket.

"You must be Louis," he said, taking his hand and holding it briefly. "Beer?"

"That'd be great," said Louis, and there was a hiss as Eddie opened it and put the cold bottle into Louis's hand. "So, what's going on out here?" Louis asked, and without hesitation Eddie efficiently described our back garden.

"We're standing on the deck, and it's just a few steps down onto the grass. The garden's about thirty long strides from here to the other end. We've got some outdoor lights, and about ten strides away we've built a bonfire."

"Look at the size of that bonfire," I said. "It's enormous!"

"Dave was already here when I got home today, had all this kindling and wood set up. Said he'd been reading up on how to make the perfect bonfire."

"He got here before you did?" I said.

"He's bored at work, too much pen-pushing," Eddie said quietly. "I think he wanted to get his hands dirty."

The bonfire wasn't lit yet, but it was beautifully erected. It looked as though shortish lengths of kindling had been used to make a central tepee, and then longer pieces of wood had been arranged in another tepee around the smaller one. This pattern was repeated, and the outermost part was constructed of what looked like six-foot-long pieces of dry wood. In between the layers of kindling was what looked like wadded-up paper. It really was an impressive structure, and higher than any bonfire we'd made before.

"Where did he get all that wood?" I said.

"Building supply shops, apparently," Eddie said, taking a pull on his beer.

"He really does have too much time on his hands," I said, laughing. "Poor Dave."

Eddie excused himself, and Louis and I followed him over to where the group was standing. I was introduced to the deacon and his wife, and Andy gave me a hug, followed by a theatrical sad expression as he held up a can of Coke.

"Oh, I'm so sorry you're driving," I said.

"And that," he said, pointing in the general direction of the house and therefore Cassie, "is *not* a pretty sight when it's got a hangover."

There was plenty of good humor, and I

was enjoying myself. I stuck with Louis, and he had my arm the whole time. The rest of our small party talked and joked as though life were the same today as it was yesterday, and the same as it would be tomorrow, but between Louis and me there was a secret, and I could feel my skin almost vibrating. We knew differently.

I closed my eyes and breathed in the cold air, relishing it. I could smell the homely smell of burning, and opened my eyes. "Have you lit it?" I said in the direction of Dave — king of the bonfire — wondering if the smell was coming from our garden or elsewhere.

"Yes," Dave said. "Baby's burning."

Louis and I moved closer to the bonfire, stopping a couple of feet away. I looked into the inner kindling tepee and saw the odd flame licking outward like a cat licking the head of its kitten. I could hear tiny pops and crackling as it gradually came to life from the inside out.

"Can you feel any heat from it yet?" I asked Louis.

"A bit, on my legs," he said, and turned his head to one side so his ear was facing the inner workings of the bonfire. "It sounds like there's someone in there crumpling a cellophane wrapper."

There was a louder pop or crack, and I tensed. I was nervous of hot embers spitting out of the fire. I squinted in anticipation that something might hit me in the eye. I'm the same when I fry bacon.

"You okay?" Louis asked, in response to my tightening grip.

"Fine," I said.

"What does it look like," Louis said.

I paused and cleared my throat. Louis didn't ask me to do this often, because it's so difficult. Colors are so important for describing fire — amber, orange, red, gold — but they mean nothing to him. I moved those descriptors to one side like so many objects along a mantelpiece, and tried to replace them with anything relevant that could be tasted, touched, or smelled.

"Imagine a dragon, cold, hard skin on the outside, it looks dead, but its heart is hot. A sharp kind of hot, a heat you would feel if you were thrown into a thorny bush. So hot that you can see it deep inside the dragon from the outside. This fire is an animal slowly coming back to life from the inside. It's the most living thing you can imagine. And the heat from its core is so powerful that it will make the whole creature move, you'll hear it roar, and it will become angry and wish so much that it could roam about and rule the world, that it will consume itself in frustration. And later tonight, it will be flat and uninspiring, but the heat at its center will be the last thing to die, and its pulse will still be beating, and deep down it has memories of a time when it could destroy you, and if you touch it then, it will still bite."

I stopped, quite impressed with myself. But then I felt Louis shaking, and worried that I might have upset him, reminded him of what he was missing by describing a thing of such violent beauty. When I looked at him properly, however, I realized he was try-ing to suppress laughter.

"Bastard," I said, and punched him in the arm, at which point he let out a whoop of laughter.

I let my gaze drift over the bonfire and couldn't help but be impressed by the workmanship. It was a shame to let it burn, but the flames were taking a good hold now, and burning was what it was made for. At eye level I noticed the details of a news-paper clipping, something about someone raising funds for a children's hospital, and an advert for a local garden center, which looked familiar. Our recycling must have been raided for this tower. My eyes rested momentarily on the edge of an old notebook I'd filled up with shopping lists and other reminders to myself, and I felt a tiny pang of sorrow to know it was going to burn, I've always been a bit sentimental about anything I've written on, even shopping lists.

My gaze traveled upward to the very peak, where it was darker, unlit by lights from the house, framed by the black sky and yet to bask in the glow of the fire's burning heart. I tried to work out why the top wasn't pointed; it looked squared off, and I saw that something was perched there at a jaunty angle, topping off the structure like an ill-fitting hat. I was suddenly reminded of a hot day last summer when Eddie had borrowed one of the girls' baseball caps to wear while he mowed the lawn, and it sat ridiculously small on his head. Whatever it was up there, I didn't envy its fate; like a Guy Fawkes effigy, it was just waiting to burn.

I could make out some letters, upside down, and found myself reading them one at a time, trying to work out what word was spelled out at the top of the pile. The flickering glow from beneath it momentarily lit the letters up, then waved them into darkness again — and then I realized, like a knife to my stomach.

Sitting at the top, like a crown on the bonfire, was my Space Hopper box.

CHAPTER 28

What had seemed like light crackling before now sounded like a car being crushed, and I trumped that sound with a scream that came from somewhere deep inside. A roar that a lion makes, or that primal scream in labor that tells you new life is on its way. Or death. Or fear of never seeing someone you love ever again.

I wrenched my arm from Louis and ran to the fire, teetering on the edge, my feet touching embers, the edges of my shoes smoking. Terror gripped me entirely as my unblinking eyes fixed on the box at the top of the fire. To my mind, of course, my mother might just as well have been propped up there, the flames beneath her thrusting upward, trying to grab at her like the burning arms of convicts swiping at a jailer's keys through the bars of their cells. I screamed for Eddie as though one of our children were in that fire. And Eddie came running.

But before he got to me, I tried to get closer to the box: leaned forward and put my hands on the wooden sides of the bonfire. The structure took my weight though I disturbed a frenzy of sparks: an electric orange snowstorm. Thousands, millions of tiny burning fragments flew upward promising something painful. But no flames could touch me yet.

There was an extraordinary beauty about being too close to the fire. It was mesmerizing in a way that only forbidden things can be, like looking into the mouth of the dragon. As I clung to the outer wood, I peered downward, and it was like gazing into hell through a crack in the floorboards. The heat on my face was like a furnace door being opened. I looked upward at the box, could see it blackening in the light of the growing flames, charring in places; I saw the surface that was nearest the flame bubbling gently, and was filled with fear.

It's strange what I recalled in the next moment: a scene from a movie where the good guy and the bad guy both spot the object of their desire at the same time — maybe a key, probably a gun — and after a stealthy glance at each other, they simultaneously make a dash for it, each hoping to get to it before the other. It was like that with me and the flames. My physical self recoiled at the thought of pressing my weight into the structure beneath me. I could have been standing on ice at the thinnest part of a frozen lake, I could have been standing on the loosest clod of earth at the edge of a crumbling cliff, and I would have felt the same. The pressure required to make a run for it was the exact pressure that was going to lead to my doom, and it was now or never as I felt the flames lick my hands, burning through my gloves.

All this took probably the best part of ten seconds, so that before I surged for the top of the bonfire, before I forced my right foot down to give me enough momentum to heave myself up onto the unstable surface, before I was able to kill myself or scar myself for life, Eddie was there.

He flew into the bonfire after me, grabbing me round the waist and throwing us both back onto the ground. I was winded but safe in his tight embrace, though all I could think about was the burning box on the top of the fire. I struggled against his grip, desperate to free myself, but he held on to me so tightly I could hardly move.

"Let me go," I said, my words like wasps, full of sting and insistence. But of course he wouldn't. I bit him on the shoulder and screamed, "Get the box off the bonfire! I need it!"

"What the fuck are you talking about?" Eddie yelled at me, not loosening his clutch one bit. We rolled on the damp grass as I engaged all of my weight in a bid to break away.

"Get that box for me, I'm begging you."

"You have got to be kidding me," said Eddie.

"Get it off before it's nothing but ashes," I said, with a quiet urgency. "That box is my life, my childhood, my mother. If you love me at all, just do it."

He shoved me away, growling, "Don't move," in a voice so angry I wouldn't have known it was his if I couldn't see him. I lay on the grass, hopelessly trying to keep the box safe by keeping it in my line of sight, and watched as Eddie took a long piece of wood from the tepee structure and made a swipe at the box, barely grazing it. He swiped again, and when it still wouldn't reach its mark, he threw the stick like a javelin, missing the precious object of my desire. Finally he yanked the clothesline pole out of the ground and knocked the box clean off the fire; it flew a little way through the air, rolled lethargically along the grass like tumbleweed, and then settled, more or less intact, from what I could see, and not burning. Then Eddie stormed toward me like a Neanderthal man, swooped me up into a fireman's lift, and marched up the garden toward the house, swearing fiercely with every step. I bounced painfully on his shoulder like a naughty child, watching our guests watching us as if we were strangers on some bizarre Channel 4 documentary. But I didn't care about that. Nothing mattered at all, nothing but the box.

"Get the box, Louis," I shouted. "Keep it safe."

Eddie stamped upstairs to the bathroom and dumped me down without ceremony. He wrenched the plug so that it nearly broke from its chain, and filled the sink with cold water, then pulled me by an elbow and pushed my hands down into the water, gloves and all. Every movement he made was so aggressive that he threatened to do damage. I wasn't frightened of Eddie; I was more frightened of what I had done to make him this way.

His hands shook as he carefully removed my gloves, worried that some of my skin might have burned and stuck to the material. Eventually, Cassie peered round the bathroom door and warily observed the angry, silent nursing that was taking place.

"Everyone's leaving," she said, directing her conversation to Eddie, now that I was presumably deemed out of my mind. "Clem's taking Louis home."

"Has he got the box?" I said, sounding — even to me — more and more like the madwoman I appeared to be.

Eddie whipped the glove off then, like a Band-Aid — his way of lashing out at my nonsense. Luckily the skin underneath wasn't too bad, raw in places and tender.

"Yes, he's got a box with him." She glanced at me, puzzled, then looked more meaningfully at Eddie, communicating what? That I inhabited a different world to them now because I suddenly existed outside of their realm of understanding.

"There will be a reason for this," Cassie said to Eddie, putting a hand on his forearm.

I was invisible.

"What reason can there be for almost killing herself for — nothing?" Eddie said.

"I have a reason," I said, as a by-the-way.

"What is it, then?" He spat out the words, turning fiercely and slopping water over the edge of the sink, piercing me with a stare as full of hatred as if I were a stranger who had almost killed his wife.

And I saw that here was the power of his love for me — the anger rising out of fear of losing me. The measure of love being loss, he had glimpsed that loss and attacked it. And my excuse for hurting me? A cardboard box. When I told him the truth, as I knew I must, I realized that whether he believed me or not, he might at least be comforted by the fact that I didn't, as he had said, do this for nothing.

"I'm going to tell you everything," I said, and then my knees gave way and weariness pressed down on me like heavy blankets falling from above.

"Look after her," Cassie said. "Do you want me to have the children for a couple of days?"

I heard Eddie say yes, and start trying to organize pajamas and overnight things, but Cassie said she had it covered. I surrendered my body to my husband, who carried me to the bedroom, undressed me as he had, on occasion, when I was too drunk to do it myself, and felt my stinging hands being wrapped in soft bandages. I pressed the clean, medicated material to my lips and tried to look my husband in the eyes, but he wouldn't return my gaze. Eddie held up a glass for me and put some pills in my mouth, painkillers, I guess, and I drifted into a fitful sleep.

At some point I woke and saw Eddie sitting on the edge of the bed, head in hands, crying. I touched his back, but he didn't move, or stop sobbing, and I sank back into oblivion.

I recall being roused, with water held to my lips, and hearing the murmur of something like a prayer, or maybe simply a word of love or comfort. It was all the same, I realized.

I don't know how long I'd been asleep when I came to full consciousness. Daylight dappled the room in a calm glow and my muscles hurt from being in the same position for too long. Parched, I took a glass from the bedside table, holding it awkwardly between two bandaged hands, then replaced it carefully; my throat was sore and I wanted some milk, my stomach rumbled like a marble in an empty can, but I couldn't imagine swallowing actual food. I rolled over, catching my breath suddenly when I saw that Eddie was asleep on one of the girls' mattresses. He had dragged it through and laid it in front of our bedroom door. To stop me escaping.

My darling husband was frightened of what I could do.

"Eddie," I croaked, my voice damaged

405

from lack of use, or maybe smoke. He stirred and opened his eyes, looking at me like a hurt animal. "Sorry," I croaked again, and tried to clear my throat.

In shorts and T-shirt, with disheveled hair and puffy eyes, Eddie sat on the edge of the bed, hands in his lap. "I want to know *everything,*" he said, his voice like the sound of a biplane in the distance on a summer's day.

"But this is the kind of *everything* I want," he continued. "I want the truth, Faye." His eyes were holding mine, kindness in them, uncertainty, and love. He shook his head sadly. "We always said we wouldn't lie to each other, and I've never broken that promise. But for some reason you have."

I opened my mouth to speak, but he held a finger up.

"Just listen," he said. "Maybe it's been easier for me than for you; I've never wanted to lie to you, never needed to. So I haven't. But I don't deserve a medal for not lying, that's just the way it should be — you should expect nothing less. You, however, have been lying to me for a long time, and I think I've been patient enough. I've tried to trust in you, and prayed that your lies are about loving me, and not about deceiving me. But the time has come to tell me what's going on." He touched my face. "I want to know how you got all those scratches and bruises when I found you in the attic. I want to know why you went into the fire. I want to know why that bloody box means so much to you. I want to know everything."

"And I'm going to tell you everything," I said, my voice hoarse and quiet.

"I'm glad to hear that."

"But it's going to be hard to hear."

"How bad can it be?" He smiled weakly, as if he already knew that it would be something terrible.

"You might think I'm crazy," I said, the salty tingle of tears threatening the backs of my eyes.

"Too late, darling, I'm already there," he said, kissing my fingers.

"Have you spoken to Louis?" I said.

"Yes. He's got your box," Eddie said with a sigh, as though the box were an old boyfriend whose name he was tired of hearing. "He says he's keeping it safe and it's not too badly damaged. He also said you had something of his, which you put somewhere safe; he asked if he could have it, but I don't know where it is."

He was talking about the box of old money. "In the bottom of the wardrobe, a

407

brown cardboard box."

"I hope you're going to explain all of this," Eddie said.

I nodded. "Can you tell Louis to come and see me tomorrow?"

"Okay," he said. "And when are we going to talk?"

I moved a lock of brown hair away from his face, and already I felt a huge sense of relief.

I thought about how Eddie's belief in God was all about faith and trust, a conviction of something that was unseeable, yet for all that, unshakable. I thought about what it was that had made me believe in the fact that I'd traveled in time to see my mother, and how I had only believed in the truth of that experience because of the evidence of my senses: the sights, the sounds, the smells; the taste of toast in the 1970s, the unforgettable feel of skin against skin when my mother held my hand to help me up into a tree. I needed that. But Eddie didn't. Eddie was no fool, and wouldn't just believe any old story. But I knew he trusted me and would recognize the sound of truth when he heard it, just as he'd recognized the lies. What he did with the truth, and what he thought of me afterward, I had to leave in his hands. I had faith in him and didn't

want to wait any longer, or make him wait.
"Now," I said.

CHAPTER 29

Eddie listened. I talked. I started with the photograph and told him about taking the box back to the attic, and everything that had happened that day, the first time I traveled back. I reminded him of my injuries that time and how the truth, no matter how unbelievable, actually made sense of everything. It fitted with him looking up in the loft when the ladder was down and finding it empty, but hearing a crash and discovering me up there later. I told him how much I'd wanted to talk to him, but that I knew he'd think I was insane. I explained how I ended up telling Louis the story, how I thought he'd believed me, but that he only became convinced later on.

I told Eddie that I'd returned to the past a second time, while he was in France, and that I'd stayed longer with my mother on that occasion. I told him about meeting Elizabeth and what had happened with the roller skates and my engagement ring. I told him how Louis and I had visited Elizabeth, how she'd lied about my ring being stolen, and that guilt had inspired her to send me an eternity ring.

I explained to Eddie my dilemma about returning to the past, how the missing ring initially made me pause and consider the consequences more seriously, and that I'd been trying to get on with my life like a normal person. I told him about my recent plans, since I'd learned from Henry that my mother hadn't died, not for certain, but had gone missing, and how it was my fault, because she'd started to think of me as a guardian angel and had gone looking for me.

I told him how I needed to go back one last time, to make amends, tell Jeanie the truth, and that after that I wouldn't go again. I told him about the old money and the ski suit, and the mattress at Louis's house. And I told him about how I'd seen the box on the top of the bonfire and had no choice but to rescue it.

And the last thing I said to my husband — in my rasping husk of a voice — the man I trusted more than any other person in the world, was that the Space Hopper box must be kept safe, because it was a lifeline. My mother's life depended on it, and while he might think I'd already lost my mind, if the box was lost, then I really would be.

And then I slept again.

When I woke, Eddie was sitting on the edge of the bed; we stared at each other, unflinching in our gaze. My mouth was dry, and when my eyes darted to the bedside table, he reached over for the glass and held it for me while I maneuvered myself into a sitting position. I drank deeply and handed the glass back to him. He silently placed it back on the table and we resumed our quiet eye contact.

"How does it feel to have a crazy wife?" I said eventually.

Eddie held my chin gently between his thumb and finger, so I wouldn't look away, and regarded me with a gravity that felt like the bass note in a song; the kind you can feel vibrating in your heart more than you can hear with your ears.

"It feels wonderful," he said, leaning forward and kissing me firmly on the forehead.

"Really?" I said, my voice tiny.

"Really," he said. "You're no different from the woman you were when I met you, no different from the woman you were

412

yesterday. I loved you then, and I love you now. Only now I can share what you're going through."

"But it's bonkers."

"Yes, it is a bit bonkers." He smiled. "But I believe in you, Faye. And whatever this is, it's crazy, but wonderful. *You're* wonderful. Don't worry, everything's going to be okay. We're just going to take things one step at a time."

I nodded. "Is the box safe?" I said.

"Yes," he said. And then slapped his legs as if to signal a change in direction. "So, are you hungry?"

I nodded again, and Eddie got up to make me scrambled eggs. It turned out I'd been drifting in and out of sleep for two days; I bathed, and Eddie redid my bandages. Although my hands hurt, there was no real damage. It felt as though I'd briefly ironed my palms on the cotton setting, and there was some blistering, but not much. I'd been lucky.

Once I'd eaten, I felt revived, and Eddie asked if I felt like seeing Louis, "your partner in crime," he said, with good humor. Then he drove me to his place, saying it would do me good to get out for a little while, and promised to collect me in an hour. After which we were going to pick up

413

the kids from Cassie's place.

Louis hugged me when I walked in, and my comrade and I spent a minimal amount of breath on niceties.

"Eddie says the box is safe," I said, as he led me into the lounge.

"Yeah, apparently he knocked it off the bonfire and it just landed on the grass. Your friends must have thought I was nuts, wanting to take it home with me. It's got a hole in the side now, and smells a bit charred and is peeling in places; I don't know how much difference the damage will make."

"It'll still work," I said.

"You haven't given up on going back, then?" he said.

"If I don't, then all this drama will have been for nothing, won't it?" I said.

"Sometimes we need to stop. Sometimes things go too far. You're lucky to be alive, from what I hear."

"I'm hardly hurt at all. I just burned my hands a bit, and that's nothing to do with time travel."

"It would have been if the box had been on the bonfire when you were coming back from the past," he said. And I grimaced.

Louis paused, his posture poised for revelation, and I waited.

"I have a little confession," he said.

414

"Go on."

"Well, I tried it myself," he said.

"Tried what?" I said, sitting more upright. "Did you get in the box?"

"I put the ski suit on and everything."

"Louis!" I said. I didn't know how to feel. *Proprietorial,* was my instant reaction. I wanted to shout *My box!* I was a bit indignant, but excited too. "What happened?"

"Well, I put on the suit — it was a bit on the tight side — and stood in the box. I waited a bit, because you told me it sometimes takes a while for something to happen."

"And then?" I said.

"Then, after about ten minutes I got out of the box, feeling like a total dick, and took the suit off and ate a Mars bar. Two, actually."

"Do you think it still works?" I said.

"Yeah, I think the box is fine. My gut instinct tells me it's your connection with your mother that makes it work, it's nothing to do with me. I don't think the box is a ticket to the seventies for just anyone."

"I have to go back," I said. "When my hands are better. Soon, though, I can't leave it much longer."

"Do you think Eddie will let you?" Louis said.

415

"I didn't talk to him about that, but I told him everything. And it went better than I expected."

"I know — he came to see me last night, said you'd told him the whole story, and he brought the money with him, the old currency I'd ordered. And took the box."

"He what?" I said, half standing. "I thought it was here." Of course it wasn't. I felt suddenly and dazzlingly deceived as I clocked that Eddie would never have left me here at Louis's place if the box were here too.

"He said you wanted the box kept safe, and that's what he said he'd do. He said there was no point in keeping it at my place now that he knew what was going on."

"Do you think he really believed me?" I said, trying to calm myself and slowly sitting again.

"He's *your* husband, what do you think?"

"I thought he did when we were actually together, but now he's not here . . . I don't know."

"When he came over, he said it was a pretty amazing tale, and I agreed, said it was hard to believe. And he said, 'But you believe in her, Louis,' and I told him yeah, because actually nothing had happened to make me think it was anything other than the truth. And that I'd met Elizabeth too."

"Anything else?"

"He said he believed you were telling the truth."

"In other words, he doesn't think I'm lying but he thinks I'm crazy."

"I don't know about that, but it's not going to be easy for him, is it, Faye? All he knows is you almost killed yourself trying to save a fucking cardboard box. Cut the guy some slack."

We laughed, but mine was a cautious laugh.

"Oh, shit," I said, my voice grating, realization catching up with me. *"Shit."*

"What?" Louis said.

"Eddie's going to get rid of the box."

"What? Why?"

"Isn't it obvious? If there were a gun in the house, he'd get rid of that. But it's the box he thinks will kill me. Oh, Louis, what if it's too late? Do you think he's thrown it away already?"

"Well, there's only two ways to think about this, so stop and calm down. Maybe it *is* too late, in which case there's nothing you can do about it."

"But my *mother,*" I wailed, my throat hurting. "I need her, I need to stop her leaving me. If I'd never gone back, she might never have disappeared."

Louis leaned toward me. "But you *did* go back, didn't you?" he chastised me in a fierce, hushed tone. "And you made some lives better. You brought peace to Elizabeth. You brought joy to Henry and Em. Who knows how much peace and joy they in turn spread because of you? You lost something, they gained. You can't have it all, Faye. You have to let some things go."

"I can't!" I wiped the tears from my face with the backs of my hands. "If I go back again," I said, sifting the logic of the thing once more, "then it's because I'm meant to go back again, isn't that the way it works?"

"I'm not sure anymore," Louis said. "But to be honest, I'm glad Eddie's got that box, because I think you're losing the plot. I'd feel bad if I let you get in it."

Eddie pulled up outside, and I grabbed my coat in a hurry. He stayed where he was, talking on his phone, and I wondered what he'd think when he saw that my eyes were red. Maybe he wouldn't notice — but then again, the eyes are the windows to the soul, so maybe it would be the only thing my husband *would* notice, seeing as he was so interested in souls.

He leaned over to open the passenger door

from the inside, and his voice carried up the pathway as I approached. I could tell he was talking to a woman. For the first time in my life I felt a pang of hatred toward him, small and sharp like a stinging nettle. He was too good-looking to be a vicar; women with problems, women with dead husbands, bakers of excellent cakes would throw themselves at him. My husband: Destroyer of Boxes.

When I settled into the car, arms folded, he finished the call and looked at me. I turned away.

"Okay?" he said.

"What did you do with my box?" I said. I couldn't look at him while he confessed.

He hesitated. Of course he did. "It's in the attic, at home. Is that okay?"

My head snapped to look at him, which hurt like hell, but I didn't care. "Is it really?" I said, unbelieving.

"Yes. I thought it was the safest place for it. I know Louis would look after it, but I guess I just thought it should be at our house."

My eyelids closed against eyes brimful of tears, pushing them over the edge.

"What's wrong?" Eddie said.

"When Louis said you'd taken the box, I thought you might have got rid of it." My

419

voice was as shaky as a ramshackle bridge, and as likely to break.

Eddie held my hand and smoothed my hair. "Yesterday you told me everything. Don't you think I understand how important that box is to you?"

"But it's so dangerous, and I really hurt myself trying to get it out of the fire — I thought maybe you'd decided to put a stop to it once and for all." I sniffed wetly and he handed me a tissue. I struggled to unfold it, with my hands bandaged so snugly.

"I'm sorry," I said, holding them up in exasperation. "Look what I've put you through."

"You've been through a lot yourself, and all of it without me. I only wish you'd told me sooner, so I could have been there for you."

"I thought you would laugh," I said. But that wasn't true, I never thought Eddie would laugh. I thought he would think I was crazy. I thought he would think differently of me, less of me. I wouldn't be the woman he loved. "I thought you would laugh," I said again, "and try to convince me it wasn't true."

"You didn't laugh when I told you that God tapped me on the shoulder and spoke to me in church. You didn't try to convince

420

me that it wasn't true."

"Isn't that a bit different?" I said. "Less extreme. Isn't it a bit less weird?"

"But you don't believe in God the way I do. In fact, you've said quite simply that you *don't* believe."

I nodded. "I'm trying."

"But that's not the point, is it? The point is, I believe that God touched me, physically, and spoke to me, with a voice. It was gentle, it wasn't a roller-coaster ride through space with an unforgiving landing three decades into the past, but it *was* real. To me. And that's whether or not *you* happen to believe it."

"So . . . you believe me."

"I believe you in the same way that you believe in me," he said, a little cryptically.

"Does that mean you think I've lost my mind?"

Eddie laughed and it was a beautiful sound. "Only if you think I've lost mine." He smiled. "Do you — think I've lost my mind?"

I shook my head, and there were no tears now. I looked at Eddie and opened my eyes a little wider, to invite him to see into my soul.

"God," he said in a whisper, "spoke to me!" He shook his head gently. "Don't you see that my story is as incredible as yours, maybe more so? I'm talking about God, and you're talking about your mother."

"So why does my story feel so incredible compared to yours?"

"I don't know, maybe because it's more dramatic: boxes, attics, fortune-telling, stolen rings, saving yourself as a child, getting to know your mother whom you haven't seen since you were a child. Everyone wants to know about that. But certainly, not everyone wants to know about my 'calling,' and yet for me, it has been an extraordinary journey."

"Why are you so good?" I asked, and he shook his head modestly. "No, really, why?"

"When I listen to other people and I find myself starting to judge, I ask myself, *Who am I?* I've heard a widow tell me how her husband stands by her fireplace smiling at her, and she was insistent that she'd actually seen him. It's not an isolated phenomenon — quite a few people have said things like that. And they all assume that I can't possibly believe them. But who am I, Faye, to say it's not true?"

"So, you believe me?"

"Who am I not to?"

"And you think we have something in common in that your thing with God and my thing with my mother are the same thing?" I said.

" 'Mother is the name for God in the lips and hearts of little children,' " he quoted.

"And grown women as well?"

"Probably," he said.

"So the box is safe?"

"For now," he said, putting the car into gear and releasing the hand brake.

"Stay where you are, vicar," I said, putting my hand over his. "What do you mean, it's safe 'for now'?"

He switched off the engine and it shuddered into silence, then he turned in his seat and looked at me.

"Listen to me, my darling. I love you more than anyone else in the world, along with the girls, oh, and God." He kissed me so softly on the lips that it was like a breath of air.

"Anyone else?" I smiled.

"And I *believe* in you. I believe your box is a bridge to your mother, a way back to her. And it's not my job to remove that bridge to the past. There are some things we need in order to help us process and keep the past with us: mementos, photographs, postcards, letters. Some links to the past are good, we hold on to them. And some links are not so good: they're the ones

423

that hold on to us. Sometimes we really do need to let go of the past. I know it's a cliché, but how else can I put it?"

Eddie's handsome face came close and he rested the tip of his nose on the tip of mine. I breathed in the woody scent of his freshly shaved cheek.

"We can't let go of someone else's past for them," he said. "We can't sever the tie for somebody else. If we did, then somehow the knot of that connection would only become tighter. If I got rid of your link to your mother, you would never get over her, never come to terms with your loss."

I put my hand to his face and closed my eyes.

"It's not my job to get rid of the box," he said. "It's yours."

CHAPTER 30

About two months later, early January, we decided that Tuesday afternoon would be a quiet time to go to the coast. Eddie had organized for the girls to be collected from school by Cassie, and they were going to stay overnight with her family. We'd probably be back in time to put them to bed ourselves, but neither of us wanted to clock-watch, not today. And it was going to be emotional. We needed to be alone, together.

I dressed nicely, made an effort as you might for a funeral, but not in black. I wore an electric-blue silk scarf around my neck that day. Eddie wore his best jeans and a gray shirt, with a black sweater over the top. We looked like people who dress nicely for the airport, which we're not, as a rule.

Looking at the map recently we had searched out a secluded cove, where hardly anyone goes so we wouldn't be disturbed, and we found one, somewhere we'd been years before.

There was a blue winter sky and I opened the window. The cold, clean air was crisp and lovely, but I shut it quickly, suddenly afraid that our precious cargo in the back-seat might blow out, like a balloon seeking escape as soon as the opening is large enough. Stupid, though: a cardboard box was never going to simply blow out of the window.

I turned to look at it, make sure it was okay, like a baby, or a puppy coming home for the first time in the car. I reached through the gap between our seats and touched it. If I was going to say good-bye, I wasn't going to bother feeling embarrassed about treating a cardboard box like a living thing.

We'd had plenty of conversations, Eddie and I, about the box and the need for me to let it go. I resisted, of course I did. It was the hardest decision I ever made in my life. But Eddie pointed out two things that convinced me in the end: one I hadn't thought of before, and the other I probably had, but had chosen to ignore. The first was that one day, Esther or Evie might find the box and get in it. Would the magic work on them too? If Louis's hunch was right and it was the link with my mother that enabled

426

me to travel back in time, then wouldn't their blood-link with her make it possible for the box to take them back to the past too? If that happened to my daughters, would they survive the journey? Would they get into trouble without me there to help them? Would they be able to find their way back?

Secondly, we kept our box safe, because we knew its power and kept it shut in the loft to protect it and to protect people from it. But who was looking after the box in the past? What if it had been destroyed at the other end, when I got into the box at *this* end? Where would I end up? What if, while I was there, it went missing, for whatever reason?

Furthermore, Eddie persuaded me that I'd already gained more than anybody else got after a loved one dies. And he was right. I had everything to lose if I started getting greedy.

We stopped at a traditional little pub, practically empty, and I quickly found a seat by a window while Eddie got himself a coffee, and a small glass of wine for me. I needed to be able to see the car at all times, just in case. *Just in case what?* Yes, just in case a burglar with a swag bag and black eye mask happened to stumble across the parking lot of a remote country pub, and break into our locked car to steal a blackened cardboard box from the backseat.

Eddie was right. I needed to let it go.

He was patient while I finished my wine, but we both knew we should get to the beach before it got dark.

We drove on a little farther, and for a short while I wondered if we were lost, maybe we wouldn't find the place. Was I glad of a last-minute reprieve, a stay of execution? Maybe it would be better to get it over and done with; hanging on to the box for a day or two longer wasn't a good idea. I needed to do it now, so I could begin to grieve.

Eddie pulled over, switched off the engine, and turned to me. "Ready?"

"Yes," I said.

When I made no move to get out of the car, he came around and opened the door for me and held out his hand. Then he opened the back door and moved to one side, letting me lean in to get the box. I insisted on carrying it, and Eddie was fine with that. He led the way and I trailed behind in the narrow parts, and when we could walk side by side he slowed to keep pace with me, his hand touching the small of my back now and then.

I hope it doesn't sound ridiculous, but this box was what made me feel closest to my mother now, and before I let her go, I needed to hold it. Don't think it didn't cross my mind to put the box on the ground and jump into it before Eddie could stop me. I visualized myself leaping in and disappearing as if there were an endless hole underneath the box.

We were in a place that required us to park in a little lane and walk past a field full of pigs and their curved silver shelters, then on through a wooded area, where the trees formed an arch overhead. Going through there felt like getting married, when the guests all join hands and cheer as you squeeze through the tunnel from the party to the car that takes you to the honeymoon. It wasn't going to be like that today. It was a departure I was reluctant to be a part of, and yet I had come to agree with Eddie that it was the right thing to do. The archway would take us to a steep path down to the beach, where the cliff would stand high, yellow and crumbling, behind us.

When we reached the path that led down to the beach, the terrain below our feet was suddenly ocher and stony. From here you could see out over a billowing sea, and I felt sick. It was windier here and our hair was whipped about; the end of my scarf flapped in my face. I held on tight to the box. Nothing was going to take it from me until I let it. It would be my choice, and in my time.

We walked onto the shore and looked out at the ocean. The sky was still blue but darkening; the water looked gray and menacing, with myriad white peaks. Choppy.

"Do you want to say a few words?" Eddie asked.

"A funeral?" I said.

"In a way," he said. "Just another way of saying good-bye."

"Could you say something?" I asked him. "Haven't you trained for this yet?"

He laughed a humble laugh. "I'll say something if you want."

"It's okay, I'll do it." And I thought for a bit before deciding it didn't really matter what I said, but I needed to say something, and then I said this. "I will never see you again or touch you again, but you will live inside me forever. You will always be in my heart and I will never, ever forget you. For every shell on this beach that once held a life, each one left something beautiful behind, just as you have done. And so, to

430

my wonderful mother, I say good-bye, and I pray to God" — I looked at Eddie and smiled sadly — "that whatever it is you went looking for that day, somehow you find it, and find peace, wherever you may be."

"Amen," Eddie said, and looked at me and held out his arms. I gave the box to him, and took my shoes off, rolling my trousers up to my knees. He gave the box back to me and did the same with his own shoes and jeans. We left our things on the sand and walked toward the water. It touched my toes and was so cold, it almost felt scalding. I crouched and held the box into a wave that lapped the shore. And then I let go.

The water took the box, and I watched as it drifted away a few feet, then came slightly back to shore, as though uncertain whether to leave or not. The orange of the box, once so bright, was mostly gone since the fire damage, and from being knocked about so much when I landed in it. But I could just see the face of the girl riding a Space Hopper on the front, and I focused on her smile for a few moments. Suddenly the box was much farther out, beyond arm's reach. The ocean had lulled me into thinking it would be gentle and take its time, but it had grabbed the box and dragged it a long way out. I watched as it started to sink, and I cried out, turning my head to Eddie's chest and clutching his sweater with both hands. I couldn't watch anymore. I felt instant warmth and protection as Eddie stood like a windbreak between me and my surroundings, muffling the sounds, the rumble of wind and waves.

I held on to him until I felt his body stiffen unexpectedly and pull away from me. I heard him gasp, and I turned to look out to sea once more. The box was still visible, just, but the water around it appeared to be churning, as though a bomb had hit it. There was magic in the box, I knew that, and perhaps it was resisting being extinguished.

Before I could stop him, Eddie ran into the sea, like a greyhound out of a starting box.

"Stop!" I shouted. "Leave it." But he carried on running, knees raised high to battle the waves that wanted to hold him back. The water around the box was still frothing and Eddie must have realized that there was something enchanted about it, because now he was as desperate to rescue it from the water as I had been to rescue it from the fire. His body obscured it from my view as he plunged on, and just before he got to the

box, he dived to get himself closer to it. I screamed out, "No." He was a good swimmer, but the waves looked unforgiving. What if I lost him now? What if he drowned? It would be all my own fault: first my mother, and now Eddie. I ran a little way into the water, until it was above my knees, the power of the water dragging at my legs, making me dig my feet into the wet sand to stay vertical.

Eddie wasn't going any farther. He seemed to be wrestling with the box, as though it were a large thrashing fish. I saw his arms held wide and then he went under again, but finally he turned, the waves colliding against him, trying to pull him under.

Ultimately he found his footing and managed to force himself upright, heaving with the weight in his arms. And there, half-drowned but alive, with wet hair hanging down and her arms around Eddie's neck as he carried her toward me, was my mother.

Eddie stumbled back to shore, battling the waves to get a more solid footing and trying not to let her slip out of his arms. I ran into the water, feeling half as though I were in a dream, while the freezing water bit me into reality. My mother looked at me, shocked, just as a wave clapped against her face, and she closed her eyes against the stinging salt and reached up to get a better grip on Eddie's shoulder. By the time I got to them, Eddie was making strides, and I touched her arm, but I couldn't help carry her; if I tried to take some of her weight, I would impede Eddie's progress. So I trotted beside them as best I could, all the while attempting contact by touching some part of her with my bluish, outstretched fingers.

Eddie's legs gave way not far from where the waves met the sand. He laid Jeanie down, and then lay next to her; his lips touched the ground, and when he looked at me, sand coated one side of his face. His wet hair was painted across his face and the whites of his eyes were pink. His teeth were chattering.

My mother's teeth were chattering too, and there was a pale-blue line around her lips, her wide eyes staring up at me. I kneeled beside her, taking off my jacket to lay over her, even though it was soaking wet.

"Is this heaven?" she said, the words chopped into pieces by her involuntary shuddering. Her whole body shook.

"No," I said. "Not heaven." I looked into her gray eyes. Like Eddie, the sea had turned the whites of her eyes pinkish. Her lashes clumped together, dark and pretty.

"My guardian angel! Where am I?"

"You know this woman?" Eddie said.

Did I know her? Not well enough. All my life I had missed out on her face, her presence, her wisdom, her warmth. And yet here she was, barely older than the last time I'd seen her, still at least ten years younger than me. And so, ultimately, it would be the case that I had not really missed one moment of my mother's life, while she had missed thirty years of mine.

I held Jeanie's hand and kissed her cheek. I let my face rest against hers and then, when I was ready I lifted my head and looked at my husband.

"Yes, I know her," I said.

He waited, the single, simple line between his brows a tiny sign of profound confusion. I looked down at my mother, and she smiled that smile that was as warm and easy as sun breaking through clouds.

"This is my mother."

I briefly looked back at the sea and saw a few pieces of cardboard drifting off, some as far away as the eye could see, and I knew there was no going back.

And then, not knowing the right questions to ask yet, and not being sure of the answers anyway, we got up off the sand. The three of us, like human shipwrecks, ascended the cliff. My mother clinging to me in disbelief. Pierced by the sword of knowing she would never see her little girl again. The unique gift of getting to know me now was a compromise she had yet to come to terms with. Eddie walked behind, his hands on our shoulders, as though we might fall backward. We climbed, taking our first steps into a new life together. The past only behind us. A life to be lived only forward.

EPILOGUE

Summer, 1979. A chest infection wasn't just a winter occurrence anymore. Jeanie could feel one coming, its early symptoms as distinct as the difference between sea and sky, its progress as predictable a story as any other — the beginning: a subtle rawness between her throat and lungs, which moved lower daily; the middle: an increasing shallowness of breath, pain breathing in, and lack of energy; the end: a cough on which she could get no purchase, until she could finally clear it, hawking up lumps of phlegm as solid as slugs. This was the end she was accustomed to, but she felt sure it would kill her one day.

It had been fifteen months since Jeanie had seen her guardian angel: the woman who looked like her mother, a mother she could barely remember, who carried the same name and the same tics and turns of phrase as her daughter. Sometimes Jeanie felt a desperation to find her guardian angel that was overwhelming; she had said as much to her friends, like-minded bohemian types whom she rarely saw these days. She had found a connection in Faye, formed a bond to the older woman, was magnetically drawn to her.

When Faye didn't return and the months passed by, Jeanie had got on with her life, but never stopped looking, quickened her pace if she saw someone similar from behind, only to be disappointed when she overtook the woman and turned to see her unfamiliar face. She knew it was foolish to miss, to mourn, a friend she barely knew. Faye had been nearly old enough to be her mother, but maybe that was it, maybe she was the mother figure Jeanie had missed out on. Maybe that's why it hurt so much. And the fantasy that this woman could look after her daughter if anything bad were to happen to Jeanie was never going to be a reality. There was no safety net; she would have to accept that.

It was time for Jeanie to let go of the idea of Faye — she had been happy before, she would be happy again — and concentrate on her daughter; she needed to get well, or her fears of dying young were going to come true, and above all else, she did not want to leave her daughter without a mother. She would never leave her willingly. Ever. God would have to take her.

She gazed at the sleeping form of little Faye, her chest rising and falling gently below the sheets, and kissed her on the forehead.

Jeanie went downstairs and flicked on the kettle, desperate for the hot water to soothe the rasping in her throat and chest, hoping it would warm and melt the infection that was taking hold, dissolve it out of her body. She leaned on the kitchen counter and absentmindedly picked up two empty glass jam jars near the window, pinching them between her thumb and finger. She walked them down to the shed; the air was warm already, even though it was still early. It was going to be a beautiful day.

Jeanie opened the shed door, wrestled with it momentarily. These jars would keep for things that didn't belong anywhere else, the things that we just don't know when the time will come for us to need them. She hadn't been in the shed for ages, perhaps years, there were a lot of cobwebs and not much else. Jeanie wondered about clearing it completely, cleaning it, painting it, and making a playhouse for her and little Faye, a place to hide, to talk and play.

There was a box on the floor, might come in handy, although it was a little broken, and beyond it just a mess of tools and other paraphernalia. As she leaned forward to place the jars on a shelf at the back of the shed, she stepped into the box on the floor, and as she did so, the bottom opened up and swallowed her.

Two glass jars hit the floor of the shed and rolled momentarily, clinking as they collided with each other, and then stopped.

Jeanie hurtled through the darkness like a bullet, until she could see something — water? Gray water. She couldn't breathe, and as she hit the ocean like a torpedo, she threw her head above the waves and took a breath as deep as her lungs would allow.

ACKNOWLEDGMENTS

It's difficult to know where the beginning really is, but, as best I can, I'd like to do this in chronological order. I couldn't have written this book without me, and so I'd like to thank my parents, Patricia Steele and Norman Graupp, for starting things off.

Thank you to Sarah Geileskey for our wonderful conversation in the early stages, which helped me create the character of Eddie. Next are three friends who read my story as I was writing it — a few chapters at a time — and told me they liked it. For their support, feedback, and patience, I give my deepest thanks to Patrick Doyle, Adam Schiller, and Amy Schiller.

When I was sick of rejections and put my manuscript in a drawer and cried myself to sleep until I came to terms with never getting published, I got a message from a friend who encouraged me to send it to one more agent. Without that nudge I may have left it locked away, so thank you, Sarah Why-and. That "one more agent" was Judith Murray, who is the character everyone loves from a novel, the fairy godmother in the story of my own life — thank you for getting me to the ball.

Thank you to Jo Dickinson and Jackie Cantor at Simon & Schuster for your moving, emotional response to my novel. Thank you to Kate Rizzo for all your work in selling the foreign rights, and Alisa Ahmed for all your help.

I thank my children for believing that I would get published just because I'm their mum, and who prayed to the universe — and everything in it — when I promised to buy them a kitten if I got a publisher.

And thank you for picking up this book. I hope you feel that reading it is time well spent.

There are a lot of people who help take a story and turn it into a book and get it out there. I didn't know about all of them until recently, but here they are, all much appreciated. Some made me laugh and were personally supportive, and some I've never met — not even virtually — but to whom I am extremely thankful.

In the US: Aimée Bell, Jen Bergstrom, Jenny Carrow (for the US cover art), Allison Green, Molly Gregory, Eliza Hanson, Lisa Litwack, Jen Long, Sally Marvin, Caroline Pallotta, Jaime Putorti, Carolyn Reidy (for her kind words of support), Jamie Selzer, and Abby Zidle. Thank you all.

In the UK: Maddie Allan, Suzanne Baboneau, Jess Barratt, Dominic Brendon, Ian Chapman, Rich Hawton, Clare Hey, Judith Long, Hayley McMullan, Polly Osborn, Gill Richardson, Joe Roche, Alice Rodgers, Katrina Scott, Francesca Sironi, Rich Vlietstra, and Pip Watkins (for the UK cover art). Thank you all.

ABOUT THE AUTHOR

Helen Fisher spent her early life in America but grew up mainly in Suffolk, England, where she now lives with her two children. She studied psychology at Westminster University and ergonomics at University College London, and worked as a senior evaluator in research at the Royal National Institute of Blind People. She is now a full-time author; *Faye, Faraway* is her first novel. She is currently working on her second.

The employees of Thorndike Press hope you have enjoyed this Large Print book. All our Thorndike, Wheeler, and Kennebec Large Print titles are designed for easy reading, and all our books are made to last. Other Thorndike Press Large Print books are available at your library, through selected bookstores, or directly from us.

For information about titles, please call:
  (800) 223-1244

or visit our website at:
  gale.com/thorndike

To share your comments, please write:
  Publisher
  Thorndike Press
  10 Water St., Suite 310
  Waterville, ME 04901